Love-40

Love-40

A Novel

Victor Cauthen

Alpharetta, GA

ISBN: 978-1-61005-743-1

10 9 8 7 6 5 4 3 2   031017

Printed in the United States of America

∞This paper meets the requirements of ANSI/NISO Z39.48-1992 (Permanence of Paper)

The TABASCO® marks, bottle and label designs are registered trademarks and servicemarks exclusively of McIlhenny Company, Avery Island, Louisiana, 70513. www.TABASCO.com.

To my mother, Betty Sue, and the memory of my father, H. A. Jr., loving, caring parents who made sacrifices for me at a young age. They allowed me the opportunity to experience the sort of athletic endeavors that teach one life lessons and ultimately mold one's character. I was lucky and forever grateful that they were my parents.

Part One

"Tennis is a perfect combination of violent action taking place in an atmosphere of total tranquility."

—Billie Jean King

Santa Barbara, 1983

"Hello, Train, this is Louie Mouton over in Lafayette. How are you liking your teaching gig at the country club in Bel Air?"

"Things didn't go too well at the Palms. I moved up the road to Santa Barbara. I'm staying at this run-down tennis camp that Irma and her husband used to have up here."

Train explained that the camp was about a half mile out toward the Santa Ynez Mountains behind the Kersh mansion near Montecito.

"How'd that happen?" I asked.

"I kinda got caught with my pants down. I decided I'd better resign. I was getting tired of the rules and pomp and circumstance at the Palms anyway."

Irma saved him on this one, he explained. She was in full view of the episode along with the club president's wife and two other ladies on the golf course in golf carts. Unlucky for him, they were playing on the same thirteenth hole where Train was giving an in-house tennis lesson to one of the lady members who desired a little extra training for a more powerful hip thrust. They were upstairs in her bedroom, and Train was fulfilling all her fantasies. She wanted to dress up like a fairy princess and use her magic wand on him.

The woman heard a door close in the driveway and said, "Oh no. He has come home early from the trip." So Train jumped up and ran down the back stairs toward the pool and across the fairway, headed back to the tennis pro shop, trying to get his pants up and shirt buttoned. He tripped over a sprinkler head and yelled, "God Almighty!" Unfortunately, twenty yards down from him was Mr. Club President's wife in the middle of her backswing, hitting an approach shot to the thirteenth green. As her golf club came down, she looked back and entirely missed the ball, swung wildly around, and fell back into the golf cart and down into the floorboard. Train tried to raise himself back up off the ground, knowing that half the buttons he had buttoned were in the wrong holes and that his pants zipper got snagged halfway up. Adding further craziness to the scene, he still had one shoe in his hand.

His composure tested, Train went with a tennis mentality — add out, trying to get back to deuce.

"Sorry, ladies," he said. "I should have yelled fore!" Inside, he was laughing hysterically.

He decided to casually walk across the fairway rather than run. The damage done, he looked back and smiled at Irma. She smiled and winked at him. He knew that Irma was also laughing hysterically inside. Irma's love for him took him back to deuce.

Not quite out of earshot, one of the two young ladies helping lift Mr. Club President's wife from the floorboard of the cart said to her other young girlfriend, "You know, girl, we ought to think about getting some private tennis lessons from him too."

Train smiled at them, waving a thumbs-up. Ten minutes after being back in the tennis pro shop, the Fairy Princess from the thirteenth hole called Train and said, "Honey, please come back over."

"Are you crazy?" Train asked.

"No, it was only the young, handsome FedEx driver, Denny."

Train asked her if she answered the door in her little princess outfit.

"Yes, I did," she said.

He asked her what she said to the FedEx driver. She said she told handsome Denny she had never been so happy to see him in all her life.

"What did he say to that?" Train asked her.

"Handsome Denny smiled and said, 'Sign for your Victoria's Secret package on line sex, I mean, line six, please, ma'am.'"

I told Train I was going to put all his escapades into my forthcoming book titled *The Second Coming of Don Juan*. Train told me he was late for some doubles lessons, waiting a beat for me to get his meaning, and hung up the phone. I leaned back in my chair and thought about the wild ride Train had been on in his life and how he got to where he was. Tennis was only the half of it.

Louie

Memorial Day was my father's favorite holiday. It was more special to him than Easter, Thanksgiving, Christmas, or, even though he never said so, my birthday and his birthday. Not that my father neglected the other holidays or my birthday. I had great birthdays: pony rides, boudin, jambalaya, beignets, and Cajun and Zydeco music. But what occurred in the great State—or the great *French* State, as my father liked to say—of Louisiana was an event that ran through every fiber of his spirit, soul, and ancestry. From the time I was six years old, my father, Dr. Roland Louis Mouton, and I made the trip from our home in Lafayette, Louisiana, to New Orleans, Louisiana, to witness a four-day-long event.

My father was of French descent, considered Cajun in Louisiana. My grandfather had named my father after two famous Frenchmen, which my father strived throughout his life to emulate. My father was a devout and serious student of French history.

King Louis X of thirteenth-century France was the first tennis player known by name. He was an ardent participant of *jeu de paumme*, which translates to "game of the palm." *Jeu de paumme* is an early incarnation of the game of tennis, as my father reminded me often when I was young. Louis X built indoor courts inside the French palace. In the sixteenth century, racquets were introduced into the game and the name of the game became *tenez*, meaning "take heed," a warning to start play. This game, played indoors in France and England, became known as "real tennis," a game of the royals. To my father's dismay, the game found more participation and enthusiasm in England than France.

Starting around 1859, Edgbaston, England, became known as the birthplace of the game of lawn tennis. Two tennis enthusiasts—Augurio Perera, a Spaniard, and Harry Gem, an Englishman—carved out the first lawn tennis court in 1859 in Perera's large backyard. My father always believed that lawn tennis should not solely be credited to Perera and Gem but to the mechanical mind of another Englishman, Mr. Edwin Budding, who should be given most of the credit for the game. At dinner parties or tennis outings, my father made this assertion to friends and patients, to which the partygoers always responded, "Who in the hell is Edwin Budding, Doc?" My father explained that only because of Edwin's inventive mind could Augurio and Harry take credit for their lawn tennis court. Edwin Budding, you see, invented and patented the first lawnmower. My father told me many times over the years—no disrespect to another of our famous and great Frenchmen—that Rene Lacoste's tennis shirts should be emblazoned with the embroidery of a lawnmower over the heart, not a crocodile, upon which my father would erupt into uncontrollable and uproarious laughter.

My grandfather, Pierre, was as devout a tennis man as Louis X.

"Without Louis X," my grandfather said, "why, hell, we'd all still be swatting little balls with our hands and breaking our fingers."

He would joke with his friends that the only differences between himself and Louis X were that he didn't have a crown, he had a little less gold, and he married a regular pain in the ass and not a royal pain in the ass.

"Only joking, my queen," he would say to my grandmother.

Roland, my father's first name, had a deeper significance to my grandfather than Louis did. Roland Garros was a famous Frenchman born in 1888 in Saint-Denis, France. Garros started flying at the age of twenty-one and flew in air races, most notably the 1911 Paris to Madrid air race, which he completed when he was twenty-three. In 1912, he joined the French Army. During World War I, he claimed to shoot down five German aircraft. This feat merited the distinction of being considered an "ace" in aircraft war battles.

"Roland Garros 'aced' those German sons of bitches," my grandfather said.

Roland was shot down behind enemy lines in Germany and held prisoner. Once Roland escaped capture, rather than quit the war, he reenlisted and was shot down in battle and killed in 1918, one day before his thirtieth birthday.

"Love-30, Roland," my father said.

I was born in Lafayette, Louisiana, and was named after my father, christening me Roland Louis Mouton Jr. My father and my mother, Evangeline, called me Louie, and I was their only child. My father occasionally reminded me with much pride that I was born in the happiest city in the country, right alongside the other happiest places: Houma, Shreveport, Baton Rouge, and Alexandria. He jokingly told me if I ever became sad I should leave the state for a couple days and only return when I was happy and smiling because he didn't want anyone in the family tarnishing our "happy" reputation. I smiled a lot.

My father attended the University of Louisiana at Lafayette as an undergraduate and attended medical school at Louisiana State University in Baton Rouge. My mother met my father when she was a nursing student at LSU, and the rest was storybook romance: love, marriage, and a baby carriage. They bought an old farm on fifty acres just a couple of miles on the outskirts of Lafayette near Carencro. The house was a two-story brick home which was reminiscent of one of the old plantation homes on the sugarcane or rice farms in Louisiana. My father purchased the home from the bank due to the fact that the heirs had no interest in returning. They forfeited it to the bank rather than spend money to refurbish it and try to find a buyer. My father said when he bought this beautiful piece of property on such a royal country setting that, like the Spaniard Augurio Perera and the Englishman Harry Gem and with the aid of Edward Budding's lawnmower, he too could make his dream come alive: The Roland Louis Mouton Lawn Tennis Court. The location of our home was perfect for my father. Interstate 10 and Highway 49 provided proximity to accommodate his regular visits to the Lafayette hospital where he delivered babies at all times and days of the week. The location also afforded the geographic proximity to the little towns to which he would make house calls to the poor. Many of these Cajun and Creole families worked the farms and factories in Breaux Bridge, Opelousas, Henderson, Crowley, Broussard, New Iberia, and Saint Martinsville.

In the first years after he started his practice, my father gained the reputation for making these house calls. These Cajun and Creole folks usually paid in some form of food, folk art, services, or, many times, just a thank-you. They named him "Dr. King de Donne un Coup de Main," the English translation being "king of giving a helping hand."

My grandfather Pierre would have been fulfilled and thrilled knowing that his son Louis had truly been crowned as royalty by those he unselfishly served just as Louis X had.

Lafayette, Louisiana, and many of the surrounding towns lay in the very southwest region of Louisiana about a hundred miles west of New Orleans. The twenty-two parishes which made up this area of Louisiana were called Acadiana due to their strong influence of French Acadian languages, culture, and traditions. The economy of Lafayette and this region primarily depended on agriculture, fishing, and the oil industry. The majority of the people in the region worked in the rice and sugarcane fields and many worked in the oil refineries and in the transportation of these products. Many of the men spent weeks at a time on the offshore oil rigs away from their families. Needless to say, the children of these families were not fortunate enough to have the money or the time to enjoy tennis, the sport of kings. The main recreation for these children as they grew up was football, baseball, or basketball because the equipment for these sports was provided by the school systems, churches, parish parks, and recreation centers surrounding Lafayette.

There were a few tennis courts around Lafayette in public parks, but because of little or no play, they were used for hop-skip-jump games or bicycle raceways by the kids, much to Dr. Roland Louis Mouton's dismay. His hopes of anyone from Acadiana ever winning the Oyster Bay Classic Memorial Day–weekend high school tournament in New Orleans mightn't ever happen unless he took matters into his own hands, which he did. This meant that not too long after being pulled from the womb, the first manmade object I touched was a tennis ball, not the customary pacifier. While most children in their cribs delightedly played with a string of little animals or bells stretched from one side of the crib to the other, my father adorned my crib with a string of six brightly colored tennis balls.

I was told in later years that I hit these balls with my right hand due to the fact that my dad gave my mother instruction to put my left hand in my diaper. This was perplexing to my mother but not to my father. As he saw it, according to his "equation factor theory," the only advantage that any left-hand-dominant athlete had in sports was the batter in the game of baseball because the left-handed batter plays closer to first base and gets there three steps quicker and faces 75 percent more right-handed pitchers than left-handed pitchers. Thus, the left-handed batter can see the balls better due to the angle of the incoming pitch. He would adoringly smile at my mama and say, "Add in lefty." As a genetically inherited footnote to this theory, upon many departures after delivering a new baby boy, my father would ask the new fathers, "By the way, what sport do you want your son to play?" And when many of those fathers answered baseball, he said, "Make sure you put his right hand in his diaper and the little crib toys in his left."

"Why is that, Doc?" these fathers asked, perplexed and finding these instructions strange.

"Lefties are closer to first base," he'd respond, upon which they would erupt into uncontrollable and uproarious laughter.

In later years, to answer my question about why there were only six brightly colored tennis balls on the string in my crib while having room for twice as many, my father only said one word: "bagel." In the game of tennis, when an opponent wins or loses a set 6-0, the term so used is "bagel." While telling this story of my crib activities to friends and patients, he smiled with pride as though I had just won the French Open.

"Before Louie could walk or talk, he was 6-0, winning a 'bagel,'" he said.

By the time I was four years old, when most children are riding tricycles, my father, sitting atop a riding lawnmower, had me in his lap with my hands on the steering wheel. Our riding lawnmower was specifically dedicated to the care and manicure of the Roland Louis Mouton Lawn Tennis Court in Lafayette, Louisiana. This exercise occurred regularly each week on Saturdays and Wednesdays. My father chose to cut the lawn twice each of these days, a high cut first and then a final lower cut, so as not to shock the lawn. He taught me that it was only appropriate to say that we were mowing the lawn, not cutting the grass because, he would theorize, it's called *lawn tennis*, not *grass tennis*, so we shouldn't ever use the word "grass."

After mowing the lawn, we replaced the net, score poles, and the umpiring chair. Although no official ever sat in the chair, it was my father's belief that I should be trained to the illusion of one being there.

"Yes, indeed, son. You do have the right and obligation to dispute what sometimes rolls off their tongues," he said. "They often confuse that chair with a throne, their *highnasses*."

My father always said that it was in the stars to buy this farm due to the fact that the rear of the house ran north and south, and the pathway that led to the court would be welcomed by the court of a north/south orientation in order for the player to avoid glare at dawn or dusk. When planning his initial design, he chose to transition the pathway to the court with two garden areas for Mama. The two gardens were separated by a pebble walkway leading to the pathway to the court. A bird's-eye view looking down on Mama Evangeline's garden would render the shape of a round tennis ball, a garden to the left and a garden to the right, centered by a parabolic pebble walkway, the seams of the ball the pathways. The end of the walkway intersecting the pathway to the court was exactly thirteen-and-a-half feet wide, the dimension width of the service box and seventy-eight feet to the tennis court, the distance from baseline to baseline.

The pathway leading to the lawn tennis court was a beautiful earth-toned clay, the same clay surface of Stade Roland Garros, home of the French Open, my father's way of walking on hallowed French ground. At exactly thirty-nine feet from the beginning of the pathway, the distance from the baseline to the net, my father had designed and erected a metal archway. One of his proud new fathers, unable to pay monetarily was—my father called him—the "Michelangelo of metalwork." He sculptured the "pearly gate to tennis heaven," which my father designed. He told me the reason for the archway was not only for aesthetic beauty but what it was supposed to represent to me mentally.

"Walk under this archway slowly, son," he said, "because it is symbolic of walking from one side of the net to the other. And as you do, you are entering the other side of the court down match point. The mental strength, focus, and determination of a true champion occur at this moment."

Above the semicircular round top of the green metal archway, there were the perfectly crafted gold-plated numbers "1927." That year was the defining moment when all the tennis gods chose to forever bestow upon France the distinction of having a royal and deserving place in tennis history. The Davis Cup was held in Philadelphia that year at the Germantown Cricket Club, and the events that transpired were shocking. The trophy was captured from the Americans by Jean Borotra, Jacques Brugnon, Henri Cochet, and Rene Lacoste, branded "The Four Musketeers."

My father preferred "The Four Pirates," and he was sure they were ready to escape the City of Brotherly Love with their heads intact. He justified their taking of the Cup as justice for Napoleon Bonaparte because Napoleon and his French soldiers had risked their lives to successfully regain control of Louisiana, which, shortly thereafter, Mr. Thomas Jefferson purchased for a mere three cents per acre from the government of France. My father, holding no unpatriotic grudge and an extremely proud American himself, argued that the price should have been one cent more per acre and been given to Napoleon and his men. After all, they delivered this grand baby to Mr. Thomas Jefferson.

There were four plaques honoring the names of the Musketeers in each corner at the baselines of the Roland Louis Mouton Lawn Tennis Court in Lafayette, Louisiana. True to my father's sense of fairness, the plaque directly in front of the umpire's chair simply read "Napoleon."

"*De rein*, Mr. President, but we French won the Cup," my father said.

Roland Louis Mouton Lawn Tennis Court
Lafayette, Louisiana

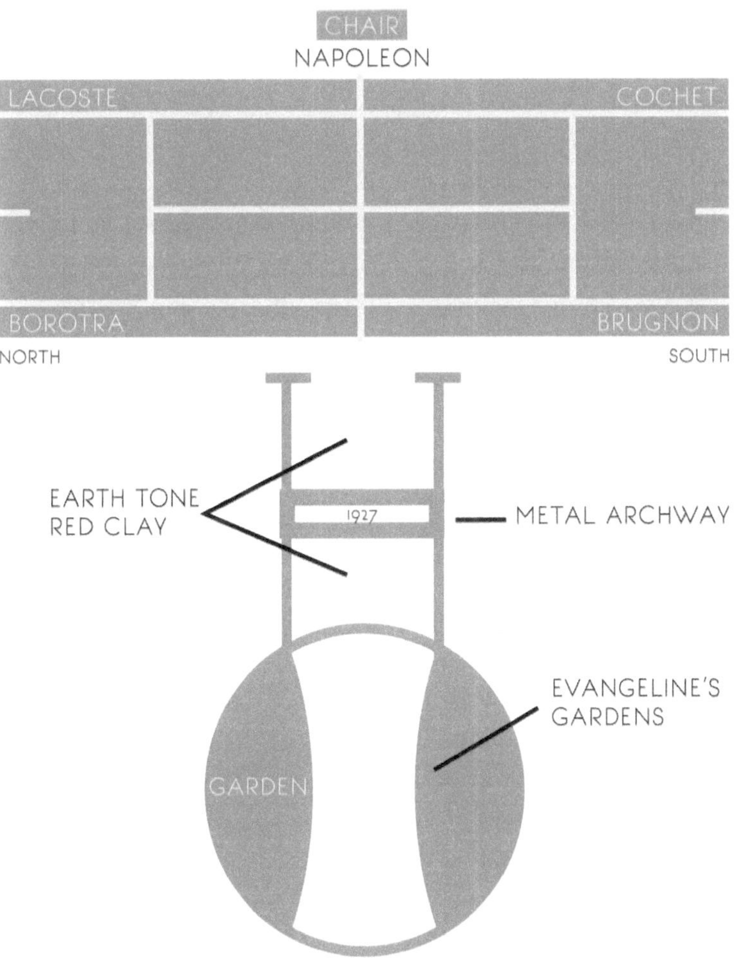

Bones

Bright and early on Saturday mornings, I was awakened by the sounds of Bones humming an old Creole song as he tended to the care of the Roland Louis Mouton Lawn Tennis Court. Bones was a Creole of African descent. He lived down in Broussard and during the week worked in the sugarcane warehouse. My father delivered by house call all of Bones's seven children and, rather than ask for money, he asked for Bones's special skills one morning a week for one year. An additional year was added for each new child. When Bones asked my father what he could offer that was more important than money, my father simply replied, "Chalk." You see, Bones, appointed by the mayor himself, bore the responsibility of laying down all the chalk lines on the playing fields at the Lafayette recreation parks. The chalk lines on my father's tennis courts were not only perfectly straight but were lined with more heart and soul than even the tennis courts of Stade Roland Garros. After lining the court, my father and Bones always shared a glass of lemonade and beignets. My mama would serve Bones Louisiana lemonade—made with freshly squeezed lemons, sugar, and water from the Abita Springs in south Louisiana—and for my father, French lemonade— with Perrier water from the Vergèze commune in the south of France. My father delighted in these moments, hearing stories of Bones's children. He told me Bones was the perfect father. As Bones was about to leave one day, my father said that Bones was the luckiest man in the world.

"I know dat's right," I heard Bones say.

"Yes sir, Bones. Lucky because you were not born with two penises. Had that medical marvel happened, you would have had twice as many kids and be lining chalk here forever."

Upon which they erupted into uncontrollable and uproarious laughter.

Several months later, in the summer of 1949, Dr. Mouton received a call from Bones late one Friday night.

"Dr. Mouton," Bones said after my father picked up the phone. "I 'pologize to ask dis of you, but would you do me du special favor of comin' down to Broussard to check up on a pregnant girl who is having a gone-wrong problem."

"You and Azalee don't leave," my father said. "Stay with the girl. I will have to pick up some things at the hospital, then I'll be right down."

Broussard was home to Bones, his wife Azalee, and their seven children. They lived in a small house by the railroad. The Louisiana and Texas railroad line made one stop in Broussard to pick up the sugar at the Broussard warehouse directly adjacent to the railroad tracks.

"The house is on East Railroad Street 'bout two hundred yawds from du sugar warehouse," Bones explained to my father, "and du faded-out name on du mailbox reads 'Lacroix.' So not to pass by it, you see du porch ceiling and du door trim be haint blue."

Painting porch ceilings haint blue was a very old custom in the South. Haints were restless spirits of the dead that hadn't left the physical world. Haint blue was to these evil spirits their boundary of no entry, and, therefore, the occupants in the house were protected from being taken or influenced by these evil spirits.

The problem with the house, as Bones saw it, was that an occupant of the house, not yet dead, was full of evil and destined to haintism. When my father and mama arrived at the house, Bones and Azalee were standing beside the bed, Azalee holding the young girl's hand and Bones softly reassuring, "Sweet Joline, evuh thang gone be awright now."

Joline was only eighteen years old. She was the prettiest cheerleader in high school. Joline's boyfriend, Jacques Lacroix, had been the beautifully handsome and extremely gifted quarterback of the high school football team and later earned a full scholarship to the University of Louisiana at Lafayette to become a Ragin' Cajun. His star had been huge. He even ended up guiding his team to the conference championship his junior year in college. Before his senior year, Jacques signed a pro football contract, but two months into training camp, he took a crushing blow to his right throwing shoulder. He had become the target of a religiously minded, three-hundred-pound defensive tackle named Jacob who cringed at every roll of Jacques's devilish tongue: "goddamn nigger," "mothafucker," "whore," "slut," "cunt." Jacob had closely minded the sermons of his Baptist preacher and took the many lessons to heart.

"It is the will of God," the preacher had said, "that if ever you have the moment to stand toe-to-toe with the devil himself, it is at that moment, and without guilt, without sorrow, and without one second's hesitation, you should use all the powers given to you by God, and I assure you at that moment—Praise God!—you will be given the extra powers of God to destroy and eliminate that devil and his temptations and evilness."

When Jacques's blocking tackle tripped and fell, Jacob had a clear shot at Jacques, only trailing him by about five yards. At that moment, everything went into slow motion for Jacob. He had come toe-to-toe with the devil, his preacher's voice ringing in his head, and Jacob propelled his three-hundred-pound body airborne, without guilt, without sorrow, and without a second's hesitation, using his power and the extra powers provided by God—Praise God!—to destroy and eliminate the temptations and the evils of the devil.

Jacques Lacroix woke up in the hospital, morphine-sedated, jaw broken, teeth wired shut, and a trapeze holding his right arm. The right shoulder had been totally separated and there was major tendon and ligament damage. The football career of the great Jacques Lacroix had come to a tragic end. Jacques's mother called the hospital from Broussard that afternoon crying. The doctor told her Jacques's football days were done. She had news for him that she thought would boost his spirits.

"Honey, congratulations," his mother said. "Everything will be okay because your pretty Joline is pregnant."

Jacques hung up the phone. His glorious star had suddenly crashed by way of an Oklahoman angel of God, praise God.

"How are her vitals?" my father asked Mama.

"We can't wait any longer," my mother said. "Her vitals are very low."

"Where in the hell is Jacques?" my father asked Bones.

"He ain't been around in du house in three days," Bones said. "He on a drunk, gambling at dat horse track down New Awleans way."

The C-section delivery was perfect. Joline had a healthy baby boy with crystal-blue eyes, golden olive skin, and curly, jet-black hair. Joline asked my father to name her son.

"I offer the name Rene Pierre for these reasons, Joline: Rene Lacoste is the name of one of the most famous athletes in French history and Pierre was my father's name."

"Oh, thank you," Joline said. "God bless you, Dr. Mouton."

"Bones, will you follow me out to the car, please?" my father asked after they walked out of the house. "Bones, give these six tennis balls to Joline and tell her these are for her baby boy's crib toys."

Bones smiled. "Winnin' a bagel, dat right, Dr. Mouton?"

"That's right, Bones, and *jeu de paumme.*"

As my father and mother were leaving Broussard, they came to the railroad tracks and the arm came down. The L&T line rumbled by, one hundred yards from the house with the faded name Lacroix on the mailbox and the haint-blue porch ceiling. It blew the whistle six times.

"Oh, what a beautiful night," Mama said. My father smiled at her.

As it turned out, the first word ever spoken by Rene Pierre Lacroix at the age of eleven months wasn't "mommy" or "daddy" but "train," and that is what his Mama Joline decided to call him.

On his travels south of Lafayette, my father dropped by the Lacroix house on occasion to say hello and check on Joline and Train. He knew that the father, Jacques, was hardly ever home, and if he was, he'd usually be drunk. Jacques was physically abusive to Train and Joline. He considered them both an exclamation point to his bad luck in life. When Train turned six years old, my father gifted him a tennis racquet.

"Bones," my father said, "you tell Joline to let Train run over to the railroad warehouse and hit balls against that wall. She can watch him from the back porch. Good exercise for the boy."

It was against those warehouse walls that Train learned to create different spins on the ball and learned to react when the ball bounced back. He painted targets on the wall to work on better accuracy. He hit the ball high, low left, low right, back spin, top spin, and back over his head.

Jacques, returning home drunk, was mad at that old doctor. He didn't have the right to name his boy, and he shouldn't be around giving Train a tennis racquet. The bile from Jacques's mouth came quick.

"Joline," he shouted, "I don't want this boy playing no girly-ass game like tennis." He grabbed the racquet and threw it out the back door and left, gone for another three or four days.

Over the following years, Train found his escape on that railroad warehouse wall with his birthday tennis racquet and the tennis balls sent to him periodically from Dr. Mouton by way of Bones. Train had actually painted on the warehouse's wooden door a resemblance of his father. His hatred for this door was his serving target. By the time he was eleven, this door was splintered, smashed, and rocked off the hinges. Jacques Lacroix's abuse to his wife and son began to spiral out of control, known all too well by Bones who would pass by their backyard on his walk to the sugarcane warehouse by way of an old logging road behind the Lacroix house. Jacques once threw young Train into a closet and, before locking the door, pissed on the floor. On another occasion, he tied Train into a chair and cut all his curly black hair off. The kids made fun of him when he returned to school.

Joline, afraid for her and Train's lives, wouldn't agree to testify against Jacques. He threatened her that if she ever said anything she would never see the boy again. Late one Friday night after a three-day gambling—and losing—binge,

Jacques returned home drunk and badly abused Joline, slapping, punching, breaking her wrist, and raping her. Joline and Train snuck out of the house at five o'clock in the morning and headed down to her mother's house in New Iberia. Jacques woke up around eight o'clock to find "that bitch" and his boy were gone. He started drinking again.

Across town, the phone rang in the Mouton household.

"Hello, Dr. Mouton, this is Sheriff Lloyd down in Broussard."

"Hello, Sheriff," my father said.

"We need your help on this beautiful Saturday, unfortunately. The coroner is on vacation, and I have a dead body I need to write a report on."

"We are headed down to the Gumbo Festival in New Iberia anyway, so I'll see you about two o'clock," my father said. "Oh, and Sheriff, why don't you pass a law that it is a felony to die on the Saturday of the Gumbo Festival?"

When Dr. Mouton and Evangeline arrived at the police station, Sheriff Lloyd was waiting beside his patrol car.

"Evangeline, why don't you go on down to the Gumbo Festival," my father said, "and I'll ride on down with Lloyd after we finish up here."

The sheriff drove the patrol car up behind the ambulance, which had no sirens going. It was just idling, waiting to take a lifeless body away. My father knew the house by its haint-blue porch ceiling and the faded "Lacroix" on the mailbox. They went around to the backyard. The two ambulance drivers were casually sitting on the broken picnic bench, eating steamed crawfish. The body of Jacques Lacroix was lying faceup at the very rear of his backyard, halfway into the old logging road. Jacques's pistol was on the ground above his right shoulder. There were two gunshot wounds, one to the shoulder and one below his right ear.

The sheriff said they received a phone call about twelve o'clock from a phone booth located somewhere up in Carencro. "A man lookin' dead gone in his backyard," the informant said.

"See anyone around?" the sheriff asked the ambulance drivers.

"Nope. Everybody's gone on down to the Gumbo Festival."

"What do you make of this, Doc?"

"There are signs of a struggle," my father said, "based on the scratch marks around the wrists, neck, and ears. In my opinion, it's not a robbery. Nothing of value to steal, anyway. Maybe an argument over a gambling debt or a husband been cheated on come to get even. He smells strongly of alcohol. He's probably been drinking all morning. Report the time of death to the coroner at about ten or ten thirty, Sheriff."

"Hey, can we take him now, Sheriff?" the ambulance driver asked. "The gumbo's getting cold down in New Iberia."

The official police report read, "Death by gunshot. Suicide or homicide undetermined. No witnesses and no physical evidence present."

When the sheriff gave the news of Jacques's death to Joline and Train, the twelve-year-old Train, without a tear in his young eyes, told the sheriff to make sure he was really dead.

"He is dead and gone, son," the sheriff said.

The coroner agreed with my father's assessment. The sheriff's report was accepted and the file closed, but one thing still bothered the sheriff.

"Why in the world did Jacques Lacroix have what appeared to be traces of white powder on the back of his neck?" the sheriff asked my father at lunch a few weeks later. He thought maybe Jacques had stumbled over to the sugarcane warehouse and was on his way back when the incident happened, supposing the substance on Jacques's neck was white sugar.

Bones had never been late on the Saturday mornings he came to our house to line the tennis courts with chalk. But on the Saturday of Jacques's death, he didn't come around until about one o'clock in the afternoon, much later than normal. Bones wanted to explain his tardiness, but my father had to leave to meet the sheriff, and Bones didn't get the chance to explain. But days later, my father had a curious thought. He had seen Bones use the pay phone outside the drugstore in Carencro before, and other than sugar, there was a similar substance that was also a white powder, but my father didn't pay it much more thought.

Two weeks after Jacques's death, two painters and two carpenters from Crowley came over to fix up Joline and Train's house. The men repaired and repainted everything and threw in new shutters, a brand-new mailbox, a new picnic table in the backyard, and a new haint-blue ceiling, compliments of Dr. Mouton's patients, payment for several baby deliveries.

Train

Several months after Jacques's death, my father was on his way back from the sugarcane warehouse in Broussard one hot August afternoon after performing physical checkups for some of the employees when the long railroad arms came down on the tracks. Glancing over toward the sugar warehouse, he saw young Train hitting tennis balls against the warehouse wall. It was now about six o'clock in the evening. He pulled across the tracks, parked the car, and walked over and sat down at the picnic table the warehouse workers used at lunchtime. He was not more than fifty feet away, watching intently as Train hit serve after serve at a wooden door. Train wasn't aware of my father's presence. My father lowered his horn-rimmed glasses. There was a cartoonish rendering of a man's face on the door, big pointed teeth, a scowling smile, red eyes, and devilish horns atop the head, with the initials J. L. below. Train's serves hit the target where the teeth were drawn every time. Each and every time, the old wooden door splintered and wood chips flew through the air like firewood being destroyed by an ax.

My father knew who was being destroyed on the old wooden door. My father eased himself off the bench and called out to Train, who kept serving and destroying the target. My father walked up behind and tapped Train on the shoulder. Train, frightened, turned and raised his racquet, but quickly recognized my father. My father saw a look in his eyes that screamed of ferocity, hatred, and intense concentration. It was the look of a grown man trying to destroy something or somebody, and in a matter of seconds the look in his eyes disappeared and the little boy my father knew came back to life behind those sky-blue eyes.

"Hello there, Train," my father said. "You sure are showing some great form with that tennis racquet for such a young boy."

"Thanks, Dr. Mouton," Train said. "I come here about every day. Have been for the last six years, practicing my serves and shots and playing those four guys on the wall and pretending I'm playing those four guys in the book."

"And who would those four guys be, Train?"

"The four guys in the tennis book that you gave Mr. Bones to give to me, the one I read over and over 'cause I get better and better. Mr. Bones wrote their names on the wall in different-colored chalk for me and said I would be a great tennis player one day if I played like the Four Musketeers from France."

My father asked Train if he would like to come up to see his backyard tennis court the next Saturday morning. Bones would bring Train up at eight o'clock and there Train would be introduced to the Roland Louis Mouton Lawn Tennis Court.

On his drive back home that evening, my father could not erase from his mind the fiery will he had just witnessed in young Train. He had witnessed this kind of will at a Wimbledon championship in his favorite player, the great Pancho Gonzales. Pancho Gonzales, at the age of forty-one, played a Puerto Rican by the name of Charlie Pasarell who was sixteen years younger. Gonzales's "cannonball" serve was dominant and overpowering, and he played a "serve and volley" style game: serve, then rush the net and hit the opponent's return before it hit the ground. This strategy was so dominant that the rules of tennis were changed so that "the ball must bounce once before the server can return." This rule would eventually be changed back. Their battle was a five-hour-and-twelve-minute epic, 22-24, 1-6, 16-14, 6-3, 11-9, Gonzales the winner. In the final set, Gonzales saved match point seven times and twice came back from Love-40. "Unbelievable," my father would say. This match would be the advent of the "tiebreak" scoring system.

My father recognized this same fiery will that Friday evening down in Broussard at the warehouse wall by the dirt road and the railroad tracks, the wooden splinters flying off the old wooden door serve after serve. He had to do everything in his power to give young Train every opportunity to take his game to the highest level. He had that killer instinct, my father knew. Train, like the great Pancho, wouldn't even blink an eye at Love-40.

Two years later my father called me and asked if I would come home and play a couple of games with young Train. He might just finally have a thoroughbred on his court, he told me. I was then in my first year of graduate school at LSU in Baton Rouge and had completed my four-year under-graduate degree at the University of Louisiana, Lafayette. My ambition and career path was to one day be the athletic director at a university in Louisiana.

I would never win the Oyster Bay Classic tournament down in New Orleans on Memorial Day weekends like my father's dream. During my senior year in high school, I made it to the quarterfinals, but my talent had pretty much peaked by then. My father would have to keep on dreaming of an Acadian winning the Oyster Bay Classic. I played tennis my freshman and sophomore years at Lafayette, but a rotator cuff injury in the conference championship ended my competitive college tennis dreams.

When I arrived at my parents' house about nine o'clock Saturday morning and saw Bones's pickup truck out to the side driveway, I knew he'd just freshly chalked the lines. I saw my dad and Bones sitting in the French chairs, sipping their French and American lemonades and savoring some beignets. I looked out onto the Roland Louis Mouton Lawn Tennis Court and saw my mother hand-cranking the tennis ball machine around and around, shooting balls across the net to Train.

This hand-and-arm-cranked tennis ball machine was the first in the history of the game and, as my father frequently announced to everyone, the machine was the invention of the genius mind of the great French tennis player Rene Lacoste.

I went directly to the courtside French table to give a big kiss to my mother and a handshake and hug to the King.

"Hello, Dad," I said. "So great to see you too, Bones."

"How dem grades at school?" Bones asked.

"All straight As, Bones. Just as straight as your chalk lines."

Dad wanted me to evaluate Train's form and movement. The Saturday morning was bright and beautiful, and a cool breeze was in the air as Train and I began to warm up. I had only seen Train hitting balls against the warehouse wall years ago on a trip I made down to the sugarcane warehouse in Broussard with my father. Train was much smaller then, but he seemed to have pretty good form. I wasn't a competitive player anymore, but I was still pretty good on the courts. The rotator cuff was okay, and I was still in good shape. After playing with Train for about thirty minutes, I first noticed his footwork. My impression of him was that he was quick and that he slid and glided and floated with the grace of a dancer.

"Okay, time to get serious, Train," I said. "We'll let those two umpires and the one umpirette judge who can win the first annual Roland Louis Mouton French Lemonade Championship today."

Train's first three or four practice serves took me by surprise: three aces and one let, all traveling over ninety miles per hour. Train won the first two games quite easily. The third game I amped up and served some ninety-plussers, but he still managed to return them. I had a lot of experience behind me, and I had home court advantage. I won the next two games. It was 2-2 then. We started to play at a higher intensity level, and he was much quicker than I was. He was running me all over the court and his serves, fast and spinning, were devastating. I won one more game and then lost the set with close scores in all three games. Rene Pierre Lacroix, Train, won 6-3. He was the winner of the first Roland Louis Mouton French Lemonade Championship.

As we approached the net to shake hands, I gazed at him. I knew that I, still a fairly young man, had not just played a young boy, but that I had just played a young boy who would quickly become a man playing against boys in a short time. The umpires and umpirette applauded Train's victory. Train smiled from ear to ear and got big hugs from his three adoring fans.

And for the record, this was not a charity match. I was playing to win. As we sat to have some refreshments, I asked, "Train, I know you like tennis but what other hobbies do you have?"

"None really," Train said. "I love tennis all the time."

"Oh, yes you do have du hobbies," Bones said. He turned to me. "He got detractifier hobbies."

"What are you talking about, Bones?" I asked.

"You know, Louie. Du ones dat have pretty legs and pretty hair."

"Bones, are you saying Train has him a girlfriend?"

"Louie, Train have so many little girls 'round Acadiana dat want him, it would take two Louisiana tugboats to pull 'em all away."

"That's all right, Train," I said. "Just take your time with all them detractifiers, son."

It was then two o'clock, and Bones and Train were headed back down to Broussard. Bones had to chalk some baseball fields and Train and Joline were headed down to New Iberia to visit with his grandmother.

My father had spent a lot of time teaching Train the different grips, and it was pretty amazing that at only fourteen, he already had a mastery of the Continental, Western, Eastern, and Midwestern. My father explained that he had spent a lot of time with Train on the importance of different grips. He was talented enough to play the one or two position on most high school tennis teams. I knew Train was way beyond his years. He had serious game and even more talent. He was going to go a long way. He was the most talented fourteen-year-old I had ever seen.

Joline and Train's house was on the north side of Broussard, and the public Beaver Park Tennis Center was about five miles up the road from there. My father sat on the Lafayette Parks and Recreation board and was aware that Mr. Cristola, the tennis director, had free tennis camps and lessons throughout the year. My father asked him to take Train as a full-time student year round. Seeing as my father had delivered his children, he immediately answered, "Yes, of course, Dr. Mouton."

Train's transportation from the Broussard middle school and back home each day was the only challenge. He was told to be at the tennis center at four thirty, four days a week, and back home to Broussard by six thirty for supper and schoolwork. Ms. Alida, who lived close to the Lacroix house on Robicheaux Road and was a friend of Joline's, just so happened to be the secretary to the general manager of the Lafayette Airport right across the street from Beaver Park, and she happily agreed to pick Train up every day at six o'clock for the ride home.

On one of his visits down to Avery Island, my father found out that a very special person who worked there left Mondays through Thursdays at three o'clock to head up the youth program for the special needs children at the Heyman Park activities building and playgrounds which wasn't far from Beaver Park, only separated by the Bayou Vermilion. The beautiful Ms. Irma Jean Boudreaux of New Iberia agreed wholeheartedly to the pleasure of picking Train up at school and taking him to Beaver Park by four thirty. Train's time at Beaver Park was the beginning of something special between him and Irma because, as fate would have it, Irma would meet a man who would change her life and reunite Train and Irma so many years later.

Irma

Irma Jean Boudreaux was born in New Iberia, Louisiana, home of the annual Gumbo Festival. She was raised by her grandfather, Mr. Maurice Boudreaux. His worthless son had run off with another woman to Florida soon after Irma was born. Her mother left two years later for New Orleans to run a bar and party scene. Irma was born with beautiful red hair and freckles that seemed to sparkle and dance on her skin. Her crystal-clear green eyes were hypnotic and enchanting. Mr. Maurice—"Mo," they called him—had a great sense of humor and loved to laugh and decided that he'd do everything in his power, and God willing he did, to make sure that Irma would grow up a happy and fun-loving child.

Upon graduating high school, she went to work for McIlhenny Company across the road from New Iberia as a tour guide and retail worker in the TABASCO Country Store where they sold their hot sauces, clothing, and other products promoting the TABASCO name. Three years later, the position of marketing and promotions director became available. During Irma's three-year management of the country store, sales had risen more than 40 percent annually, a record for the company. Irma was asked by the board in her interview how she had accomplished this record feat. She simply said she acted friendly and gracious, and when she thought a customer might leave without buying something, she'd say, "If you don't buy one of our sauces today, there may not be any spice in your life tomorrow." Upon which the board broke out into uncontrollable and uproarious laughter.

While working the country store one day, a young college student about her age came in around four o'clock for the tour. The boy's name was H. A. Kersh Jr. The tours had ended that Friday afternoon at four o'clock, but good-hearted Irma said, "It's fine. I'll take you on a tour. I have no plans for later anyway."

TABASCO-brand original red-pepper sauce, Irma explained, was created from the 1868 recipe of Mr. Edmund McIlhenny and was aged up to three years in old Jack Daniels whiskey barrels. The recipe included red tabasco peppers grown on the island, vinegar, and salt from an old Avery Island salt mine. Avery Island's salt dome structure was a geologic formation of the earth rich with pockets of oil and gas deposits.

As it turned out, H. A. Jr.'s livelihood was all about oil and gas. He was from Santa Barbara, California, the son of an oil engineer who invested in an oil-drilling operation off the Summerland pier in California, the first offshore well in the world. His father hit the mother lode and made millions. He sent Junior to the University of Louisiana, Lafayette, for an advanced degree in petroleum engineering. He demanded that each summer Junior remain in Louisiana and work some weeks out on the offshore rigs in the Gulf of Mexico.

"You ain't gonna be no silver-spooned kid," his father's mantra went. "You gotta earn your way to the top of the company."

The beautiful red-haired Irma told me that upon leaving that Friday afternoon, H. A. Jr. asked her, "Of all your pepper sauces, which is the hottest?"

"Why, the red one, of course," she said with a wink and a smile.

H. A. Kersh Jr. had been pierced by Cupid's red-hot-pepper arrow.

Before heading over for Train's afternoon match one day, Irma picked up H. A. and went to one of her favorite lunchtime places down on St. John Street in Lafayette, Johnson's Boucaniere, a meat-smoking and butcher store. She was excited to introduce H. A. to their famous boudin, a spicy pork mixed with onions, cooked rice, herbs, and stuffed in a sausage casing developed by Johnson's Grocery in 1937 in Eunice, Louisiana. She told H. A. they measured the original recipe in small Dixie cups. H. A. loved the pork boudin and Mrs. Lou's gumbo. They also had a special treat, the bread pudding with praline sauce. Irma had her favorite, the Zydeco Special, a mixed beef and pork sandwich with mayonnaise, mustard, lettuce, and tomatoes.

After lunch, they drove over toward the Bayou Vermilion, which flowed between Heyman Park and Beaver Park. The Beaver Park tennis complex was quite impressive. It had thirteen lighted courts and was surrounded by the beauty of Louisiana palm trees. There were hundreds of people there from all over the state that day. Junior State champions would be crowned in both the boys' and girls' singles and boys' and girls' doubles divisions. When H. A. and Irma arrived, they were told that the semifinals boys' match would take place on court six. It was between Train, seeded fourth, and a fifteen-year-old from Baton Rouge, seeded second.

The number-one seeded boy was a sixteen-year-old from New Orleans who held a top ten juniors national ranking. He defeated his semifinal opponent, 6-3, 6-4, and 6-2 in straight sets. Train's first two sets with the fifteen-year-old from Baton Rouge were not very tough for Train, but they were hard fought. The score in the first set was Train, 6-4, and the second set, 6-3, but by the third set, the kid from Baton Rouge had been worn out by Train's short volleying and power serves. During five of these games, Train's service had gone to Love-40, all but one of which he would come back to win seemingly at will. Between sets two and three, my father had Bones deliver a message to Train.

"Tell him I said to get out of the 'tank' now," my father said.

"What does that mean?" Bones asked.

My father explained he meant Train was losing some points on purpose, playing around with the opponent. Train got the message—doctor's orders—and in a hurry, finished the third set quickly. The kid from Baton Rouge only won one game. Train, 6-1. Train's serves rocketed with power and precision, and his winning points were decisive and accurate.

The championship match began later in the afternoon between Train and the heralded number-one seed from New Orleans. Train, like his father, was blessed with a very large and statuesque build. At fourteen, he was already six feet tall and weighed a chiseled one hundred and sixty pounds. He had quick feet and a strong upper body from years of pounding tennis balls against the warehouse wall and working weekends lifting fifty-pound sacks of sugar, loading them onto the L&T train cars. The New Orleans kid was six feet one inch tall and weighed one hundred and eighty pounds. The first set was hard fought and Train lost 6-4. Two service games went to Love-40, and Train came back to deuce but lost both games, the deciding points in the first set.

The second set through game six, at 3-3, had the same tempo and volleying as the first set. The seventh game, Train went to Love-40 again but served four straight aces to add out. The next serve went wide and his second serve, unlike the rest of the day, had some speed taken off. The sixteen-year-old return served to the corner baseline. Train raced over to make an impossible return, a baseline high lob. His opponent returned the lob and moved forward to the net. Train had anticipated the volley and raised his racquet. He smiled and hit a smashing ball between the legs of the sixteen-year-old. Train, 4-3.

These five points changed the whole tone for the opponent. He began playing defensively. In game five, Train broke serve and was 5-3. He won his serve, 6-3, and had beaten the heralded sixteen-year-old, the kid's only set loss since entering the tournament. The third set started all tied, 4-4. The two were exchanging courts and walking down the net.

"You just got lucky in that second set, you Lafayette trash," the kid said. "I'm gonna whip your ass like I'm your old man, you swamp gator piece of shit."

When Train got to the baseline to take serve in game nine, he faced the rear toward the Bayou Vermilion and, in that instant, he saw the door of the warehouse wall and his father's face.

"Mr. Lacroix, are you ready to receive serve?" the chair umpire called to Train twice.

"Yes sir," Train said quietly.

Train ran the sixteen-year-old all over the court at will. He had a hard and stoic face, bearing no smiles and no expression as he broke serve.

Train, at 5-4, served for the championship. The first two points were aces and the third, a double fault, 30-15. The fourth point was a lob volley over Train's head which he seemed to give up on, deuce. The fifth point was another double fault, giving his opponent 40-30.

Next Train hit a powerful serve, impossible to reach, ace. The next point, another ace, add in, Train. Train took the ball and turned toward the bayou again. He got set and served right into the strength of the opponent. Train hit and spun shots at will. He had studied the moves and knew that a shot straight back to the middle baseline would bring the sixteen-year-old toward the net and that the speed of his shot would only get him a little past midcourt and that this shot would set him up to deliver a smashing overhand not just to win, but to take him down.

As Train's racquet came down, it sent his most brutal power shot at the perfect location. He had hit that shot hundreds of times at the warehouse wall. As the sixteen-year-old just barely got by midcourt, the ball came at him like it was shot out of a gun. He was handcuffed. He jumped to get out of the way, but the ball hit him right in the stomach, a "brutalizer." The kid fell and grabbed his belly. Train waited at the net. The sixteen-year-old only came within five feet of the net so as not to shake hands. Train showed no reaction to the victory. He looked into the eyes of his highly ranked opponent and said, "Next time don't come up to the swamp, you Big Easy piece of gator bait."

The crowd went crazy. A player from the Acadiana region had never won a junior state championship before and Irma was screaming and crying with joy.

The trophy remained in the trophy case at Beaver Park for a year. People at Beaver Park went crazy over Train's victory. It was great to see the joy and excitement of all the friendly people witnessing one of their own capture the first junior state championship ever. H. A. commented to Irma that he had only seen a combination of size, power, speed, and smartness on a tennis court once before, and for that kid to handle such an advanced game was unreal.

"It was like Train played a combination of styles of two players I used to watch in California, Pancho Gonzales and Pancho Segura," H. A. said. "Train looks like he might be just as good as them one day if he keeps at it. He has a bright future."

H. A. invited Irma to dinner that night, just the two of them. As the couple waited for their food, H. A. directed the table conversation into the direction of where Irma's life was taking her, her wishes, and her happiness. She said she was quite happy but knew there would be a big void in life without her grandfather—her grandfather had died a week prior, and H. A. went to the funeral, which was well attended—but that she'd have much more time to spend with her children's foundation.

After dinner, as they were driving away from the restaurant, Irma turned on the car radio which was set to the local station. Clifton Chenier was singing a song, "Eh, Petite Fille," that to H. A. was all about Irma. Shortly after H. A. first met Irma, he was getting to liking Zydeco music. She explained to him "Zydeco" was French, meaning, "You's too poor to afford salt meat for the snap beans."

Clifton Chenier was to an accordion what Picasso was to a paintbrush, Irma's grandfather Maurice once told her. Her grandfather told H. A. he didn't know which the doctor delivered first from Clifton's mama's womb, the accordion or the baby. Irma told H. A. that Clifton thought up the vest frottoir—a metal washboard that hung over the shoulders and played with spoons—for his brother Cleveland who played in the band. It was fabricated by Mr. Willie Landry of Port Arthur, Texas, and the vest frottoir was now proudly on exhibit in the Smithsonian in Washington, DC.

Listening to that song of Chenier's in the car, H. A. asked Irma to drive to the Cathedral of Saint John the Evangelist on St. John Street, probably the most beautiful church he had ever seen. A week earlier, the funeral of Mr. Maurice Boudreaux of New Iberia, Louisiana, Irma's grandfather, had occupied the grand cathedral.

As they walked toward the archway and entrance to the cemetery, H. A. reached for Irma's hand. The sunset was turning the beautiful colors of a painted sky. The softness and soothing colors of the sunset had turned from a brilliant orange to a bright pink, the waving arms of white clouds brushing the majestic painting of the Almighty. They slowly approached the headstone of Irma's granddaddy at the back of the graveyard. H. A.'s heart pounded. He stood facing Mr. Maurice's final resting place and went to one knee, touched the headstone, bowed his head, and said a short prayer. The sunset shifted to a deeper pink and a radiantly deep-blue sky above. He turned to Irma who had tears in her eyes.

She placed her hand on her grandfather's name on the headstone and whispered a prayer. She stood and put her arms around H. A. and her head on his chest. She stepped back and kissed him on the lips as tears flowed from her eyes.

As they walked out of the cemetery underneath and beyond the archway leading into the St. John's cemetery, H. A. turned Irma around for the stillness and beauty of one last look at the ceremonious sunset. This was the moment he told her he loved her and could not live without her and asked her to marry him. He had found his soul mate, the woman he wanted to live with forever.

They married in the Cathedral of Saint John the Evangelist, and they happily went on their way to Bellagio Road in the Bel Air Estates in Southern California.

Simone

Train started tenth grade. He practiced and played tennis all the time he could. He had a friend named Claude who he met at the Beaver Park tennis courts a couple years earlier who played on the Lafayette High School football team.

Claude was not a tennis player, but his mama, Simone, and sister, Betsy, played at Beaver Park. Betsy had been a pretty good junior player and won a tournament, so she was often at the park. That year she was a sophomore at LSU. Claude's mom played in the afternoon ladies league year round, so Train saw her often in the fall and spring during his after-school lessons and practices. She played tennis very well. She was a lefty. Simone and Betsy were both very pretty. Simone had been a homecoming queen, a cheerleader, and won the crown at some Acadiana festivals. Betsy had been a cheerleader in high school too and had a reputation of really liking the boys a little too much. Train had often practiced and played against Betsy and even one time played a set against Simone. Claude's daddy, Von, was not much of an athlete. His thing was hunting and fishing, which he and Claude did a lot of in the fall.

One Thursday afternoon early in Train's first tenth-grade semester, Claude came to pick up his mama at the Beaver Park tennis courts, and Train was over hitting balls on the blue wall, practicing drop lob shots.

"Boy, why you practice so much?" Claude asked. "You just won the junior state championship this summer."

"Always trying to get better, Claude," Train said.

"Hey, what you doin' tomorrow night?"

"Nothing," Train said. He lobbed a few more shots.

"Why don't you spend the night with me and come watch my high school football team play Friday night?"

Before Train could answer, Claude hollered over to his mama on the court and asked, "Can Train spend the night tomorrow night, Mama?"

"Sure, honey. Just make sure his mom knows," she said with a raised voice.

Betsy had gone back to LSU her sophomore year, a cheerleader for the football Tigers, no more tennis, but she was coming home that weekend and bringing her new friend to the football game at Claude's high school. Her friend was a cutie from New Orleans and their names matched, the two Betsys. They all took off from Claude's house about six o'clock Friday night—Train, the two Betsys, Simone, and her husband Von—to do a little tailgating before the seven o'clock kickoff.

Claude was a fast defensive back. He had two interceptions that night and ran one back for a touchdown. Train was sitting between the two Betsys when Claude ran into the end zone. They started screaming and jumping up and down. They both hugged Train and kissed him on his cheeks.

Train hadn't seen Betsy in about two years since she had gone off to LSU, but she was really pretty now and blessed in a way she hadn't been in high school. Train himself had grown about two inches to almost six feet tall, big for a tenth grader. Claude's team won the game 21-20, the other team having missed a two-pointer going for the win. When they got back to the house, Von said to Claude and Train, "We just had two guys cancel on us for our hunting trip. Do you guys want to go over to the hunting club in Mississippi with me tonight?"

"Shoot yeah, Dad," Claude said. "Let's go, Train."

But Train knew he couldn't.

"I have matches with some college guys from Tulane tomorrow," Train said. He told them that it was all right, that they should go ahead and go on without him.

"Train, you're going to spend the night with me and the girls anyway," Simone said, joining the conversation. "Your mom went out dancing and won't be home till late. It'll be fine if you stay with us."

Claude and Von got their hunting gear together and took off for the hunting club over in Mississippi. Simone and the girls decided to watch a movie with some pizza and popcorn. The Betsys had gone out across town to rent the movie, leaving Train alone in the house with Simone.

"They won't be long, Train," Simone said. "You can go in the den and turn on the TV, or I have a new tennis magazine on the table you can read. I'll be right back." She left the room and walked down the hall.

Sitting in their living room, Train wasn't really happy that Claude decided to take off hunting with his dad and leave him all alone with two college girls and his mother to watch a chick flick. He was flipping through Simone's new tennis magazine and decided to go to the kitchen and get a drink. The Betsys should have been back by then, but they probably ran into some high school friends. The kitchen was at the back of the house. As Train walked down the hallway, he saw the door to Claude's parents' bedroom was open and heard Simone humming. He wanted to ask her if it was okay to grab a root beer out of the refrigerator. He stuck his head in the door and noticed the bathroom door was wide open. He froze. Across the room, he saw her in the shower. He stared at her naked body.

Train's mama had asked him a couple of years ago to go up into the attic and get some news articles about Jacques because there was a reporter there doing an article on him. When Train picked up the old articles, there was a *Playboy* magazine underneath. He had never seen a naked woman before that moment. He took his mama the articles and took the magazine to his room. He looked at that magazine often. He had never seen any girl or woman with all their clothes off, only models and women at the park pools in little bathing suits.

He stood there in the hallway in Claude's house hypnotized. Simone's body was as beautiful as any naked woman in that *Playboy* magazine. Her legs were long and slender, her shapely butt a perfect peach with little tan lines, her back and shoulders tapered down to her thin waist. She bent over to put more of the body wash on her knees. The lather and the water mixed, a white, creamy river streaming slowly down between her rounded cheeks and between her legs, a milky waterfall all the way down to her feet. She was still humming a song. He couldn't move. She turned around. Her eyes were closed. She squeezed the wash bottle with both hands and began massaging the lather onto her breasts. The milky white lather, cascading like teardrops down her body. She kept squeezing her breasts. She moved her other hand down to her stomach and between her legs, slowly moving her fingers back and forth. She was moaning and groaning, in a world of her own. He couldn't move. He stood there watching her. He was frozen in a childlike trance.

Train heard car doors slam. The Betsys were back. He quickly returned to the den, sat down on the couch, and picked up Simone's tennis magazine and put it over his lap. The girls walked in.

"Did you miss us, Train?" Claude's sister asked.

"Just been reading some tennis magazines," Train said.

"You need some distraction from all that tennis," the other Betsy said. "Maybe a girlfriend or two."

"Maybe like us," Claude's sister said. "Where's Mama?"

Train choked. "Uh, I guess she must be back in the kitchen," he said. "I don't know. She's been back there since y'all left."

"Mama," Betsy called out. They started walking down the hall toward the kitchen. "Did you take a shower, Mama?"

"Yes, honey," Simone said from the other room. "I was a little hot and sticky from the ball game. I feel much better now."

"Okay, let's watch the movie now," Claude's sister said.

Train remained sitting on the couch. Simone came in the den and sat down beside him. He picked up a flowery scent. She was wearing a pair of pink shorts and a skimpy T-shirt with the golden flashy letters of LSU Tigers. He pictured the perfume fragrances flowing from her braless breasts.

"I'm sorry the guys took off," Simone said. "They love hunting." She put her hand on his knee, squeezed it, and patted his thigh. "We can have some fun with the movie and those crazy girls." She squeezed his leg again. Train had no control over what was happening. He was excited, hard as a rock, and he didn't want it to go away. The Betsys came back from the kitchen with the popcorn, and Train had trouble getting the private movie in his mind to go away. The actual movie started, and Simone curled her legs up on the couch beside him. Her shorts rode further up her thighs and tighter between her legs. Luckily, the tennis magazine was still across his lap.

Once the movie ended, Simone said, "Train, I hope you had a good time with our little slumber party tonight. We enjoyed having you. You can come spend the night any time. You're always welcome."

Train promised he would definitely visit again as soon as he could. He told the Betsys goodnight and closed the door to Claude's bedroom. The vision of Simone in the shower was fresh in his mind. He had never experienced that kind of sexual excitement before. As he slowly drifted off to sleep, a fantasy awakened.

The door opened.

"Good morning," Simone said. "Ready for a little breakfast wake-me-up?"

"Yes ma'am," Train said.

Simone still had her nightgown on and a pink blindfold around her neck. Claude left his dirty football uniform on the floor, and when Simone bent over to pick up the uniform, the top of her nightgown fell open. There they were again. Train was looking at her beautiful breasts. She rose slowly back up and smiled, her silky gown falling against her body. Then she asked Train if he had any sweet dreams. *Yes*, he thought, *it was all a sweet dream*. The sweetest dream he ever had.

"Breakfast in about thirty minutes, honey," Simone then said.

Train didn't understand what was happening to him.

"All right, girls," Train heard Simone call down the hall. "Get some showers and breakfast. You two need to be back in Baton Rouge by ten thirty for the game."

Train heard the girls murmur some sign of acknowledgment through the wall.

"Train, you can shower after the girls leave," Simone said. "Use my shower. Betsy's has clothes all over it, and Claude's has some football-field mud in there from last night's game, and I haven't cleaned it yet."

Train was breathless. *Her* shower. His match was at eleven thirty. It was only nine thirty, plenty of time, he figured, before he needed to be at Beaver Park to turn in his registration form. Simone was in the kitchen, cleaning, still in her nightgown. Train wrapped a towel around his waist and walked into her bedroom to the glass-walled shower. He walked slowly through Simone's bedroom. He could hear her humming in the kitchen. Her bed was still unmade. He could see the wrinkles in the satin sheets where she had slept. He touched the sheets with his hand and could smell her perfume. There was a candle on her nightstand and a paperback book beside it titled *The Passions*. There was a bottle of perfume next to the bed with the word "Delicacy" calligraphied across the front.

Train dropped the towel from his waist to enter the shower. He looked over and saw on her vanity chair a pair of pink bikini panties with white lace on the front and white hearts on the back. He could still hear her in the kitchen. He put the silk pink panties in his hands. He put them down and went into the waterfall shower. He used the same jasmine and vanilla body wash she used. He had it all over himself, his eyes closed, excited, imagining he was about to—

"Train, honey, here is a fresh towel for you," Simone interrupted. "I will lay it right here beside the sink. Do you need anything else?"

Train's eyes shot open. "No ma'am," he said hurriedly.

Once she was gone, he turned around. The pink panties were gone. She had been in the same room with him only three feet away. He had left the bathroom door open. Had she seen him? He rinsed off and got out of the shower and put the fresh towel around his waist. Walking through her bedroom he saw the nightstand drawer was open. There inside the drawer was one of those things he'd seen advertised in the *Playboy* magazine. It was purple and long and rubbery and curved, the advertised magical wand with five different speeds. He picked it up and flicked the switch. The large round head began vibrating. He turned it off quickly and put it back.

In Claude's room, he dropped the towel to the floor, completely naked, before noticing Simone right there in Claude's bathroom, cleaning still in her nightgown. He watched her bending over the sink, the fantasy awakening even more. He quickly dressed and packed his bags. Simone came out of Claude's shower.

"Ready to go over to Beaver Park?" Simone asked.

"Yes ma'am," Train answered. "I think I'll hit some practice balls before my match."

"Let me slip on my shorts and a T-shirt and I'll run you right over," Simone said.

"No ma'am, that's okay. I think I'll jog over and get my legs going. Tell Claude thanks. I hope they saw something, uh, I mean, killed something."

"I will," Simone said. She stared into his face. "I have a match today about five o'clock. Claude will bring me over around then. I hope you had a good time even without Claude here last night."

On his one-mile jog over to the park, he thought about the tennis article he had seen the night before in Simone's magazine, a story he dreamed would be his own one day. It was about a rising pro tennis superstar, a twenty-five-year-old Spaniard nicknamed Jamey. The article went into his early childhood, the poverty and abuse he endured, and his storied determination to rise to stardom.

A full-page color layout accompanied the article, a photograph showing Jamey in his underwear. He was six feet tall, two hundred pounds. He had tanned olive skin, and his muscles rippled like those of a Greek god. An Italian designer underwear company had signed Jamey to a contract. He was photographed beside an Italian pool and a tall springing fountain. He was wearing sunglasses and a pair of royal-blue bikini underwear and was lying back on a pink lounge chair, his legs spread while holding a tennis racquet between them. The racquet rose from between his legs and there were two tennis balls on either side of the base of the handle. It wasn't exactly subtle. Jamey was awash with golden glistening oil all over his body. Train thought his face was much like Jamey's, same smile, same curly jet-black hair and olive skin, but Train did not have the muscle definition Jamey did. Not yet, anyway.

Train was inspired to reach that level. He couldn't wait to get into his high school gym to start weight training. One day he would look better in the designer underwear than Jamey did and Train would do it before he was twenty-five years old. They would pay him more, and he wouldn't need a racquet between his legs.

When Train got to Beaver Park, he couldn't find his registration form. He went through his racquet bag and clothes bag, but there was no registration form. He thought he put it in one of his bags the previous day when he left to go to Claude's house before the game, but then he remembered. Damn it, he'd pulled it out the night before and laid it somewhere in Claude's room when he got his sleeping shorts out to go to bed. It was about ten thirty then. He ran back to Claude's house and knocked on the door and rang the doorbell. No one came to the door. A couple of minutes went by and still no one came to the door, but Simone's car was in the driveway. He didn't want to miss the tournament. It was the big fall regional qualifier. He figured nobody was home. Simone must have walked over to some neighbor's house after breakfast or had gone for a morning run. He had to find that registration form and fast.

The hidden door key was under the porch rail. He let himself in and headed back toward Claude's room. There his registration form lay right on top of the dresser. As he walked out of the door, he heard music coming from Simone's room.

He walked down the hall. Her bedroom door was open. He walked in. The nightstand candle was burning, *The Passions* lay open beside her on the bed, and her tennis racquet was at her knee. Simone lay on her back. She had on the pink-lace-and-white-heart panties from her vanity chair, a pair of thigh-high, royal-blue silk stockings, white lacing at the thigh. Her pink blindfold Train had seen around her neck earlier that day covered her eyes. She was wearing a strand of pink pearls around her neck. She had a bottle of lotion in her hand. She was massaging the glistening oily lotion onto her body and massaging the pearls in a circular motion.

Train just stood there. She could not see or hear him. She massaged the lotion on her stomach and onto her thighs. She put her hand down inside her panties and gently patted herself. She moaned softly. He looked directly at her. She straightened her legs. She slowly massaged the oil with her fingers between her legs and on her thighs. She moved her left hand over beside her hip. There beside her was the tennis magazine opened to the full-color photo shoot of the tennis superstar, Jamey. Between the pages lay the purple-and-gold magic wand. She picked it up, moving down from her breasts and cleavage and across her stomach. She was moving the wand through her legs, slowly back and forth. She moaned louder. She started whispering.

She flicked the switch, and the wand vibrated. The head revolved as she put it between her legs. She quivered. She moved the wand slowly in a circular motion back and forth. She moved the wand faster with long strokes. She became louder. Her legs trembled more and her hips bucked, throwing her breasts from side to side. Train unbuttoned his tennis shorts and pulled down the zipper. They fell to the floor.

She was loud, almost screaming. Train was in rhythm with her motion, his hand moving faster. He was sweating. She squirmed and moaned, moving the vibrating wand faster and faster.

She screamed. She was in ecstasy. Minutes went by, then still and quiet she held one hand on her stomach, the other hand across the page of her tennis magazine and Jamey the tennis superstar. Train went quickly to Claude's room and got dressed.

As he went to the front door, he could hear the soft music and Simone's humming, her bed a stage, her body a symphony of moaning ecstasy. He ran back to Beaver Park and his mind raced, imagining—hoping—that one day his story too would be one of an exciting tennis superstar that was every woman's fantasy.

Tournament Qualifier

Train got back to Beaver Park right at eleven o'clock and turned in his registration form. He only had fifteen minutes to warm up, but, heck, he was already so warmed up, he could barely concentrate on tennis. A college kid from Tulane killed him the first set, 6-1. Train was incredulous. The kid had dealt Train his first "breadstick." Of any tournament he had ever played, he'd never only won one game in a set.

Train lacked energy. Stroking tennis balls was not on his mind. He lost the second set, 6-4. He came out of his fantasyland and back to reality, but the first match had already been decided. He lost the third set, 7-5. Of the people in the bleachers that morning, 90 percent were women and girls. All the sons and boyfriends and husbands were out hunting or gone to LSU or Louisiana, Lafayette, for Saturday football. There was disbelief in the stands. Their own junior state champion and tennis phenom, Rene Pierre Lacroix, had just lost in straight sets, something that had never happened before.

The qualifier was a one-day double elimination contest for a tournament in the spring at the LSU tennis complex. If a player lost two, he was out. Win one or two and he was in. Train had to win his second match. His second match started at three o'clock against a freshman from Tulane. Another pairing with someone from New Orleans. He shook hands with the Big Easy player and wished him good luck. The kid smirked. He was cocky.

"Hey, you ever been in New Orleans, kid? Ever been out of these sticks and this ratty little tennis center?" he asked Train.

Kid. Who was he calling "kid"? Who was he calling Lafayette "the sticks"? Train's old man used to beat him up with words. He got used to it. He could handle it. He woke up every day being beat down by Jacques. He wasn't going to get beat down by his old man or nobody, no way, no matter how old or how mean. A smile came across Train's face. When he glanced back at the kid from New Orleans, he saw his father. All the energy came back to his body. The vision of his father, all those memories, changed his entire being. His brutalizing shots aimed at his father would be foremost in his approach to this opponent.

"Win your morning match?" Train asked.

"No, I lost in four sets," his opponent said. "But I'm not too worried playing a tenth grader from up here in the backwoods swamps."

"I think I'm just going to go ahead and knock you out of the tournament, Big Easy," Train said. "I could do it in three sets, but I'm going to string you out. I'm going to give you a couple tanked sets 'cause I'm gonna win either way. You will walk off a loser to a tenth grader from the sticks. Pray to the saints you don't get hurt today."

At the end of the match, knees and elbows bloody, the kid doubled over the net on Train's winning point. Train gazed at his opponent with the devilish vision of his father still in his mind. *Fuck you, Jacques Lacroix*. The crowd cheered him wildly. He smiled up to them, held his racquet between his knees, and blew a kiss with both hands. He felt naked in the moment except for a pair of royal-blue designer underwear and sunglasses. He walked out of the court and headed up the wooden patio deck to the Beaver Park pro shop when he saw Claude and Simone walking toward him.

"Hey, boy, that was a hell of a war out there," Claude said. "You really kicked his butt. His coach is back there bandaging up his knees."

Simone walked up behind Claude.

"Congratulations," she said. She gave Train a big squeezing hug. "That was a spectacular and incredible show you just put on. Wow, I'm exhausted from watching you."

Train stared at her for a minute. Little did she know he thought the same of her early that morning.

Train's mama came over and congratulated her son and thanked Simone for letting him spend the night.

"I'm sure he had a good time," Train's mama said. She was more right than she could ever have imagined.

Claude told Train he was sorry he had to go hunting with his dad, leaving him with his mom and the two Betsys.

"Don't worry about it," Train said. "I had an okay time." Train asked Claude why his dad wasn't there to watch his wife's match.

"He ain't been out here in years," Claude explained. "His thing is outdoor stuff and hanging with his card-playing drinking buddies. They even have separate bedrooms now. He goes to bed early. He's out the door early morning driving that oil tanker, gone for two or three days at a time."

Train went back to the court to get his wristbands which he'd left on the court bench. Simone was there alone, stretching and getting ready for her match, her tennis uniform pulled tight, the golden letters across her breasts.

The next day after Sunday lunch, Train went to practice his serves at Beaver Park. He went to the lower court, court thirteen, by the Bayou Vermilion where it was always quiet and peaceful. He could concentrate back there. He was working on his "cannonball" shot, a hard and fast flat serve with no spin on it. In the qualifier the day before, that shot had cost him about fifteen points in two matches. After about a half hour, he heard his name called out.

"Hey, Train, do you ever stop?" It was Claude.

"You ever play tennis, Claude?" Train answered.

"No, ain't ever played. My daddy wouldn't let me. My mama bought me a tennis racquet one Christmas when I was about seven years old. The next morning, I went into the den to get my racquet from underneath the Christmas tree, but there wasn't no racquet there. I asked Mama where my new tennis racquet that Santa Claus brought me was and she said, 'Claude, you'll have to take that up with your daddy when he gets back.' Daddy came back later that afternoon. He had been with his drinking buddies at a bar over in Maurice. I asked him if he had my tennis racquet in his truck, and he told me he took that damn racquet back down to the sporting goods store where Mama bought it."

Train hit a few hard serves from the left side.

"Train," Claude continued, "he told me that him and his brothers and their boys played football and baseball and went huntin' and fishin'. He said no son of his was gonna grow up to be a little queer playing a skirt-wearing pussy sport like tennis. My daddy became a dumbass redneck in my eyes that Christmas day and I didn't believe in Santa Claus no more."

Train never did go back to spend the night with Claude after hearing that story. There was no way he was going to go sit with Big Daddy Von at any football games, much less go back to his house and watch him drink beer and flick the TV on a Friday night between hunting shows to reruns of the best of Louisiana fishing shows. No way in hell. Not Train. Not this queer skirt-wearing tennis pussy. Over the next hour or more, Train hit over a hundred serves. He only had ten cannonball misses, a new target in mind he figured. He sat by the fence, alone, exhausted, listening to the rhythmical flowing sound of the Bayou Vermilion.

Betsy

Train played and practiced hours upon hours his tenth-grade year, preparing for the high school state championship at LSU to take place the second week of June. He only lost one match that year. Everything kept rolling right on down the tracks. He lifted weights, ran, biked, and regularly swam to increase his upper body strength. Train's mama and one of her girlfriends, Brittany, drove him over to LSU for the tournament. They stayed at a friend's house. Thursday's rounds went well, and Train beat two seniors in straight sets. At the end of his second match, as he was walking off the court, he heard his name.

"Famous Train. Haven't seen you in a long time." It was the New Orleans Betsy, Claude's sister's friend. Train asked her what she was doing still hanging around campus during the summer.

"I had to stay and take two make-up exams to avoid summer school," she explained. "One Friday and one Saturday. I'm not leaving until late Saturday. Do you play tomorrow?"

Train explained to her that he had made the quarterfinals and would probably start the second match around three o'clock.

"I'll drop by and see if you've still got what it takes," she said, winking.

Train played the morning match and won. It went four sets: 6-1, 6-4, 3-6, and 7-5. He slid into the back wall in the third set at 3-3 and twisted his ankle. He was in pain and lost three games in a row. He battled like crazy in the final set, using all his tricks and antics to finally outlast the guy.

By the time he got to his afternoon match, his ankle was pretty swollen, almost no jump in his serve.

He had a lot of double faults. He just couldn't get to the balls and had no base of power.

The quarterfinal match became his second three-set loss in a year. He hoped he hadn't torn anything or cracked a bone. They checked him over at the LSU clinic. It was just a bad sprain.

Train went back to the court and sat down with his mama and Brittany. They were going to watch a friend of Train's play his match, a pretty good player from down in Abbeville. Into the first game, Train heard his name. It was Betsy again, walking toward him.

"Sorry I missed your match," Betsy said. "The professor showed up an hour late." She sat down beside him. "You must be Train's mom." Betsy extended her hand. "Nice to meet you, ma'am."

"Just how do you know Train, Betsy?" Train's mama asked.

"Train and I spent the whole night together this fall over in Lafayette at my sorority sister Betsy's house," Betsy said. "We had a ball. Train was so much fun."

Train couldn't believe what he was hearing.

"Did you win your matches today?" Betsy asked.

Train's mother explained that he lost the last one. Sprained his ankle.

"We're here watching to see if his friend can win and go on to the semis tomorrow," Train's mother said.

"Will you watch him tomorrow if he wins?" Betsy asked.

"No," Train said. "We're going back after his match today."

"Why don't you stay tonight if he wins?" Betsy asked Train. Then she whispered in his ear. "I'm all alone in the sorority house. Please stay and ride back with your friend tomorrow."

Joline overheard the first part of what Betsy said.

"Honey," Train's mama said, "why don't you stay and watch your friend play tomorrow if he wins today. I'm sure he would appreciate that. You can just stay in the dorm room they assigned you. I'm sure it will be okay. Betsy, if you have time tonight you can show Train some things around campus. I'm hoping he will play here one day."

It was decided.

Train's Abbeville friend won his match and would play the semis the next day. Train asked him if he could catch a ride with him the next day, and Train's friend said yes. Betsy had already gone to her car so that everything wouldn't be so obvious to Train's friends. She pulled up to the dorm parking lot and told Train to go in and get his things.

"You're going to spend the night with me in the sorority house," she said. "All my sorority sisters are gone for the summer. Only the house mom is there, and she goes to bed at ten o'clock every night. I have my own side entrance, so it's all okay."

They went to a funky little pizza joint and talked about everything, laughed about all her sorority stories and Claude's wild sister Betsy. When they got back to her room, they sat on her bed and looked at her high school yearbooks. She was the homecoming queen and a New Orleans debutante. She was high society.

"You been out all day and night," Betsy said. "Go jump in my shower. You'll feel much better."

When Train finished showering, there was no towel for him to use. Before he could call for one, Betsy opened the door with a towel in her hand. He stood still. She had on a blue silk spaghetti-strap top and a pair of black lace underwear. Betsy toweled Train's face and hair. She toweled down his neck and chest to his waist. She pulled him toward her and kissed him softly.

"Feel better?" she asked.

She kneeled down and toweled his thighs and calves. She teased him to a torturous throbbing. Then on her knees, she dropped the towel and looked up at him. She put her hands on his knees.

"I missed a little spot," she said. "All dry now."

She took his hand and led him into her bed. He had never stayed all night with a girl. As a matter of fact, he had never been with a girl like this, only a little making out here and there. They played and played. Betsy told Train what to do.

"Put your hand under my top. Slide my panties to the side. Touch me there. Not yet. Don't take them off yet. Kiss me here. Pinch me there. Squeeze me. Lower. Higher."

Train thought if this was always going to be what foreplay was all about, he didn't want to hear the chair umpire say, "Game, set, match, end of play." Oh no, umpire, he'd stay right there in the match point forever. In the middle of all the kissing and whispering and touching, he let out an "oh" sound when her hand moved between his legs. He was ready.

"Wait," Betsy said. She reached over to her drawer and pulled out a little package. "I picked them up at the drugstore when I left my exam today."

She rolled over and slowly guided Train into a place he had never been before. She had gloriously taken his virginity.

Afterward, Train lay motionless on top of Betsy. She ran her hands softly across his back, kissing his ear. It was his first time, never to be forgotten. The beautiful Betsy from New Orleans. They finally went to sleep around four o'clock. They woke up before dawn and made love again until the sun rose.

She drove him back over to the courts. She was on her way back to New Orleans. She walked a little way with him and said she felt something special for him.

"I have a little something for you, Train," she said.

She handed Train a box. He opened it. Inside there was a silver necklace with a pendant, a half-opened oyster shell, and inside the pendant there were two small pearls.

"It's a lucky charm," she said. "I heard your mother talking about this, your dream of one day winning the Oyster Bay Classic." The necklace was a miniature version of the Oyster Bay trophy. "This is your lucky charm for two years from now when you are a senior in high school, a lucky necklace for you when you come down to New Orleans on Memorial Day weekend and win. If you're lucky, you can take the oyster shell trophy back to Acadiana."

She gave Train a long hug and kissed him on the cheek. He couldn't speak, his heart was beating so fast. She walked a few steps away and turned around.

"Train," she said, "next time you come over to LSU and need a shower, remember to leave your towel at home."

Señor Matador

Train was determined and disciplined the summer of his tenth-grade year to work out and practice daily. He rode with Bones up to my father's court on Wednesdays and Saturdays, and the rest of the week he practiced at Beaver Park. My father and mother spent many hours with him.

My mother cranked the Rene Lacoste ball machine for him every training visit. But most all of his mental approach and strategy of play were born of my father's intense interest and knowledge and genius concerning the game of tennis. My father had an uncanny ability to bring analogous understanding of his teachings to Train. The analogy which had the most impact on him was that of the bullfighter. Aware of Train's Spanish heritage, my father addressed Train many times over as "Señor Matador." As Train and Bones approached the court, my father would say, "Here comes the famous and fearless young matador, Rene Pierre, and his loyal picador, Señor Bones."

My father explained to Train over and over that the test between two opponents on the tennis court is much like the test between the bullfighter and the bull. The matador controls and entices all the movements of the bull. He unnerves the bull to make predictable and errant lunges and eventually wears him down to defeat. From that moment forward, when Train entered a tennis court, he would close his eyes briefly and see a round coliseum filled with people and a half-ton bull standing on the other side. This vision allowed him the mental ability to control the ebb and flow of all his matches.

"Always the matador, Train," my father would say. "Never the bull, *comprende, señor?*"

"Sí, señor," Train answered. "Bring on the bulls."

Train went undefeated his junior year and won the high school state championship. The next summer of practice was more of the same. His senior year bore the possibilities of things never done in tennis by anyone from Acadiana before. Again, he went undefeated his senior year. He slept tennis. He drank it, ate it, and dreamed it. His life, body, and soul were tennis. He grew to six feet two inches tall and one hundred ninety-five pounds—almost zero percent body fat—and had the strength, muscle definition, and look of a Greek god.

The championship took place in New Orleans. Train's opponent in the championship was the same guy who had defeated him two years earlier in the Baton Rouge match when Train had a sprained ankle. His name was Guillermo, and he was part Spaniard just like Train. Two matadors in the match that day and no bull.

Train won the championship in straight sets, 6-3, 6-4, 7-5, though the last set was hard fought. Train remembered Guillermo's compassion when Train lost in the tournament because of his sprained ankle. When they shook hands at the net that day two years earlier, Guillermo showed dignity in his victory, and Train never forgot that.

Train had made history. An Acadiana boy had won back-to-back high school state tennis championships. The trophy was not only for him but earned by all who had helped him, my father and mother, Bones, everyone at Beaver Park,

Irma, and especially his beautiful mama, Joline Lacroix. I even like to think I played a small role in his success that day.

"Train, keep rollin' down dem tennis tracks," Bones said that day.

But the most important thing to Train at that moment was the fact that he could possibly make a dream come true for someone special to him. The senior high school state champion from Louisiana did not have to qualify and was an automatic entry into a very elite event, the Oyster Bay Classic, held each Memorial Day weekend in New Orleans. The event was open to qualifying high school seniors only. It was also an event exclusively for seniors from the states bordering the Gulf of Mexico, Texas, Louisiana, Mississippi, Alabama, and Florida.

Train had heard all about the Oyster Bay from my father over the years and from me who told him how much my father loved that tournament and that his biggest wish and dream was for someone to bring that trophy back to Acadiana. Train knew he had the talent and the game to win the Classic. He wanted it more than anything for all of us and all the people of Acadiana, but the person he wanted to win for more than anyone else was the "King de Donne un Coup de Main," my father, Dr. Roland Louis Mouton.

During the fall of his senior year, Train was grappling with the very hard decision of which college tennis scholarship he would take. He could go anywhere he wanted, UCLA, Texas, UGA, Alabama, LSU, even Yale or Harvard. His determining factor had nothing to do with the schools or their tennis programs. His determining factor was the well-being of his mother. He was still very close with his mother, and she still had not been serious with anyone or even dated anyone much since Jacques died.

Her social calendar pretty much only included Train or going out with her friend Brittany on their usual Saturday night *fais do-do*. In French, fais do-do was something mothers told their children, meaning "go to sleep quick," because the mother wanted to get back to the dance before another woman danced with her husband. Joline danced with other men at these parties but never did steady up with any of them. Jacques had stripped away her self-esteem and youthful exuberance. Train didn't want to leave her. He had pretty much decided to stay close by and attend the University of Louisiana at Lafayette. He could see her every day if he wanted. He needed to commit to Lafayette before Christmas.

He wanted more than anything for his mama to find happiness in life. He'd give back all his trophies to return Mama Joline's *joie de vivre*.

Back in the eleventh grade, my father had arranged a weekend night job for Train. The job not only made a little extra money but put Train in an environment that would continue to inspire his tennis. He worked as a busboy at Pamplona Tapas Bar, a restaurant on Jefferson Street in Lafayette named after the bullfighting city in Spain. Their logo was a charging bull. Train's uniform at work was a pair of black polished shoes, black pants, a white ruffled shirt, a red vest, and a gold sash around his waist. He was dressed like a matador. This was, after all, my father's entire plan. There were bullfighting pictures over all the walls, images of matadors and bullrings and Ernest Hemingway. One of the finest restaurants in Louisiana, Pamplona Tapas Bar was always busy. Train got to know a lot of new people and regularly saw many people he already knew. He worked there into his senior year in high school.

Often Train's manager, James, would embarrass him in front of all the waitresses.

"Hey girls, did you know we have a hundred and fifty reservations tonight? And guess what one hundred and forty-nine women wanted to know? Which tables are assigned to Train."

"What happened to number one-fifty?" one waitress asked.

James smiled. "It was a man. Wrong number."

Joline called Pamplona one Friday night during Train's senior year and told James to tell him to come down to The Filling Station when he got off work, only a few blocks down from Pamplona on the corner of Jefferson and Lee. It was a cool little restaurant built from an old gas station with a large patio. It stood in the apex of the two streets with neon lighting casting over the front.

After work, Train went there and walked up to the hostess, a longtime friend named Juanita.

She explained that his mother and Brittany were over in the back corner of the patio. Train walked around the side, and there were Brittany, his mama, and a guy who had his hand around Train's mother's shoulder. They were all laughing hysterically. His mama and a guy. The only time he had seen a man touch his mama was at a fais do-do. Train tightened up. Brittany stood up and gave him a big hug.

"Hey, sweetie," his mother said. "Good night at the bull-ring?" She liked to tease Train about the restaurant. She smiled with a smile Train hadn't ever seen before. She even hugged Train a little tighter. "Honey, I want you to meet a new friend. His name is Russell."

Russell smiled. He stuck out his hand.

"Nice to meet you, Train," Russell said. "They have been telling me all about you."

"Sit down, honey," Train's mother said. "Russell just moved here a month ago from New Orleans. He is working down at the bank with Mr. Coteau and has been picked to take over the bank when Mr. Coteau resigns this coming spring."

Train sat down but didn't say anything.

"He was also assigned the administrator for our trust accounts," Train's mama continued. "He is originally from Tampa, Florida, and still owns a beach house there. Brittany thought it would be nice for her and myself to introduce Russell around a little bit tonight to some of our friends. There are two really good Zydeco bands playing over at the Blue Moon Saloon tonight."

As he stood up to leave, Train looked at Russell. He was a real nice-looking fellow and about Mama's age. Russell asked Train to come down to the bank on Monday after school about four thirty for a meeting.

"You and I need to make some decisions concerning your trust account," Russell said.

Train felt Mama was safe with Russell and hoped she would have fun that night.

"I'm gonna teach Russell how to Zydeco line dance tonight," his mama said.

She invited Train to go with them, but he decided not to cramp their style. He asked his hostess friend Juanita for a ride home. He didn't have his own car. Train liked Juanita a lot. She was pretty and real sweet, and they'd been out a couple times before, just a friendly kind of thing, though, nothing serious. But Juanita had some steady boyfriends on and off. All the girls around Acadiana knew that Train was not the steady-going kind of guy. They thought it was his tennis that kept him from committing, but that wasn't the case. Train had a psychological barrier to ever being real close or staying with one girl, afraid that he might have a drop of that mean Jacques gene in him. He couldn't become what his father became, then or ever. But Juanita was the girl Train liked being around the most. He invited her to all the big dances, and she even went out with him, Mama, and Brittany to a couple Saturday-night fais do-dos.

Juanita pulled into Train's driveway. Train invited Juanita to come in for a little while and asked if she wanted to watch a movie or something. They ended up watching an old Hitchcock movie about a murder and a tennis player, *Stranger on a Train*. The phone rang. Joline told Train she was going to spend the night with Brittany. Train recognized an exciting new tone in her voice.

Train got up the nerve to ask Juanita to spend the night with him, and she did. She never had before but had always wanted to be a little more intimate with him. She just hadn't ever had the chance.

Joline got home about one o'clock the next day. She was like a different person, smiling, talking nonstop about how much fun they all had the previous night.

"You weren't worried about me were you, Train?" she asked.

He told her he stayed up all night long. She laughed and kissed him on the cheek. Juanita had only left minutes earlier. Before she left for college that fall, Juanita told him that was her first time, and she was so happy it was him. She would never forget it.

Train asked his mother for the story on Russell. She told him that Russell was from Florida, that he graduated from Florida State University, and that he had a masters in finance from the Wharton School of Finance. He'd never been married. She explained he'd had a couple of serious relationships, but the magic wasn't there. He got tired of Florida and wanted a change, so he moved to New Orleans. He wanted a small-town way of life and heard many people talk very favorably about the lifestyle in Lafayette.

"Mr. Coteau told me in confidence," his mother said, "that Russell was qualified to run any banking entity in the country, and the bank got served a superstar from the heavens. He even volunteers two hours of his time every Saturday afternoon handing out pamphlets down at the Lafayette Visitors Center."

She said Russell made her feel real happy. Train listened to his mother without saying anything.

"He invited me out to dinner tonight," she said. "Is that okay with you, honey?"

Train gave her his permission on one condition. She had to go downtown at three o'clock and meet Ms. Evangeline. Train said my mother dresses prettier than any woman he knew. She would help Joline pick out a brand-new dress, new cowgirl boots, and new makeup, get her nails done, and even get Joline a last-minute Saturday hair appointment— my father had delivered the hairdresser's babies, of course. Train said he was paying for everything. He explained that all the ladies down at Pamplona tipped him very well.

"Oh, Train, you are so wonderful," Joline said. "Son, I love you so much."

Train told her to quit crying and get on downtown to meet Ms. Evangeline. Train wanted Russell to see the prettiest woman in all of Louisiana.

When Joline came out of her bedroom later that evening, Train couldn't believe his blue eyes. He got chills. She was beautiful. The dress, the hair, the nails, the makeup, the jewelry, and the new red-and-gold alligator-skin boots. There was a knock on the door, and Train went to answer it.

When Russell and Joline left for their evening out, Russell bent his right arm with a slight bow, and out the door they went, arm in arm.

Train met with Russell at the bank the following Monday afternoon. Russell informed Train that he could begin to draw five hundred dollars a month from a trust that had been set up for him by an anonymous benefactor. The trust money, in combination with the money he'd saved from waiting tables, paved a way for Train to buy a car. He was even happier knowing he could take the burden off his mama for driving him all over town and to his tennis matches.

Train stood up and looked at Russell for a moment. In a humble but serious tone, he said, "Always be nice to my mama, Russell."

As they shook hands, Russell looked him in the eyes and said, "As God as my witness, you have my word. I hope to make Joline even happier than you can imagine, Train."

Russell and Joline became a steady couple by the Christmas holidays. Train could see the happiness they brought each other. He wasn't worried about his mother anymore.

In the summer after his senior year in high school before leaving for college, Russell proposed to Joline. A week earlier, Russell asked Train to meet him down by the Bayou Vermilion. He told him how much he loved Joline and how much he cared for her and how happy he wanted to make her for the rest of her life. He asked Train for permission to marry his beautiful mother.

Train knew his mama was happier than she had ever been in her life. She smiled and laughed and sang like he hadn't seen her do before. Russell would make her happy and love her forever. Train and Russell hugged. Russell left and Train sat down on the bank by the Bayou Vermilion and hummed an old Cajun love song his mother taught him a long time ago.

The Oyster Bay Classic

Train still made weekly visits to the Roland Louis Mouton Lawn Tennis Court and practiced daily. The Memorial Day Oyster Bay Classic weekend tennis championship for graduating high school seniors was approaching. After winning his second straight state championship, he had that final trophy in his sights. He had that one goal to accomplish for himself and for my father, Dr. Mouton, before he finished his high school career. My father knew that his long-awaited dream of someone bringing back that trophy to Acadiana was now a very good possibility.

The Classic was four weeks away. Train had to play one more event before Memorial Day, the Acadiana Amateur Championship Tournament at Beaver Park, which he'd already won twice.

No one had ever won three straight. Train lost in the finals of that tournament. He got beat by a thirty-year-old amateur named Phillipe who played out of Red Lerille's Health and Racquet Club in Lafayette. Phillipe had been a college champion elsewhere, but he never turned pro. Train got a taste of the real deal that day. He went the full five sets. He had a chance to win, but Train made a mental mistake during the last point to lose. After he lost, Train did something he'd never done before. He threw his racquet.

It slid back behind the fence. He could see the neck had cracked. He was too embarrassed to go get it. He apologized to Phillipe and the umpire. He was the last to leave.

His mama drove off and Train decided to go back and get his racquet. It was special to him. The train engineers coming through Broussard by his practice wall had given it to him one Christmas when he was very young. It had been too big for him then, but he eventually grew into it and began using it every time he played. When he went back behind the fence, the racquet was gone. He looked everywhere, even in the trash cans, but it wasn't anywhere. Who would have wanted a broken racquet?

The 1967 Oyster Bay Classic was the year the game of tennis went metallic. Train was heading into the tournament without his favorite racquet, and my father couldn't have been happier.

My father and mother had vacationed in Paris in 1953. My father went on a visit to Stade Roland Garros that week and heard that Rene Lacoste, the tennis player and innovator, had designed a metal racquet. He heard it was very light and resilient resulting in a *trampolining* effect, adding much more power to the shot. Lacoste patented the racquet some years later, named the T2000, and Wilson Sporting Goods Company began to produce it in the US not too long after. The 1967 US Open Women's Singles Championship at Forest Hills, New York, was won with the Wilson T2000 in play before a stunned and surprised audience.

My father knew Bones had an older brother who moved up north years ago and worked in the Wilson factory. The Wilson T2000 arrived at my father's house three days later and quickly found itself in the hands of Train.

For the four weeks before the Oyster Bay, Train did nothing except practice, play, and sleep tennis. He called his new racquet "Baby T." He was determined. No staying out late, no high school parties, no fais do-dos, no sex, no detractifiers. Only tennis.

He followed my father and mother down to New Orleans early in the week. I was busy over at LSU recruiting and would only come down if Train made it to the championship round. Joline, Russell, and Brittany were coming down that Sunday, hoping to see him make the championship round on Monday. The final round would be played on center court at the New Orleans Lawn Tennis Club, the very first lawn tennis club in America. Some British cotton merchants and New Orleans businessmen formed it back in 1876. It rested on Phillip Street.

"Why couldn't it have been French businessmen?" my father asked. "Damn those English."

Train was not a fan favorite at the tournament. He had been heavily recruited by Tulane University, the mighty "Green Wave," a tennis powerhouse. Train's decision to go elsewhere even made the front cover of the sports page in the local paper: "Lacroix turns down Tulane for LSU," the headline read. "What's he thinking?" the reporter wrote in the article.

Train was only three sets away from accomplishing both his and my father's lifelong dream. Train made it to the championship round.

His opponent was the younger brother of "Big Easy" who Train had defeated two years previous at the high school championships. Train was in the dressing room changing into his tennis clothes and getting ready for the finals. He opened the locker on the top shelf and found the purple-and-gold box. He opened it and put the charm—the oyster-and-pearl necklace given to him by Betsy—around his neck, her special good-luck charm to him, some magical voodoo gris-gris. He had not seen her at the tournament. She was probably still back at LSU.

Baby Easy, as Train took to calling him, was as bad mannered as his older brother. They were from a wealthy family and had always attended private schools, living in those private little bubbles.

Baby Easy and Train approached the net.

"Hey, swamp boy," Baby Easy said. "My brother said you would need luck today. How is everything up there in the Lafayette sticks? Any raccoon-eatin' coonasses been doing your mama lately?"

This made Train furious, but he possessed a strong discipline of mind. He stayed calm. He would brutalize the boy on the court. Train decided to give Baby Easy the Rene Lacoste crocodile approach. Slow and methodical. He'd run him all over the court with precision shots and no gambles. He'd wear him out and run him into the walls. Train looked in the stands and gave his crocodile strategy sign to my father who smiled and nodded his approval. He'd taught Train well.

It wasn't Train's favorite style of play. Train loved to attack and to attack mercilessly.

After the first set, it was Rene Pierre Lacroix, 6-4.

"A close match, ladies and gentlemen," the announcer said. "We are in for a long day."

Train took the second set, 6-2, only one game to go in the third set. The score was 5-0 in games. He was serving game six, 40-30, game, set, match point. Train looked up into the stands at my father and mother, who were cheering. Train turned toward them, his feet together, his arms at his sides, his head rising. He smiled and pointed his racquet toward them and gave them a salute and a bow.

"Your serve, please, Mr. Lacroix," the umpire said.

"My pleasure, Señor Umpire," Train said.

Baby Easy was exhausted. Train set him up for his final winner just like he did to his brother Big Easy two years ago. Baby Easy took the bait. He rushed toward the net. Train visualized on the warehouse wall door Jacques Lacroix's face. The ball came down from the sky. Train's back was totally arched, his racquet touching the ground behind him. Kill Jacques. The ball struck Baby Easy in the crotch, and he doubled over in pain. Train raised his arms in victory. He looked up in the stands. My father and mother, Train's mother, Russell, Brittany, Bones, and I were all standing and clapping and yelling. Train went to the net to shake the hand of the opponent, but Baby Easy was already being helped off the court. Train went back to his chair to put his racquets back in his bag.

"There's no reason for that kind of play," a man behind Train said.

Train turned around. It was Baby Easy's father, Mr. Bratteur.

"You had a match with my other son just like this one," Mr. Bratteur said. "You play like some kind of backwoods animal. If I was your father I'd whip your ass."

"Sorry to deny you the pleasure, Mr. Bratteur," Train said, "but my old man beat you to the punch years ago."

Everyone was at courtside for the trophy presentation. It was so beautiful, a big half-open silver oyster shell with two golden tennis balls inside. As Train walked off the court, he heard his name called.

"Congratulations, Train." It was Betsy. Train hadn't seen her in two years. "I love your necklace. A lucky charm, I suppose?" She had been up in the press box with her dad. He had been on the tournament committee for years. "Why don't you stay in New Orleans tonight, Train?" Betsy asked. "Come up to the press box right after you tell everyone goodbye."

Train handed the trophy to my father and told my parents that the trophy was as much theirs as it was his. He asked them to do him the honor of placing it in their home, where it remained for years to come. Train thanked everyone for coming and said he would be back to Lafayette in a couple of days. He then made his way up to the press box.

Betsy introduced Train to her father who congratulated him on a great victory and the achievement of being the first person from Acadiana to win the trophy. Her father also explained to Train that the winner was entitled to a full scholarship to Tulane University in New Orleans. If Train had other college plans, he had the option to award the scholarship to any other player in the tournament as long as the player finished in the quarterfinals round. Train said that he did indeed have other college plans, but he also had a friend perfect for the scholarship, Guillermo Santos, his friend and opponent from the high school state tournaments. Guillermo came from a farming family in Louisiana and could certainly use the full scholarship.

"Betsy," her father said, "I have to run, sweetheart. Your mother is waiting on me at the airport. I need the Bahamas after this tournament."

"Y'all have a good trip," Betsy said.

Her father stopped and turned. "Betsy," he said.

"Yes sir?"

"Why don't you bring a boy like Train home to your mother and me one day?"

Betsy looked at Train and gave him a wink.

"I'll get right on top of that for sure, Daddy," she said. Her father smiled and left. Betsy kissed Train.

"Let's go make Daddy happy, Train," she said. "You did forget your towel, didn't you?"

After their erotic shower, Train and Betsy went down to The Oyster Palace and ate nothing but dozens of celebration oysters. Train sure needed their extra magical powers for the rest of his Oyster Bay Trophy Celebration night with Betsy. The silk sheets. The naked and beautiful body of Betsy. Train only wearing his lucky charm, the two pink pearls close together. Train and Betsy still close together.

The next day, as he was leaving around lunchtime, he thanked Betsy for the lucky charm and the great times they had spent together.

"It's all about you, Train," she said.

"I guess I'll see you when classes start at LSU this fall," Train said.

"No, Train, you won't. I graduated in the three-year program. I'm going to study in Europe for a year."

"Don't forget me, Betsy," Train said. He kissed Betsy on the cheek.

"Never, Train. I promise. Couldn't if I tried."

Sweet Betsy, Train's lucky charm, his first lover, his first love.

Train left New Orleans and went to Baton Rouge to finalize his full tennis scholarship application with me. I was, by then, an assistant athletic director at LSU. Train had decided to stay a little closer to Lafayette and his mother. He knew it would only be a short ride over for my mother and father to watch some of his college tournaments. Train's signing was a big feather in my cap. After winning the Oyster Bay Classic, he was ranked as a top-five college prospect in the country.

Train's three years at LSU went by like a Texas tornado. He played first man and won three straight conference titles and the NCAA individual championship his junior year.

He reached all his goals. He knew that tennis would be his livelihood. He wasn't going to be any banker or doctor or lawyer. He wasn't going to do any more school. It was time for him to move on, and he was anxious and ready.

He decided to cut his teeth on the European tour. He lived in Paris for a while. He even visited Pamplona, Spain, to run with the bulls. He moved back to the US after his third year and bought a home in Florida and lived there for the next ten years. He still ranked in the top ten on the pro tour and earned quite a bit of money playing and even more with his many endorsements. Fortunately, his stepfather was a banker. Russell and Joline got hitched and Russell invested wisely on Train's behalf.

Train went on to only win one grand slam, the Australian Open, but he had numerous other wins. He especially enjoyed playing at the Spanish Open in Barcelona which he won in back-to-back years. He earned runner-up in the French Open, the tournament he wanted to win the most for my father. As he grew older, he began to lose his drive and passion for the game, and the life of a jet-setter wore on him, the five-star hotels, limousines, yachts, casinos, women, a princess here, and a celebrity there. He had an affair with a duchess in England. He nicknamed her his "Cyclops Princess," after the device used at Wimbledon that made a loud audible sound when the serve went long past the service line. He told me she was his number-one royal screamer, and he went past her service line many times.

But it all became too much for a kid from the sticks.

His last professional event after a successful thirteen-year career was the New Orleans Open, a final tribute to Dr. Mouton and Ms. Evangeline, another championship trophy for their home. Train was in his midthirties by then. In another month, he would be on his way to a posh, celebrity-laden LA country club to become the head teaching tennis professional, thanks to Irma Jean Boudreaux, formerly of New Iberia, Louisiana. Before heading to California, though, he made one last stop: two weeks at home in his beloved Lafayette and Acadiana. How very sweet it was.

Final Exhibitions

Nothing much had changed since Train had been on tour. My father was still delivering babies. Bones was still working at the sugar warehouse and lining chalk at all Lafayette recreation fields and my dad's tennis court. Mr. Cristola was still at the Beaver Park Tennis Center, and all the fais do-do dance halls and bands were still going strong, *joie de vivre*.

Train's first stop driving back into town was lunch at Pamplona to catch up on some more news with the manager, James. They sat a couple of stools at the end of the bar. It was midafternoon and the restaurant was very quiet. James had time to sit and get him up to date. Juanita married a New Orleans banker, had two kids, and became president of the Garden District Ladies Guild. Claude rented a hunting club over in Mississippi and was a hunting and fishing tour guide. Claude's sister, Betsy, was living over in Biloxi with husband number three, children by each of them. Claude's daddy, Von, was ordered gone and done with by Simone a couple years back. She had not remarried and had no steady boyfriend. Von became the caretaker at another hunting club over in Mississippi and an unfortunate thing happened to him, James explained.

One night, as part of his duties, he was checking to make sure the eight members of the all-male hunting party from Key West were okay, satisfied, and settled in the cabin for the night. Von was surprised when he walked in to find that they were all covered in oil and aglow with the light from scented candles. Two of the hunters were wearing skirts and high heels. Unable to control his anger, Von screamed, "This ain't no place for a goddamn bunch o' skirt-wearing queer pussy faggots."

Von was found early the next morning by the camp guide tied to a chair, a front-row seat most likely for an all-male revue, panties wrapped around his neck and a pair of high heels lying near his side, the scented candles still flickering.

Train fell backward off the barstool, erupting into uncontrollable and uproarious laughter. After raising himself back onto the stool, Train heard laughter from around the bar down in the Hemingway room. He knew by the laugh that it was Simone.

"Yeah," James said, "Simone and some of her tennis lady friends are having a fundraising meeting for a tennis event they are planning."

James had to take a phone call and told Train since he knew almost all the ladies at the meeting, he ought to go down and say hello. As Train turned the corner to walk down the steps, the ladies were all very surprised to see him. They all had watched him grow up at Beaver Park; he knew all of them. He was a favorite son and legend at Beaver Park. The first to leave her seat was Simone who gave him a big hug and kiss on the cheek. After speaking to each of them, they asked him to join their meeting. They thought he might have some ideas for the fundraiser.

As chair of the committee, Simone explained that they were two weeks away from a fundraiser for two of their lady tennis team members who were diagnosed with breast cancer. They were short of meeting their goal by about five hundred tickets and needed to come up with a plan to sell the additional tickets. Train listened intently and knew from his days on the tour that pro exhibitions were big spectator draws. Train had an idea. He told the ladies to hold on because he needed to make a phone call back in James's office.

"Be right back, ladies," Train said. "I think I can 'ace' this one for y'all."

He dialed the phone and called Guillermo Santos, his old high school and college tennis opponent, the recipient of Train's Oyster Bay tennis scholarship to Tulane University. Guillermo had also spent time on the pro circuit. He and Train had played in several doubles matches as partners and had ranked in the top five for a while. Guillermo was then the head tennis coach at a private university in New Orleans. The touring lifestyle was not to Guillermo's liking either. He wanted a family, a dog, a fence, and a quiet home life. Train asked him to come up to Lafayette. He and Guillermo would put on an exhibition for the fundraiser at Beaver Park. Train knew that his local celebrity and Guillermo's connections down in New Orleans would surely fill the stands and sell more than five hundred tickets.

"Anything for you, amigo," Guillermo said on the phone. "I can probably bring up about three busloads from the Tulane Alumni group and most of the lady members from some of the New Orleans tennis clubs."

Train had one more call to make to seal the deal. That phone call was to Train's reporter friend, Scratch. Scratch was Train's age. They'd grown up together in Broussard. Scratch was a natural-born sportswriter, now a syndicated freelance writer signed on by most all the papers from Florida to Texas. Train had given him his early break, granting Scratch exclusive access to himself and some other touring pros.

"What's up, glamour boy?" Scratch said. "When you ever coming back to Lafayette?"

"I'm here now," Train said.

About half an hour later, Scratch strolled into Pamplona.

"Hello, all you beauty queens," Scratch said to the tennis ladies, who all adored Scratch. "Why are you ladies slumming with this tennis bum? What the heck are you doing back in town, Train?"

Train told Scratch that the beauty queens of Beaver Park needed some of his magic words and ink to talk up a fundraiser at the tennis club. Train explained that he would be playing an exhibition match with Guillermo Santos.

"It needs to hit all your papers," Train said. "And there's going to be a little icing on this cake. We're going to hold an auction, my services to the highest bidder, a series of tennis lessons, dinner, and dancing."

"An all-day-and-night train ride, huh?" Scratch replied. "You got it. We'll pack 'em in, ladies, don't you worry."

All the ladies were in disbelief and overjoyed. It was a sure bet that the fundraiser would meet its goal thanks to Train. Simone was so excited that she jumped up and hugged Train and told him how wonderful he was. She asked in what special way she could ever show her appreciation and gratitude to him. She wanted to do something extra special for him.

Train whispered to her that it would be most special to him if she would join him for a night of dinner and a little dancing before he left town. Little did she know that she was still his number-one fantasy.

"Anytime you want, Train," Simone said. "I'd be so excited to spend an evening of dinner and dancing with you." He looked at her and winked. Dinner and dancing weren't the only thing bubbling behind those crystal-blue eyes of his.

Scratch's article hit all the Gulf Coast papers. The phones were ringing off the hook over at Beaver Park and the Chamber of Commerce. Tickets sold out in three days, and they even sold an extra five hundred seats. There was another reason so many tickets were sold. Other than to watch Train and Guillermo put on a show, Train had signed a contract as part of his farewell tour to do a photo shoot and model a pair of underwear for a well-known American designer. The photo set Train did was the centerfold in a major tennis magazine prior to the exhibition match.

A four-woman production crew did the shoot. They posed Train on a gold lounge chair in purple-and-gold underwear. He told the wardrobe lady those were his loyal royal colors. He had a tennis racquet laying across his chest. The prop lady put oil all over his body, and the golden boy glistened under the camera lights. Train was more than well endowed, and the erotic shot of his body and that handsome face and wavy, shoulder-length, jet-black hair had those tennis magazines flying off the shelves. It was the designer's number-one ad sales campaign for the year.

The fundraiser and the exhibition at Beaver Park turned out to be a huge success. Over $100,000 was raised. Train drove over to Baton Rouge a couple days later and told me all about the exhibition and the fundraiser and couldn't wait to tell me about the winning bidder of the dinner and dance with him. He said her name was Crystal. He told me she said she was from New Orleans and wanted him to come down the day after the exhibition.

Train drove down the next afternoon to the Hotel Ponchartrain and waited in the Bayou Bar, a popular hangout for celebrities in New Orleans. He asked the bartender if she knew a Crystal. The bartender Missy said she did and explained that Crystal was in the middle of a nasty divorce from a powerful and wealthy man from New Orleans, a Mr. Bratteur. Train asked if they had any kids. She said they had two boys, tennis players back in the day, both spoiled rotten. They had torn up a couple rooms there one night at a bachelor party.

"The old man blamed it on me for overserving," she said, "and said the security guards were worthless as gator shit."

Train smiled. Unbelievable. She was the mother of Big and Baby Easy, the two guys he'd beaten years ago. She was the wife of the man who threatened to whip his ass.

"You just made my day," Train said. "That was a great story and worth a big tip." Train threw Missy a twenty.

She shrugged and said, "Thanks, but what's this for?"

Train only winked at her.

Crystal Bratteur came into the bar wearing a soft pink cotton dress, white high heels, and Tiffany jewelry. She had beautiful tanned legs and the body of a *Playboy* centerfold. She had blonde hair and bright blue eyes and a devilish smile on her face. She was in her midfifties, very elegant and regal. Train had an intense fascination for older women. As they sat at the bar, she told him her winning bid was never intended for tennis lessons or dinner, much to his surprise but certainly more to his delight.

She escorted him up to the presidential suite. Sweet-smelling magnolias floated in water dishes and rose petals rested on the silk pillows. Soft music. She led him to the spa tub in the corner, brimming with bubbles, and told him to undress her. She slowly eased into the spa, the bubbles covering her beautiful body. She ordered him to undress and enter the spa. After a little time of her playfully blowing bubbles, they entered the shower, and she massaged every part of his body and he did hers.

They made love long into the morning hours. She was erotically adventurous, and her passion for any kind of sex was insatiable.

As he left her room the next morning, Crystal said, "Train, honey, let me know when you are on the auction block again. I'll raise my bid. You were more than I imagined."

"Of course," Train said. Before leaving, Train asked Crystal why she picked the Hotel Pontchartrain.

"It has special meaning," she said. "Ever heard of Tennessee Williams?"

"Yes, the famous author," Train said.

"It was here in this very room that he wrote his classic play *A Streetcar Named Desire*, so I had my desire come true here, my ride on a streetcar named 'Train.'" And with a wink and a smile, she pulled on an imaginary cord and said, "Ding ding."

A week had gone by since the exhibition fundraiser. It was Saturday, Train's last full day in Lafayette. He would leave for Bel Air early Sunday morning. Simone had signed Train up as her partner in a mixed doubles match for a high school cheerleading fundraiser. She volunteered as coach for two cheerleading squads. Simone was fifty-six then and more beautiful than ever. She was still very sexy and had a great body which she kept in great physical shape. They started the tennis matches around one o'clock. Train and Simone were having a ball together, high-fiving and hugging. They laughed all day long. The matches ended around five o'clock after raising two thousand dollars. Train donated an extra two thousand dollars. *Like a bid for Simone,* he thought.

After leaving her husband, Simone moved into a condo in downtown Lafayette right off of Jefferson Street. Train invited her out that night for the dinner and dancing she had promised him for putting on the exhibition. He told her he would pick her up at seven sharp and asked her to dress in his favorite royal colors.

"My pleasure," Simone said, "but only because it's you, Train."

He knocked on her condo door. She wore a purple strapless dress, a gold necklace and bracelet, and red high heels.

"Purple, gold, and red," she said. "Royal enough?"

She gave him a tour of her condo. It was decorated with contemporary art, Lichtenstein, Warhol, and a painting of a blue dog wearing a sheriff cap and badge over the headboard of her bed. Her watchdog, she called him. Train also took notice of her floor-to-ceiling glass shower, rimmed in soft pink neon lighting. As they were walking back out of the bedroom to sit on the balcony, Train glanced over and there on her bedside table was the tennis magazine, the one with his underwear centerfold photograph.

After dinner, they went back to Simone's condo. She went into her bedroom to change into her jeans and cowgirl boots for a night of waltzing and Zydeco dancing. Train had been fantasizing about Simone for over twenty years now, and his fantasy was unfolding before him. Two things could happen, he figured. His fantasy could come to life or he could get slapped all the way to Bel Air nonstop.

He walked into her bedroom. She was standing at the closet, wearing a purple silk blouse, barefoot, and only a pair of silk panties. She held her jeans in her hand. Train walked slowly and quietly up behind her and put his hand on her shoulder and turned her around. He was looking into her beautiful green eyes. His hand slid from her shoulder to her waist. He pulled her close and kissed her, and the jeans fell from her hand. He began to unbutton her blouse slowly, the gold-and-diamond tennis racquet necklace still around her neck. Her blouse fell like a leaf to the floor, revealing a black lace, low-cut, see-through bra. She looked at him, no motion, the seconds going by. He wondered where she was at that moment.

She pulled him to her and gently kissed him. She unbuttoned his shirt and pushed it off over his broad muscular shoulders. Without saying a word, she took his hand and led him to her bed. She unbuckled his belt, still no words, then unfastened and slowly took off his pants. She opened the dresser drawer and pulled out her pink blindfold. She covered her eyes and lay back on the bed.

He walked over to the vanity and opened the bottle of oil, pouring it onto her chest, the oil flowing between her breasts down to her navel. He started massaging in a circular motion over her breasts. He moved across her stomach to her legs, teasing her with his fingers. "Again," she asked. He moved down her body, sensually kissing her all over. She was moaning and breathless. He removed the blindfold, wanting to drift into her beautiful green eyes. She rolled over and sat up on top of him. His wish came true, his fantasy unfolded, the reality was beautiful ecstasy. She lowered herself to him and they lay still for a while, no words. Their embrace captured the moment.

She took his hand and led him into the shower. Train's memory went back twenty years ago to that Friday night after the football game when he first saw her in shower, the lather, rivers and streams flowing and dripping down her beautiful body. He'd fantasized since then about her in the shower with him, together with those rivers and streams of lather washing over them.

He walked out the door onto Jefferson Street and looked back up to see her standing on her second-floor balcony. She blew him a kiss and disappeared into her bedroom.

He needed time to savor the moment. He walked down Jefferson Street. It was about four in the morning and everything was closed, deserted streets, just him and his departing thoughts. He would truly miss the southwest Louisiana culture. He'd miss the food, the music, the fais do-dos, but his waltz had seen its time there. It was time for him to waltz in a different place: Southern California.

On Sunday morning, his last morning in Lafayette, he met with my father and mother at their favorite breakfast place, The French Press, across from Parc Sans Souci on East Vermilion Street. Bones met them there also. Train ordered his usual, the Cajun Benedict, toasted French bread, Hebert's boudin, two poached eggs topped with chicken and andouille gumbo and fresh scallions. His emotions built, and he teared up as they were leaving the restaurant. He said his good-byes to Dr. Mouton and Evangeline and Bones.

"Come back to see us soon, Train," my mother said. "We've always loved you like a son."

Train was silent.

"Okay, let's go, Bones, before I change my mind," Train finally said.

Bones drove Train to the Lafayette Airport in his official parks and recreation pickup truck. The Lafayette Airport was directly across Surrey Street from Beaver Park. Train asked Bones to cruise by Beaver Park. As they got closer to the tennis courts, Train could see her.

"Stop here, Bones," Train said. "Don't go no closer."

There she was on court one, the beautiful Simone. She played with the movement and grace of a goddess. Train was hypnotized. She was his first love in many ways. She stirred his first instincts of pleasure, excitement, wonderment, and thrill. He couldn't take his eyes off her. Bones knew who he was looking at.

"Sure is a fine-lookin' woman, that Miss Simone," Bones said. "Train, wanna go say goodbye to her? She goin' miss you mighty much now."

"Naw, Bones, but Lord I can only wish she was mine."

But Train didn't say goodbye. He'd already said goodbye as well as he knew how.

Part Two

"Every time I hit the ball on the wall I used to pretend I was there—Wimbledon. When I went to sleep I used to pretend I was there."

—Evonne Goolagong

Marcel

My father delivered a baby boy up in Carencro to Mr. Mel and Mrs. Marlene Jackson in February of 1962. They named their son Marcel Girard Jackson. Marlene worked as a music teacher in the Acadia Parish School System, visiting different schools throughout the week. Mel was from North Carolina and left UNC-Chapel Hill his junior year to play some music festivals in and around Lafayette. He met Marlene while playing with a Zydeco band at the Crawfish Festival in Breaux Bridge. He never returned to college and stayed in Lafayette, marrying Marlene a year later.

Mel was now a part-time musician playing in a Zydeco band on weekends. He supplemented his income through the week by working as a cook at a restaurant in Lafayette, real close to his house in Carencro. Mel had been doing his music gigs for a while, and the cooking job paid all right but not enough to support a wife and new baby boy. He'd hoped to buy a house. He got a call from his buddy named Keith, an offshore oil rig worker. The Kersh Oil Co. of Santa Barbara, California, was operating three offshore rigs out in the Gulf of Mexico and was looking for a cook with a culinary certificate. The job paid well, but all the men worked several weeks at a time on the rigs—not the greatest thing for a proud new father. But the money was necessary. Keith told Mel if he wanted the spot he had to decide quickly. Keith's lady friend at Kersh Oil, Juliette, owed him a big favor, and he'd put in a special word for him.

Mel was off a week for Christmas about six years after starting his job. He was doing well working for Kersh Oil. Mel and Marlene loved to dance, sing, and play music, and little Marcel was always right there with them. Mel made that Christmas special. He gave his son a guitar from Santa Claus and promised to teach Marcel to play.

About two weeks later, after Mel left to go back out on the rig, Keith dropped by unexpectedly and visited Marlene and Marcel. He came to the house in Carencro with the Kersh Oil chaplain. He had some bad news to deliver, he said, but had a hard time speaking. The chaplain stepped in and explained, regretfully, that Mel had died in an oil rig explosion.

A gumbo and crawfish boil reception followed the funeral down in Girard Park. Mel and his Zydeco band had played festivals in that park many times over the years, and it was one of his special places.

Mel and Marlene had never been able to buy a house. It was going to be difficult for Marlene to juggle her schedule and get Marcel around while living up in Carencro. A week after the memorial, Juliette, the Louisiana-based secretary for Kersh Oil, and Irma came to pay Marlene a visit. Irma expressed her condolences and told Marlene she was the wife of Mr. Kersh, the owner of Kersh Oil. Irma explained that she lived in Santa Barbara, but she was born and grew up in New Iberia. Irma told Marlene she had a check from the Kersh Oil Co.'s life insurance division for fifty thousand dollars. She also presented Marlene with a ten-thousand-dollar interest-bearing municipal bond which would mature after ten years and cover a good portion of the costs of Marcel's education or any necessary expenses. They had chosen Mr. Coteau down at the bank to act as Marlene's trustee and handle all the financial due diligence. This brought tears to Marlene's eyes.

Irma went on to explain that years ago, Kersh Oil bought three houses down near the airport. They were on a little street over behind Heyman Park right on the Bayou Vermilion.

"Just across the bayou is Beaver Park," Irma said. "Marcel will enjoy living near the parks."

They would be within walking distance of the elementary and middle schools and the park. One of the houses had been vacant for over a year and sat right on a little lake, the Petite Bayou. They had gifted one of the houses to a couple, William and Viola, who took care of the properties. Marlene knew Viola. Viola worked in the cafeteria at the middle school and Marlene met her when she traveled around teaching music. Irma explained to Marlene that if Kersh Oil had a steady tenant in the vacant house, they would be able to get the necessary insurance. Irma offered the house to Marlene rent free. All Marlene had to do was sign a lease and it was hers. Irma said that if she and Marcel stayed in the house for ten years, it would be deeded over to her and written off by the Kersh Oil Co. This was a dream come true for Marlene. The parks and schools were so close by.

The house would be so perfect for her and Marcel. The only thing missing was Mel.

Marcel started the first grade at Paul Breaux Elementary School on South Orange Street right across the road from Heyman Park. Marlene and Marcel lived at the south end of Heyman Park on Gauthier Street close to the baseball field and the basketball court. But right across from his new school at the other end of the park was the recreation center, a picnic pavilion, a tennis court, and a tennis wall, a wall that a kid could hit tennis balls against to practice if that kid couldn't find anyone to practice with, which turned out to be Marcel's good fortune.

The tennis courts were mostly used for hopscotch and bicycle riding and were mostly unattended, as there was no activity on these courts. Every day Marcel would ride his bike to school and pass by the tennis courts and tennis wall. Marlene and Marcel walked down the road one Saturday afternoon to meet their new neighbors, Viola and William, both of Creole descent. Their house overlooked the Petite Bayou pond which was fed by a little stream off the Bayou Vermilion. William was employed at the local Chevrolet dealership where he worked in the body shop.

When they walked up to the house, Ms. Viola, as Marcel would call her, was sitting on the front porch. She got up and smiled brightly and started clapping her hands. Viola was a petite woman of boundless energy, a constant smile, and was maybe one hundred and ten pounds. Her words had a rhythmical, songlike quality. Her husband William often called her his "Violin." William had a handsome face and a smile as beautiful as a glowing southwest Louisiana crescent moon. Most days when not working, William would dress in a pair of pressed jeans, black-and-gold alligator cowboy boots, a collared white shirt, his signature red vest, and a wide-brimmed black hat.

"Why, Marlene, who is this fine-looking young man you be showing off today?" Viola asked.

Marlene nudged Marcel to introduce himself and shake hands with Viola.

"It's so nice to meet you, Marcel," Viola said. "Why, you such a handsome young man. Did y'all get moved in up the road okay? Everything awright now?"

About that time, they heard the sound of an accordion coming from the back porch. It was William, sitting in a rocking chair playing an old Cajun waltz about an alligator. Viola put her finger over her mouth and smiled for them to be quiet. When William finished, he put his accordion down and said, "I hope you enjoyed your concert today." Viola pointed out to the small pond not more than fifty feet from the back porch, where a small alligator lay on the bank facing William, who'd named the animal "Tabasco Joe." Viola started clapping. William was wearing dark sunglasses and he turned toward them.

"William, we have some new friends for you to meet," Viola said. "This is Ms. Marlene Jackson, the music teacher at the schools I've told you about, and her young son, Marcel. They moved in just up the street into the Kersh Oil house. Irma set it all up for them."

"That's one fine woman, that Irma," William said.

After Viola's introduction, William said it would be fine for them to just call him "Blind Willie."

He had been blind since birth.

"Blind Willie?" asked Marcel.

Blind Willie told him he got off work from the body shop job every day at five o'clock. Mr. Robicheaux, the owner of the Chevrolet dealership, told his customers that Blind Willie could feel all the dents in the cars with his hands and fingers better than a man with 20-20 vision. Every time Mr. Robicheaux sold a new car, he would tell the customer that he would have Blind Willie drive it right over. Everybody in town knowing he was blind would burst out laughing.

"What you like to do for fun?" Blind Willie asked Marcel.

Marcel explained that he liked to practice playing his guitar a lot after school. "My daddy gave me a guitar last Christmas," Marcel said shyly.

Blind Willie told Marcel that he was always home 'round five thirty every day and Marcel would be done schoolin'. Willie told Marcel to ride his bike over and ole Blind Willie would teach him to play that guitar real good. And every day in the fall of his first-grade year, Marcel went home after school, did his homework, got his guitar, and rode over to Blind Willie's house. They played a little musical game. Marcel would park his bike on the front porch, and as he walked around to the back porch, he would stop and play a couple of notes on his guitar. Then Blind Willie would play the same notes on his accordion, and they would trade notes for a couple minutes, and Marcel would go around the porch and sit down on the steps beside Blind Willie's rocking chair. Blind Willie always had some lemonade and a snack for Marcel.

As time went on, Marcel got to play guitar some at Blind Willie's church and at little festivals around town with him. He even got to play with Blind Willie in the band at the Christmas concert at the Vermilionville Performance Center at Beaver Park. They were like father and son. Blind Willie taught him more things than just how to play a guitar.

One day after the end of his first school year, Marcel was riding his bike to Blind Willie's house for some more guitar lessons and on the way he saw a big sign out on Surrey Street for the Acadiana Amateur Tennis Championship Finals that Saturday at Beaver Park. Marlene was going to be at a band festival over in Opelousas all day that day, and Blind Willie had to catch up on some work at the dealership, so Marcel decided to ride his bike across the Surrey Street Bridge to Beaver Park and see what this tennis tournament thing was all about.

When he got there, he couldn't believe his eyes. There were hundreds of people. There were cars everywhere and boys and girls dressed in tennis clothes with their high school names on them. Marcel stayed at the back of the fence, watching in amazement at the tennis battles being fought. A loud voice came on the microphone.

"Ladies and gentlemen, the championship match will take place in five minutes on court one," the booming voice said. The match was between a player from Red Lerille's Health and Racquet Club and a player from Beaver Park.

Marcel was awestruck. He couldn't take his eyes off the game. He had never seen a tennis match before. The championship match was the last match taking place. Hundreds of people sat in the stands to watch the two finalists play. The announcer kept saying words and numbers that Marcel didn't understand. It was all jumbled up. *Love-15, 30-40, 15-all, 40-all, deuce, add out, add in, Love-40.*

"Game, set, match," the announcer said. "The Acadiana Amateur Championship trophy will now take its place in the trophy case at Red Lerille's Health and Racquet Club."

The two players went to the net and shook hands and a man in a white coat and pants came out and gave the guy named Phillipe a big trophy. A lot of people came over and shook hands and everyone started to leave, but the Beaver Park player who lost just sat there and Marcel watched him. The player had thrown his racquet toward the back fence after he lost the match. It hit a pole and slid underneath the fence, and the player left.

Marcel looked around, and everyone was gone. He looked down at the racquet. It cracked at the top of the handle. The letter T was broken by the crack. There were other letters carved deeply into the wooden handle. Marcel picked the racquet up. All of a sudden he heard a voice.

"Hey, young man."

Marcel started to run because he thought the man would think he was stealing the racquet. He turned and looked back. It was a black man. It was Bones. Marcel started to cry.

"I wasn't going to steal it," Marcel said.

"What's yo name, son?" Bones asked.

Marcel didn't answer.

"It's all right," Bones said. "You keep that racquet. Take it on home and get it taped up. Be as good as new."

Bones gave him some balls that had been left around the courts and told Marcel to start hitting tennis balls with somebody.

"If you can't find nobody," Bones said, "just find a tennis wall and hit them balls against that wall. And if anybody happen to say anything to you 'bout dat racquet, you just tell them I give it to you."

Marcel rode straight over to Blind Willie's house and told Viola all about his adventure and the broken racquet, the tennis balls, and the nice man named Bones. Viola taped up that racquet right then and there, good as new.

Marcel was out of school for the summer, and Marlene was going to start taking summer classes over at the University of Louisiana, Lafayette, to finish her master's in music education. Marcel spent his summer days playing around Heyman Park. There were many parks and recreation workers around, and there were all kinds of summer activities going on in the park: flag football, youth basketball, art classes up at the recreation center, cheerleading camps. Heyman Park was a very safe place for him. Marcel was still too small and not old enough to participate in any of the summer team sports at the park. He was not interested in painting trees in art class either. He remembered what Mr. Bones told him over at Beaver Park: find a tennis wall. Lucky for Marcel, there was an old tennis wall at Heyman Park and he had never seen anybody use it. The white paint was peeling off a little bit. A blue line went across the middle of the wall. Marcel figured that was supposed to be the net. Hit it over the net, he told himself. Marcel would go up to that wall every day after he and Marlene had breakfast and she left for school. He would hit balls until lunchtime, then ride back home, eat the sandwich and cookies his mama made him, then go right back out to the wall.

One day he had only been back at the wall for about fifteen minutes when a pickup truck pulled up on Orange Street. It was Bones in his Lafayette Parks and Recreation truck.

"You fixin' to be du next Acadiana Amateur State Champion, Marcel?" Bones asked.

Bones started to drop by every day and check on Marcel and tell him how great he was getting and to keep on working hard. Bones also kept Marcel supplied with the old tennis balls he found lying around the Beaver Park Tennis Center. Bones had been hired as the new maintenance supervisor for the Lafayette Parks and Recreation Department in charge of Heyman Park and Beaver Park. The previous guy had reached retirement age at the end of the year.

The search committee included several board members including my father and Sheriff Lloyd and others. Bones had been working part time for the parks department now for twenty years, so my father spoke up.

"Why don't we just go ahead and hire Bones as the new supervisor?" my father asked.

The director of the Lafayette Parks and Recreation Department, Ms. Hollier, explained that would not be possible due to the qualifications for this position. Bones did not have a high school degree from the Acadia Parish School System. My father countered that Bones had taken care of all the school fields and park fields in and around Lafayette for years and was more qualified than most people with a degree. He asked for a continuance and in the meantime asked the Acadia Parish school superintendent, Mr. Thibodeaux—who, by the way, had three children delivered by my father—to award Bones an honorary degree from the Acadia Parish School System for loyalty and hard work and for time served in the interest of the Parks and Recreation Department. Mr. Thibodeaux did indeed grant my father's request and formally signed the document, granting the honorary degree to Bones, thus qualifying him for the position.

My father, the genius.

Bones was now fully employed by the Lafayette Parks and Recreation Department and was able to leave his job at the sugar warehouse with full retirement and benefits after working there for more than forty years. When Bones stopped by to check on Marcel, he noticed Marcel was getting better every day. Hard shots, drop shots, lob shots, high shots, low shots—Marcel was learning everything on his own. Hours and hours of hitting that tennis wall.

Bones figured that Marcel had the same natural talent that Train had.

Marcel left the tennis wall every day that summer about five o'clock in the afternoon to make his special trip over to Blind Willie's house with his guitar.

In a couple years, I would happen to enter into Marcel's life thanks to Bones.

Being the assistant athletic director at LSU required many road trips to interview potential high school athletes for our athletic scholarships. I had seen Bones occasionally in and around Lafayette but had not been down to Beaver

Park in about five years, having no reason because scouting and recruiting tennis players to LSU had been delegated to another assistant in the athletic department. I traveled through Lafayette down to Abbeville one spring in the early '70s, I think it was, to watch a baseball player who our coach wanted very much to become a Tiger. Just before leaving my office that Friday morning, I got a call from Bones asking me to drop by and see him sometime over at Beaver Park.

"Just so happens I'm coming your way this weekend, Bones," I said.

After leaving the baseball game early that Friday evening, I decided to drive back by way of Surrey Street through Heyman Park. I had a little time to kill and wouldn't see Bones until Saturday for lunch. It was getting dark then as I drove though Heyman Park. A raccoon came into my headlights, and I swerved and ran into a ditch. The car stalled.

I got out to see if everything was okay. The lights still worked. Nothing was smoking. All appeared good. All of a sudden I heard a young voice carrying from the park. The park lights were still on.

"Jackson wins the second set, 6-4, to force a third set with Lacoste!" the voice exclaimed.

I heard the sound of tennis balls hitting a wall.

"Jackson, add-in. Jackson, game, set, match," the voice said. "Rene Lacoste down in defeat. Marcel Jackson, the new Wimbledon champion!"

I went around the tennis wall, and there stood a young boy holding his racquet in the air, bowing to a make-believe crowd. So, why not, I began to applaud. The boy turned toward me, startled.

"Oh, hello, Mister," the kid said.

"Hello, son," I said. "Don't be afraid. My name is Louie Mouton."

The kid told me his name was Marcel Jackson and that he and his mama Marlene lived just on the other side of the park.

It turned out that I knew Marlene because we'd gone through school together. It was getting dark, so I decided to follow Marcel home and say hello to Marlene.

Marlene was surprised to see me and said she and Marcel were doing great. She was still teaching music and studying for her masters, and Marcel was now twelve years old and in the sixth grade. She told me that Marcel practiced his tennis every day but had not yet taken any lessons. I told her I would drop by in the morning and take him with me over to Beaver Park to see Bones and that I would talk to Mr. Cristola about some tennis lessons and maybe a junior tournament or two. She was excited, knowing how much Marcel loved Bones and that he would have a chance to play on a real tennis court.

I picked Marcel up at twelve o'clock, and we had lunch with Bones right there in Beaver Park at the Vermilionville Historic Center restaurant. Bones told me how much and how often Marcel had been practicing tennis for the last six years. After lunch I winked at Bones and asked Marcel if he would like to go hit some balls with me at the tennis courts.

"You can show me what you got," I said.

At the courts, as we began to hit a few, I was amazed at his strokes and footwork. It was like he stepped out of *Tennis for the Advanced Player*, a tennis book which sat fat in the middle of my father's bookshelf. Watching Marcel, I was reminded of years ago when I went home to hit balls with Train and saw his potential. Marcel showed the same stuff, a lot of talent. Mr. Cristola agreed with me and signed Marcel into the junior league and agreed to give him lessons, free of charge, whenever he came to the park.

Blind Willie

Marcel practiced and played in the junior tennis league on an almost daily basis for two years, though never on Sundays. On Sunday he went to church and in the afternoons played with all the musicians around Acadiana.

One Sunday afternoon Marlene and Marcel were going through some old trunks and boxes in the woodshed out back they had moved down from Carencro years ago. Marcel saw an old trunk behind a wooden wicker chair with a lock on it. Marlene said she had no idea what was in there. Mel had brought that down from North Carolina when he first moved to Lafayette, and she figured it was some old high school yearbooks and stuff. Marlene rushed off to choir practice and left Marcel in the woodshed. He kept eyeing that trunk and fantasized he was going to find out what was in that secret pirate's chest—full of gold, he fantasized. He found a mason jar full of keys on a shelf in the shed and after thirty minutes of trying a bunch of different ones, a key finally slipped in. He turned it, and the chest flew open with a loud pop and bang. Marcel fell back on the floor, terrified, as if the old dead pirate inside was waiting for someone to steal his treasures of gold.

He raised himself up and looked in the chest. It *was* full of gold: golden tennis trophies, old tennis shoes, and newspaper articles all about his daddy, Mel. Five trophies bore the inscription "North Carolina Junior State Champion Melvin Jackson." When Marlene returned Marcel excitedly took her back out to the woodshed to show her his treasure find. She was in awe, explaining to Marcel that Mel never talked about his early years very much, only that he played a little bit of tennis when he was a kid. No wonder Marcel liked tennis so much, Marlene explained. She said he was going to be just as good as his daddy was and make him real proud. He was going to win a lot of trophies too, just like his daddy Mel. He would start practicing and playing more than ever. He wanted a trunk full of gold one day too.

Marcel earned a number-four junior ranking in the state. The Louisiana Junior State Championship was held at Beaver Park, and Marcel upset the number-one ranked player from New Orleans, only the second time a player from Lafayette had won the junior title, the first being Rene Pierre "Train" Lacroix. As Marcel stood at center court with the trophy in hand, he looked up into the stands directly at Bones and me and raised and pointed his racquet toward us. He took a bow just like he did two years ago at sunset at the Heyman Park tennis wall. He looked like he had just won the French Open. He went on to win the junior state title two more times.

Marcel's high school tennis career was superlative. He became another big-time player from Lafayette. He was only five feet, ten inches tall and weighed only about one hundred sixty-five pounds, much smaller than Train, his famous predecessor. Marcel patterned his game after the great Rene Lacoste: control, patience, study, persistence, and, most of all, the intellectual analysis of the opponent. I'd describe Marcel's game as one of planning and an almost ballet-like attitude of movement. When I think about his stroke, the word that comes to mind is *finesse* and more finesse. The art of it all. Totally opposite of the great Train, a swashbuckling, slashing, purely instinctual player who liked to play the cat-and-mouse strategy. But Train had the rage to eliminate his opponent, the instinct to survive at all costs. To him, the winner lived and the loser died with pain. Train's killer instinct told him to punish. He was dangerous. Not so with Marcel.

Marcel won the Louisiana State High School Championship his junior year, opening up the possibility for back-to-back high school championships for Lafayette, inching closer and closer in on the footsteps of the legendary Train.

Through the years, Marcel spent time in the afternoons with Blind Willie, playing their music and listening to Blind Willie's lessons about life. Blind Willie told Marcel at an early age to close his eyes, hear the note he was going to play, and then play it on the guitar. And after Marcel starting getting good at tennis, Blind Willie told him the same thing about tennis.

"Close your eyes," Willie said. "Think about where you want to hit that serve, or return that serve. Think about if you want to hit it hard or slow, long or short. When your mind sees what you trying to do, it lots of times will happen. All in the mind's eye. There's lots of power in the mind's eye, Marcel. I know this all my life."

This became Marcel's way of thinking. Playing guitar or playing tennis, he would close his eyes, think through the situation, envision the events as they would happen, and program his physical actions with a mental picture, a movie in his head.

Marcel spent his eleventh-grade summer thinking less about tennis and more about his guitar. He put a band together that summer to pick up some extra money. He played in only two tournaments that summer and only advanced as far as the semifinals. The band was working about four nights a week and traveling around Louisiana. He dropped by Blind Willie's about twice a week then and sometimes played with Willie in one of the church bands on Sunday. Marcel had become an accomplished songwriter and singer. One of his songs had even been nominated for a Grammy. "In the Mind's Eye," the song was called.

The band gigs during Marcel's senior year were usually just one-nighters on the weekends and a couple of junior/senior prom dances. He picked up his racquet again and was on a disciplined track to begin training for his senior year of tennis. He hoped to claim a second high school state championship, but that didn't happen. He lost, 6-4, 7-5, 4-6, and 7-5 to a player from Baton Rouge. Two days later he dropped by Blind Willie's for some music, but also because his confidence was in need of restoration after losing the state championship. He figured maybe Blind Willie had the answers.

Marcel was worried. The Memorial Day Oyster Bay Classic was in another two months and he wanted that trophy more than anything. Blind Willie had some simple advice. He told Marcel to put down that guitar, quit playing in those bands, and think and do nothing but play and practice tennis until that Oyster Bay Classic started.

Blind Willie's advice was right on. Marcel put his music way out of sight and out of mind. Not even on Sundays did he play. Nothing but tennis all day, every day. Blind Willie called Marcel a week before the Oyster Bay and said he wasn't feelin' too good. He must have caught him a bad cold, maybe a little flu or something. Marcel wanted to drop by and see Willie before going down to the tournament.

"Betta not, Marcel," Willie said. "You might catch sick and miss du tournament. I don't want dat to happen now.

We need dat trophy back up here in Acadiana. You play hard and see dat trophy in yo mind and after you get back up here to du bayou with dat trophy, we can start playin' some music again. Evuh thang gone be awright now, Marcel. Yes suh, you play good, son."

Marcel's daily practice and the talks with Blind Willie aligned all the stars in his game. Marcel won the finals of the Oyster Bay Classic against the reigning high school state champion who had defeated him earlier that year. Marcel won in blistering straight sets, 6-3, 6-2, 6-4. The Oyster Bay trophy was on its way back to Acadiana. Marcel now stood in the vaulted and celebrated company of the legendary Train.

Marcel had to stay around New Orleans a couple days for the awards ceremony, press interviews, and to announce his decision to accept the full tennis scholarship at Tulane by virtue of his Oyster Bay Classic win.

It would have been great for Marcel to play for us at LSU, but Tulane had a strong tennis program as well and a great coach. And I knew the richness of the music culture in New Orleans and Marcel's desire to continue his musical journey, making it the perfect fit. Marcel's hardest decision to make was leaving his mama, but she tried to make the decision easy. It was a great opportunity to experience a whole new world, she told him, and he could become a great tennis player or a great musical talent, whichever he chose. He could find out all on his own. He'd make his own way in the world.

Marcel couldn't wait to return to see Blind Willie and show him the Oyster Bay Classic trophy. At their usual time, five thirty, that Friday afternoon, Marcel walked onto the front porch and around to the side porch and played about four or five new notes on his guitar. But that afternoon no accordion echoed his guitar. Marcel played his guitar notes again. Again, no accordion. Marcel walked around to the back porch. There in the chair was the accordion. The screen door opened. Viola walked out, put her hand on his shoulder, and told Marcel that William had died the previous night in his sleep four days after hearing that Marcel had won the Oyster Bay Classic. He had developed acute pneumonia a week earlier.

Marcel began to cry. He walked out to the bench by the Petite Bayou where he and Blind Willie had sat many times before. As he peered out across the water, thinking of how much he would miss Willie, he saw Blind Willie's old friend, Tabasco Joe, gracefully gliding toward the bank.

On the day of the funeral, Heyman Park was closed for the afternoon for the throng of people and to accommodate the march of the funeral line. Blind Willie's wish was to be buried out back of his house just down the way near the banks of the Petite Bayou. His other final wish was that Marcel would play one of their old favorite Creole songs on his guitar.

Marcel, remembering the years playing guitar with Blind Willie, spent more time with his music that summer and very little with his tennis. His heart was with Blind Willie and all the music they had played together. Marcel started a band and named it "Blind Willie's Bayou Boogaloo Band." Viola wanted to have a big crawfish boil for Marcel the Saturday before he left for college and invite all their friends. The party ended around five o'clock, and Viola led Marlene and Marcel around the side of the house toward a little wooden clapboard building. Viola took a key out of her apron and unlocked the door. The afternoon sunlight shone on a sparkling red car.

It was Blind Willie's pride and joy, a 1959 Mercedes-Benz roadster.

"Mr. Robicheaux gave this car to William years ago for his long service and loyalty to the Chevrolet dealership," Viola explained.

The car was traded in for a Chevy Corvette convertible by a lady passing through from Texas. The car needed some bodywork and a new paint job and Mr. Robicheaux knew just who could fix it and restore it back to perfect condition. Never once was the car taken out for a drive. Old Willie would only start it up once in a little while to keep it running smoothly, saving it as a graduation present for Marcel. Willie nicknamed the car "Tabasco Cat" and said Marcel would be the hottest red cat cruising around Louisiana.

> *"I believe in the power of the mind and visualization, which is a big part of my everyday life."*
> —Novak Djokovic

The Big Easy

Marcel, Marlene, and Viola took off early Sunday morning for New Orleans. Marlene and Viola followed Marcel down the highway. He was driving his vintage red Mercedes-Benz roadster with the top down and his guitar case and tennis racquet sticking out above the backseat, a head-turner for sure, that little red Mercedes roadster. The fact that Marcel had those boyish good looks and that golden mane of curly blonde hair added to the high attention factor from all the young coeds on campus. He was every Louisiana girl's delight, a handsome red-hot gumbo.

Marcel played number three his freshmen year. The coach thought that the more wins and experience Marcel got under his belt, the better prepared mentally he would be to slide into the number-one or two slot his sophomore year. Marcel destroyed his opponents while the number-two player, a junior from right there in New Orleans named Carson Bratteur III, struggled. Carson's grandmother, Ms. Crystal Bratteur, was usually at all of Carson's matches. She often asked Marcel if he ever saw Rene Lacroix back in Lafayette. Each time, with a look of curiosity in his eyes, Marcel answered no. All he knew was that he was on tour all the time and he'd actually never met him.

Early in Marcel's freshman year, just three weeks into the spring season, Carson Bratteur III tore his right ACL, requiring two surgeries and rehabilitation, which everyone later learned did not go well. His college tennis career had ended. The tennis team decided to visit Carson at the Bratteur home. It was a three-story mansion in the Garden District of New Orleans on St. Charles Avenue.

Marcel Jackson had never seen such a place. A uniformed maid greeted them at the front door, and an elevator transported them up to Carson's bedroom on the third floor. The guys wished him well and wanted him to return with them the following season as the assistant trainer for the team.

Marcel glided effortlessly into the number-two spot. After only two losses his freshman season, he was named MVP of the team and selected first team All-Conference.

Marcel aimed to be number one by his sophomore year, which he earned after an intense summer and fall training and practice regime. He usually drove home on Sundays to go to church with Marlene and Viola, eat some jambalaya and etouffee, then swing over to the park performance center for the Sunday afternoon dance, the Bal du Dimanche. His sophomore year was golden, an individual conference championship and a team championship playing number one, all the while maintaining a top-twenty national ranking. Things went differently in the NCAA tourney, however. His game wasn't a great match against the super elite, and he was eliminated before the quarterfinals.

In Marcel's junior year, he exited as a runner-up in the Southeastern Conference Individual Championship and finished fourth in the NCAA National Championship.

I attended most of his championship rounds and readily saw the difference between him and Train. Train had no major distractions away from his complete focus on the game. Marcel didn't have Train's focus. Marcel felt the pull from his love of music, playing the guitar and writing songs. Marcel had a weakness in his game, the backhand, but the most important thing that Train had that Marcel didn't was a killer instinct, the desire to completely destroy the opponent, the desire to brutalize the opponent, the desire to win at all costs. Marcel's game was one of artistry and a calm demeanor, almost a *counterpuncher*, not much of an attacker as was Train.

During the fall of Marcel's senior year, he began to drift more toward the music. He was writing songs, playing more gigs at fraternity parties on weekends, and traveling in and out of town to play the many festivals taking place around Louisiana. He still attended the team practice sessions but didn't practice on the side to improve his game, especially his backhand. He also earned extra money giving private tennis lessons in and around New Orleans, especially down in the Garden District to all the rich kids. Between all the admiring Tulane coeds and his tennis students, he had little time left for extra practice. He even made fewer trips to Lafayette on the weekends due to his busy schedule playing gigs on Friday and Saturday nights and giving tennis lessons.

But again Marcel's heart shifted focus. He made himself a New Year's resolution to give it his all. He wanted to win an individual and team championship for the mighty Green Wave.

Marcel achieved another super record his senior season with only three losses. He finished runner-up in the individual Southeastern Conference Championship, another bridesmaid finish.

The final tournament of Marcel's college career would be the NCAA Championship. His last shot to cap off a great college career. The tournament seeded him third going into the championship. He ranked in the top ten nationwide all season. He made it to the championship round against a player named Andy, a USC Trojan from the "vineyard of tennis," Southern California. Andy, like Marcel, learned his game on the public parks and tennis courts of Los Angeles. Andy upset the number-one seed, a *stopper*, the term used in tennis to define an upset. Marcel won the first set, 6-4. Andy was a baseliner and a percentage player, constantly hitting shots to the baseline. The second set went to a tie-break with Andy the victor. In set three, Andy discovered a weakness in Marcel's game, his backhand, and Andy won the set, 7-5. The final set was a war on many occasions. With a chance to hit a *putaway* to win the game, Marcel tried a finesse shot which backfired. Andy again went to Marcel's backhand.

The final set Andy won, 7-5, another *stopper* by the fourth seed. The NCAA championship trophy headed back to Southern California. It was yet another bridesmaid finish for Marcel. He'd had enough runner-up and top-ten finishes in big tournaments over the years.

Marcel didn't want to finish in the top twenty or as a perennial bridesmaid on the pro circuit. The NCAA tournament had been hosted by the University of Texas at Austin, a hotbed of great musicians and songwriters. *Why not*, Marcel thought, *lay down the tennis strings and pick up those guitar strings and have some fun?* He stayed in Austin for a couple days, pulled his guitar out of the trunk, and mixed it up with some old musician friends in and around the music venues of the city. Marcel had a blast, pure joy. He hadn't picked up his guitar in months, and what fun. No pressure, no thinking, no intensity, just the sheer enjoyment of playing his music.

Marcel headed back to New Orleans and graduated three weeks later. He took some time to consider whether or not to join the tour. While considering it, he was invited to sit in with a band and play over the weekend down at a Bourbon Street honky-tonk. The owner of a bar named Papa Mojo's Roadhouse about fifteen miles just on the outskirts of New Orleans was in that night and was blown away by Marcel's guitar riffs and offered him a gig in his house band. Papa Mojo's wasn't a place where the typical tourist would care to venture, but the locals hung out there where things got a little wild sometimes. It sounded like a good gig to Marcel, playing music four nights a week and writing songs every day, chilling a while away from tennis.

Marcel accepted the job and said he would be back in a week. He had to go home and spend some time with his mama. Around that time, Marcel began to notice a little change in her. She often seemed tired. She slept longer than usual and had occasional headaches. She assured Marcel that nothing was wrong. He told her of his plans to play and write music for the summer down in New Orleans and she was very happy for him. She knew he had the gift and a talent for music.

Marcel moved into a swamp house about a half-mile down the dirt road from Papa Mojo's Roadhouse with the other guitar player, "California Mike." Swamp houses were pretty much one- or two-room houses that sat right on the bayou and swamps. They were built from the wood of bald cypress trees, a perfect place for Marcel. He had the solitude to write songs and to think about the future, whether music or tennis. Papa Mojo's Roadhouse sat about fifty yards off the highway down a dirt road, bordered by the swamp and cypress trees.

Papa Mojo's was constructed from wood and cinderblock and a ceiling of rafters and had concrete floors. It held about two hundred fifty people, and there was a whole lot of drinking and dancing. On Wednesdays through Saturdays the doors opened at eight and the band started at nine thirty. Closing time was two o'clock sharp, hotel motel time. The crowd on any given night consisted mostly of locals, but on the weekends sometimes some college kids from New Orleans showed up to raise a little hell. Marcel loved the gig. The owner Roy okayed Marcel to play some of his original songs.

There was never any real trouble at Papa Mojo's and for two very good reasons. One, the front door bouncer was a six-foot-two, three-hundred-pound ox of a man named Gator Jaw. He'd usually eliminate any problems within minutes after receiving the caution signal. As a backup, sitting by the band stage, was a man named Snaketooth Sam who hadn't been long out of prison for killing a man with his bare hands.

Marcel's position was on the left of the stage near the dimly lit hallway to his side that led to the bathrooms and around the corner out the back to the swamp.

Things were going great one hot summer Saturday night in Papa Mojo's. The band was smoking, the dance floor rocking. Marcel looked toward the front door when in walked ten beautiful college-aged girls all dressed to the nines. High heels, short dresses, jewelry. All beauty queens, but totally in the wrong place and certainly not in the normal dress code for that swamp joint. They immediately went right on to the dance floor. Marcel's eyes fixed on a redhead with a sparkling green dress. She glanced up and winked and hit the target.

There was a kid named Jasper in the bar that night. Jasper had been in and out of juvenile and foster homes and often abused. His parents were perpetual criminals—drugs and bad checks—in and out of prisons. They dropped him off on the State's doorstep when he was five. Marcel knew he was bad news. He had a reputation for being rough on women. He'd been in jail for assault before, out on probation then. Jasper slowly slid onto the dance floor and starting dancing with the redhead. She smiled and kept dancing. She'd probably had a couple shooters and didn't seem to notice him. Two songs later, Marcel looked down the hallway. Jasper had the redhead by the arm. He was taking her around the corner past the bathrooms.

Marcel asked California Mike to take his lead on the guitar for the next set. He needed to take a quick leak.

"Be right back," Marcel said. He walked down the hallway past the bathrooms and around the corner. The redhead let out a scream. She told Jasper to leave her alone. Marcel heard him call her a little bitch. He said she needed some of his gator meat. Marcel told him to let her go.

"Fuck off," Jasper told Marcel. "This ain't none of your business."

Marcel started toward him. Jasper took his hand off the redhead, stepped within one foot of Marcel, and began to raise his right arm. Jasper's fist came toward Marcel's head. Marcel ducked and dropkicked Jasper behind the knee with a forearm to the chest, slamming him to the floor, an old fighting move taught to him by Blind Willie when some of the kids bullied Marcel about his tennis when he was young. Marcel had his knee on Jasper's throat and Jasper's elbow turned backward.

"I'll break it," Marcel said.

Jasper couldn't breathe. He gasped for air. Marcel got up and took the redhead by the arm and told Jasper he was going to get Snaketooth Sam. Jasper bolted out the back door into the night. Marcel took the redhead by the hand back into the bar and told her that she and her girlfriends needed to leave because there could be more trouble. Marcel led them out to the front parking lot to a black limousine. Their driver, Maurice, rolled his window down. Marcel knew Maurice from the Garden District where he often chauffeured the rich kids to him for tennis lessons. He told him to take them back to New Orleans.

"What the hell you bringing these chicks out here for, Maurice? You crazy?" Marcel asked.

"They pay the cost to be the boss, Marcel, everything cool," Maurice answered with a wink.

As Maurice pulled away, the back window rolled down, and the redhead thanked him for saving her. She said her name was Annie. The limo sped away, and Marcel didn't have time to tell her his name. Her magic dust had entered his soul; how beautiful she was.

Marcel went back to the front door and asked Gator Jaw where the girls were from.

"Don't know," Gator Jaw said. "Probably some rich sorority girls from New Orleans."

Marcel looked down the road.

"Dat redhead," Gator Jaw said. "Boy, she was sho nuff a beauty queen."

Marcel couldn't sleep all that night, thinking about the beautiful green-eyed redhead Annie, whom he'd think about often.

Marlene

I didn't see or hear from Marcel from the beginning of that summer. It was late November, and I was told he was still working at Papa Mojo's and writing music. The LSU Tigers were playing their last conference game late that November on a Saturday, and it was then that my father told me something that would send me down to New Orleans to break some bad news to Marcel.

Bones and I sat out in front of the LSU Athletic Museum late that Sunday afternoon when we heard my father's voice.

"Time to head back to Lafayette, Mr. Bones," he said.

My father, Sheriff Lloyd, the Lafayette coroner, the district attorney, and Mr. Eikenberry—the owner of the Lafayette funeral home—always attended all of the LSU home games. They were all alumni. Bones always drove them over in Mr. Eikenberry's stretch Cadillac limousine used mostly for more sacred trips. But inside the limousine, the napkin holders, flower vases, and ice coolers were custom made for boudin, cracklin, Abita beers, and Louisiana's own bourbon liqueur, Southern Comfort, proudly christened, "None genuine but mine," by the McCauley's Tavern bartender, Martin Heron.

There was another occasion that would require an extra day's stay by my father and the others: a vote on Sunday for the deceased Jacques Lacroix to enter the Louisiana State

Sports Hall of Fame. His death was still a mystery. Bones and I had a chance to sit just outside the hall in the patio garden. It was a beautiful midafternoon fall day in Baton Rouge. Bones seemed very quiet for a while, nervous.

He told me he needed to lay a burden down. I knew this sometimes was an expression of guilt and told him to talk to me. Nobody knew how Jacques died and what white powder was on his neck, but Bones knew. He knew it all, he said.

He was walking up the railroad tracks that Saturday morning to the sugar warehouse to close the doors after the L&T line had finished loading earlier. He was walking back down the road, when he heard some loud cussing and saw a pickup truck parked at the Lacroix's back gate. He knew it was Jacques. Jacques was bad drunk, accusing a man of taking off with his bitch wife and little bastard down to her mama's house. The man accused by Jacques said he hadn't seen Jacques's wife and kid, but Jacques pulled out his gun and pointed it at the man, who ducked.

"They was on the other side of the truck," Bones said. "A shot went off, and they fell to the ground and then another shot went off and then it got quiet."

Bones said he thought they were both dead. He went around to the other side of the truck, and the man was kneeling over Jacques. He turned to look up at Bones and said, "He's dead." The man's hands had white powder on them. He'd tried to do CPR to no avail.

Bones told me many times before he'd seen this man come up behind the Lacroix house. Joline and Train would come running out, and he'd take them down to New Iberia to Joline's mama's house. The man told Bones he wasn't going to tell the police because he knew how it looked, but it was self-defense. He was getting older and he wanted to spend the rest of his days with his granddaughter.

Bones said he knew it was self-defense and agreed not to say anything.

"Ain't no reason to tell 'cause the devil Jacques better off dead," Bones said. "Better for Joline and Train."

He told me the man's hands were white because he delivered a pickup full of white salt every Saturday to the sugar warehouse for the train pickup. Bones told me I could help him lay his burden down if I would be kind enough to let him say the good and godly man's name.

"Yes, Bones," I said. "You can tell me. Your secret is safe. You are like family to me."

"Mr. Louie," Bones said. "It was Irma's grandfather, Mr. Maurice. He God's angel that day, hallelujah. I know God have him do His work."

I didn't need to ask if Jacques Lacroix had been voted into the Louisiana Hall of Fame. My father carried the plaque in his hand as he made his way to the limousine. We were all in a great mood, but not about Jacques. LSU had defeated Alabama the day before, and beating Alabama deserved more than one day of feeling good.

Before they left, my father took me off to the side and told me that Marcel's mother, Marlene, had been diagnosed with a brain tumor, a glioma. She would need surgery, then chemotherapy and radiation treatments that could last anywhere from four to six months.

I asked if Marcel knew yet, and my father said no. The results only came back the previous Friday. My father told me he would call Marcel on Monday.

I had a scholarship signing with a high school football player on Wednesday down in New Orleans, so I decided I would rather break the news to Marcel in person. My father said that would be great. He gave me a big hug.

As Bones opened the limousine door for my father, he handed Bones the plaque that had been awarded to Jacques Lacroix and told him to put it up in the front seat. Bones looked at me as though he had seen a ghost.

I smiled at him and pointed toward the heavens and whispered to him, "Lay your burden down, Bones."

He took a deep breath and smiled back at me. "Thank you, Mr. Louie," Bones said, and they headed back to Lafayette.

I walked in Papa Mojo's around eleven thirty that following Wednesday night after the football scholarship signing. The place was packed. I stood at the bar and ordered an Abita Amber, my favorite beer. The bartender told me the band usually stopped playing around twelve thirty during the week. I waited till then to talk to Marcel. What a band. Marcel burned up that guitar much to the delight of all the young and adoring ladies in the house. He spotted me out in the crowd and pointed toward me and smiled. The band stopped at twelve thirty, but the crowd called for an encore. They hadn't had enough. "More! More!" they chanted. The band closed out the night with a rocking Zydeco classic about a boy who can't dance 'cause he had ants in his pants.

Afterward, Marcel came back to the bar.

"Great to see you, Marcel," I said. "You work the strings on that guitar as good as you work the ones on a tennis racquet, and the girls seem to like it just as much. Your little black book must be brimming."

Marcel told me he had two black books, but none of the girls in those books hit his magic button quite yet. We went around the bar and took a booth near the back door, away from the crowd. Once we sat down, I didn't waste any time. There wasn't any point dragging it out. When I told Marcel his mother had been diagnosed with a rare form of cancer, he was, of course, in shock and disbelief.

He slumped back in the booth and put both hands over his eyes.

"I was just with her a couple of weeks ago out for dinner and some dancing," Marcel said. "Other than being a little tired, she seemed fine. The doctors must be wrong."

I told him the doctors weren't wrong. My father had checked the diagnosis himself.

"Get another opinion," Marcel said. "There's no way this can be. She's never one to get sick."

I told him my father had gotten more than two opinions, and they were all the same. I explained that two different cancer centers ran the tests at my father's orders. "My father wanted to make sure the results came in the same and they did," I said.

Tears began to well in Marcel's eyes.

"Can they help her?" he asked. "Is she going to die? How long does she have to live? Do I need to move back home right away?" He leveled questions at me nonstop. "This can't be happening to my mama," he said. He stood up out of the booth and threw his beer bottle. It crashed against the cinderblock wall. He banged his fist onto the Formica tabletop.

I stood up and grabbed his arms. He kept saying "no" over and over and over. I had never seen Marcel show that kind of emotion before.

"Please calm down," I said. "Marcel, let's slow down here a little. Let me explain everything about what we know right now of your mother's condition. She will have surgery soon—very soon—then chemotherapy and radiation for several months."

Marcel didn't understand. His face showed confusion and anger. "Just go ahead and take out all the cancer now, damn it," he said. "Cut it out. Get it over with. Make her well now. Just make her well."

"That's just not the way it happens, son," I said. "These are fine doctors, and they are going to do all they can for your mama in the best way they know how."

Marcel still doubted and disregarded my words of comfort. "Can't be happening to her," he muttered. "She doesn't deserve something like this." He didn't know what to do. "What can I do?" he said over and over.

Unfortunately, I had more bad news for him. What I told him next unsettled him further.

"Marcel, her insurance policy will only cover half the cost of all the treatments, tests, and surgery," I said. "The balance will be a little over one hundred and fifty thousand dollars. We have already raised about fifty thousand, so another hundred thousand or so will have to be paid somehow."

Marcel put his head in his hands and kept repeating, "No way, no way. This can't be happening."

But I didn't come to Marcel unprepared. I didn't want only to bring him bad news and leave. I talked to my father about solutions, about how to come up with more money. We brainstormed on it until my father's mind went to the place it always goes—tennis—and then came up with the answer.

"Marcel, listen to me," I said. "There is something you can do to help your mama."

Marcel paused his lamentations for a moment to listen to me, his eyes still wet and wide open.

"There is a tournament," I said. "A tennis tournament. The Pacific Palisades Open in California. It's in about five months. It's for amateurs planning on going pro, and it pays two hundred thousand dollars for first place and one hundred thousand for second place. I talked to some of my connections in athletics and your college record meets all the qualifications to enter."

Marcel gave me a skeptical look but didn't say anything.

"This is what you can do for your mama," I said. "Enter the tournament. Win the money. That's what you can do for her."

"I don't know if I have the skill to win," Marcel said. "I don't know if I can beat the top players in the country. Those guys grew up in tennis camps and country clubs with full-time instructors. They were much better instructed and had more access to things than I did growing up."

"I know you have some missing pieces in your game, but we know who can prepare you and fix those missing pieces. You need to take some time off from here, go up to Lafayette Sunday, and spend a week with your mama. Come over to LSU on Tuesday to my office, and I'll lay out the plan for you. We can make this happen, Marcel. Trust me. We're all going to do everything we can for your mama, and we're going to hope for the best."

I sensed that Marcel had at least a small sense of relief and hope that everything really might turn out all right. He hugged me. He told me he appreciated hearing the news from me in person. Marcel and I walked out to the parking lot of Papa Mojo's. When I closed the door, he said he didn't know if he could've handled the news over the phone, and I said, "Neither could I, Marcel. Neither could I. Let's hope for the best. See you on Tuesday." I headed back to Baton Rouge that night.

Marcel drove up to Lafayette early Sunday morning and went to his house. Marlene lay in bed and Viola was at her side, reading the Bible. They were both surprised to see him. He hadn't called to tell them he was coming. Marlene asked him what on earth he was doing home. He had just been home a couple of weeks ago. Marcel walked over to Viola and gave her a big hug and sat on the bed next to Marlene. Before he could ask her about the cancer, she wanted to know all about how he was doing down at Papa Mojo's.

"I've been doing a lot of writing," Marcel said. "And I have enough songs to start recording an album." Marcel said he was going to dedicate the album to her, Viola, and Blind Willie.

Marlene was so happy to see him.

"Why, we ought to go out for some fun this Sunday afternoon," Marlene said. "Listen to some Zydeco music and do a little dancing. Viola, you go home, put on dancing boots, and we'll pick you up in thirty minutes and go over to the festival in Parc Sans Souci."

Marcel couldn't believe his ears. She didn't know that I had driven down to Papa Mojo's and told Marcel about her cancer. Marcel told her that he knew, but she only shrugged.

"I told Louie Mouton not to be worrying you with this little old problem," Marlene said. "I'm gonna be just fine."

So they went dancing that afternoon and stayed out until about six. Viola told Marcel that his mama was getting tired more often and was sleeping a lot. They went back home and had dinner around seven thirty, and Marlene made her way to the bedroom an hour later. Viola gave Marcel a little more information than I had available when I visited him at Papa Mojo's. The doctors were going to perform the operation at the LSU Medical Center, and my father was taking care of all the appointments and meetings. He came by the house many days during the week to check on her.

Marcel told Viola he might be going to California. He told her about the tennis tournament and the money for the operation. He said he was going to tell his mama he was going out for a couple months to work on his music. He didn't want her to know his real reason for going. He thought it might upset her, knowing how much he enjoyed being back into his music and him giving that up for her. Viola assured Marcel that she would be visiting with his mama every day and taking real good care of her and would call him every week to let him know how she was doing with all the tests and treatments.

Marcel came over to see me Tuesday afternoon in my office at LSU. I thanked him for coming and began to tell him more about the Pacific Palisades tournament. He said he appreciated all we were doing for him. He told me to thank "Dr. Mouton" for all he was doing for his mama. I told Marcel that he had a shot of winning or at least finishing second in the Pacific Palisades Open. I really believed that. He said he still wasn't confident in his game to finish in the top five. He had too many experiences in college tournaments to justify his doubts. He asked me if I really thought he had a chance.

"Absolutely," I said. "The missing pieces you need to win can be learned." I went on to explain that tennis, like any other sport, is a game of constant improvement, practice, preparation, and hard work. "I have all the confidence in the world that you can take your game to the next level," I said, "if you have the best training and the right teacher, someone who has been at that higher level."

I asked him to walk over with me to the Athletic Museum in the Alumni Center. We walked down the hall into the tennis trophy room and stopped in front of the center case. I read to him the name off many of those trophies: "Rene Pierre 'Train' Lacroix."

"He is your answer, Marcel," I said. "He can find your missing pieces. He can take you to a higher level of play and competition."

Train was about thirteen years older than Marcel. Marcel was six when he rode his bike over to Beaver Park for the first time and came away with the cracked racquet. Train was a senior in high school playing in the Acadiana State Amateur Championship that day, but Marcel had no idea who Train was. Train had been long gone on tour traveling the world. Marcel did know of Train's reputation. Marcel had seen all of Train's trophies in the trophy case over at Beaver Park and had once, when he and Marlene had been invited up for dinner to my father's house, seen the Oyster Bay Classic trophy that Train had given my parents. I told him the tennis gods were working in our favor. He'd come along at just the right time. We had the perfect opportunity available to us because Train had retired from the tour and was at a posh Southern California country club, the Palms, working as the head tennis teaching pro.

"It just so happens the finals of the Pacific Palisades Open are taking place right there at that club where Train teaches," I said. "Train has the whole game: power, quickness, grace, finesse, intelligence, a chess player's mind when to tank, when to volley, when to brutalize, the forehand, the backhand. A pro baseball scout once told me that if Train had been a baseball player, he would have been a Hall of Famer."

Marcel asked me if Train had any weakness in his game.

I laughed. "Yes," I said, "but Train's weakness isn't between his ears. His weakness is between his legs. The beautiful Train is every woman's desire. Queens leave their kings in a minute with a flick of his racquet to sit on his throne. Had he been born an ugly man, he would have won a hundred tournaments and more grand slams, but there were far too many distractions and conquests off the court. What he did have was what most great champions have: a killer instinct. When the greatest of champions play at any sport, their mindset is survival. Destroy the opponent before you are destroyed. Fight to the death. In their minds, winning is only a result and not the focus of the battle. Some have it, some don't, but sometimes an athlete can have a circumstance arise that will push him into that mindset."

"Train was the victim of an abusive childhood," I said. "Like he told me one time years later, he woke up to the feeling of Love-40 every day, beat down mentally and physically by his dad. When he got into competitive tennis, his mindset involuntarily and automatically placed the image of his father across the net with the desire to destroy, the desire to kill."

I hoped that when Train started working with Marcel that maybe he could take him to that arena of thinking because I knew Train could teach Marcel all the necessary physical maneuvers to win. I warned Marcel if he decided to go work with Train, he'd take Marcel with great intensity into a war zone.

"He will work you until there is nothing left," I said. "He won't have any mercy for you on that tennis court, but off the court you will have the time of your life. He is the thorn, and he is the rose. If you stay the challenge for the next four months with him, you will have a huge chance to win the Pacific Palisades Open."

Marcel told me his game was never about brutalizing or destroying the opponent. His style was built on the premise that the player with the better game, finesse, and strategy would win. But he realized that there were other means of motivation to win a contest, and he had another more important desire and motivation to win now. This was just not a game to him anymore. It was a battle for life, Marlene's life. I asked him if he needed to go back home to Lafayette and take a little time to think it over.

"No," he answered without hesitation. "This needs to happen now. The tournament is only four months away."

Marcel had to do this for his mama. He had to make it happen for her sake. He wanted me to call Train as soon as possible.

"Tell him a warrior is on the way," Marcel said. He went back home to Lafayette that afternoon and spent the rest of the week with his mama and Viola. It was hard for him to leave.

"I play each point like my life depends on it."

—Rafael Nadal

Part Three

California Train

It was late Friday afternoon when I finally made the call to Train in California, thinking he would be finished teaching for the day. The coveted tennis pro teaching job at the Palms Country Club had landed his way compliments of his longtime friend from Acadiana, Irma Jean Boudreaux, formerly of New Iberia, Louisiana, now Irma Jean Kersh, who years ago married the oilman H. A. Kersh Jr. They had moved into the Bel Air Estates. She had driven Train to the Beaver Park tennis courts every day after school and watched him play tennis all through high school and college. Irma, in her late sixties now, had long been a member at the Palms and was well liked and respected by everyone. When the teaching position became open, Irma, aware that Train had retired from the tour, offered his name to the search committee. After reviewing his record of achievements on tour and seeing the photo portfolio of the handsome thirty-seven-year-old bachelor, the majority of the search committee, including seven women, quickly made their decision, and Irma made the call. Train hadn't spent much time in California. He had enjoyed his beach days while living in Florida and playing the tour, so he decided, hell yeah, why not Southern California?

The phone rang. Train, not knowing it was me, asked me to hold on. I could hear him in the background.

"That's good," I heard him say. "You're getting better but bend over a little more and spread your legs a little wider apart. Now bend at the knees. Pivot around as though you were headed toward the baseline. Sweetheart, move a little closer toward me. Don't apply so much pressure with your fingers. Hold it a little more gently. There you go. That's the grip that works best. Now you have much more feel for the perfect stroking action."

I silently waited on the other side.

"Hold on, girls," Train said. "Stay where you are."

I heard him come back to the phone.

"Hello, this is Louie Mouton over at the LSU tennis center," I said. "Can I speak with Train please?

"You got him, Louie," Train said. "I didn't recognize your voice at first."

 "Do you have a moment to talk?" I asked.

"Well, Louie, I'm in the middle of a lesson, teaching doubles strategy to two girls, and I need to get back with them."

He covered the phone, and I heard him tell the two girls to keep moving and doing what they were doing. He was starting to feel really good about them. They were showing so much promise and talent. He asked if he could call me right back. I said yes, but he forgot to hang up the phone. I started to hang up, but I heard two girls talking to him in the background.

"You are amazing, Train," one girl said. "You have such great concentration and discipline."

"Yeah," the other girl said. "We've been in bed with you all afternoon."

I heard him say, "You slide closer, and you turn around. Now talk some nasty tennis. We need to end this party."

I figured out the doubles strategy he was teaching these girls. A few minutes later, I heard them moaning and groaning.

He must have left the phone off the hook right beside his bed. I guess I lost track of time because my reverie was disrupted when Train finally said, "Lesson's over, girls."

"Do we really have to go now, Train?" one girl asked. "Can we have an extra hour? We'll pay you quite handsomely."

"Girls, girls," Train answered. "Too much training in one day is not good. It takes more than one session to massage a smooth tennis game. Now be good little girls and put your tennis skirts and tops back on, and we'll pick up where we left off next week."

I hung up the phone. Within minutes he called me back.

"You forgot to hang the phone up, Train," I said.

And with no embarrassment in his voice at all, Train asked me if I enjoyed hearing the show. All I could do was laugh.

"Damn, Train," I said. "When are you ever gonna learn?"

"I am learning," Train said, laughing. "I'm still trying to get it right."

Train let me get to the reason for my call.

"I've got a special situation over here in Louisiana," I said. "It's somewhat of a health-related financial emergency. I think we stand a chance of making this come out all right if we can get your help."

Train stayed silent on the other end.

"Marcel Jackson is the boy," I said, "and his mother is having a bout with cancer that will require surgery and treatments over the next four to six months. There is a need to raise more money for her operation, about a hundred thousand dollars. Train, if you can, I want you to work with Marcel. He is a talented and seasoned tennis player from Lafayette who just graduated from Tulane. You have about four months to take him to the next level. He qualified to compete in the Pacific Palisades Open for amateurs going pro. The finals are being held at the Palms Country Club, and the purse is two hundred thousand dollars first place and one hundred thousand dollars second place."

Train didn't hesitate. He told me he knew he could take the kid to the next level if I really thought he had the tools and had what it took to work hard and handle the practices and workout sessions that he would be putting him through.

"Four months preparing for a big one is a grind," he reminded me.

I knew Train could take Marcel to the next level and I was hoping Marcel could handle the intense training that was about to happen.

"Send the kid on out," Train said. "I'll have a cabin all fixed up and waiting on him. Consider it done."

"Train," I said, "I'll call you back in about a week to fill you in on all the details of when he's coming."

Then I made the mistake of asking him a question that would keep me on the phone for another hour. Train loved to tell me his stories and escapades with the excitement of a little kid who just took his first pony ride or got that first bike from Santa Claus. I asked him, simply, just how did he end up at Irma's run-down tennis camp in Santa Barbara?

Match Point

The story started after the thirteenth-hole incident with the Fairy Princess that he'd told me about months ago. Train packed up all his things out of the tennis pro shop and passed through the upstairs outdoor patio dining area of the Palms Country Club, overlooking the center court. Irma saw Train as he was leaving and motioned him over to the table with her two young lady golfing friends, the same two who helped Mr. Club President's wife up off the floorboard of the golf cart and said they wanted some private lessons with him.

Irma asked Train why he was carrying all his tennis gear with him. He said due to the unfortunate events she had witnessed on the unlucky thirteenth hole, rather than embarrass her anymore, he thought it best to move on. She wanted to know where he was headed. He had no idea, he said. He was just going to take it easy for a while. She asked him to go to Santa Barbara and put something very special back into her life.

Irma's husband, H. A. Jr., had passed away about three years earlier. They'd been Train's financial sponsors all through his college days and when he first went onto the tour. They opened a tennis camp on their one-hundred-and-fifty-acre ranch in Santa Barbara named Match Point. The camp had been opened some fifteen years earlier for the sole purpose of allowing underprivileged and special needs children of all ages a chance to develop physically and mentally and, most importantly, to build self-confidence in their value in society. Train had first visited the ranch about ten years ago for two weeks during a break from the tour.

Irma had invited Train out to help teach some of the children and to put on an exhibition fundraiser for the museum. He hadn't been back since then, but he had very special feelings and memories of his short time there. Irma told him that the camp had been closed and not used since the passing of her husband. It would be wonderful if he would move up and live there for a while and bring it back to life for her and all the kids. How great it would be for the community, she said.

A calming and great peace came over Train. His mind went into the zone where tennis battles had often taken him. He saw and knew and remembered that place and knew that he was going to make it happen. It was time for him to give back. He was the living story of the prince and the pauper, born into poverty in an unstable and tragic family life and saved and treated like a prince by the good graces of Irma. His was the epic fairytale story. His answer was yes. He would revive Match Point.

He sat down with Irma and her two young lady friends and asked her to promise him that whoever he chose to help him with the tennis camp would be taken care of.

"Absolutely," Irma said, "of course, my dear."

Train had no idea of who was going to be his right hand man for the rebirth of the magical Match Point Tennis Camp of Santa Barbara, California, but at that moment a series of coincidences occurred which solved his problem. As Train was talking with Irma and the ladies, they heard a loud voice down below. Mack, the grounds superintendent, was cursing loudly below on the adjacent tennis court. He had

Roberto, a maintenance worker, standing against the back baseline. Mack was spouting words of abuse at Roberto, including some choice words concerning Roberto's Mexican identity.

Train's mind raced to his childhood memories and the devilish visions of his father's vile. He stood up, forgetting the distinguished guests of the club patio area, and hollered down to Mack to shut his motherfucking mouth. Train raced down the steps onto the tennis court and approached the two men. Mack's face turned into that of Train's father's. Mack had his finger on Roberto's chest pointing and pushing. Train's tennis mentality switched on, like rushing *ghosting* into the net when his opponent least expected him to. The next thing Train knew, three country-club security guards were pulling him off of the superintendent.

Mack stood up with a bloodied nose, a black eye, and a broken wrist. He looked at Roberto and said, "You're fired."

"Fuck off," Train said on Roberto's behalf. "You ain't firing nobody because Roberto just quit. I'm taking Roberto to Santa Barbara with me. I need a great groundskeeper for my new tennis camp."

The security guards escorted Train back up to the patio table where everyone was in shock, except Irma who knew what ignited Train's inner rage. As Train picked up his things, Irma asked him to sit back down. The head security guard, politely and with some amount of fear, told Irma that they had to escort Train off the property. Irma, then the chairman of the governing board of the club in place of her deceased husband and wealthy enough to buy ten Palms Country Clubs, responded, "Mr. Rene Pierre Lacroix will leave shortly after he is personally admonished for this act by me."

The guards left. Irma asked with a reassuring mother's touch on his knee if Train was okay. He told her he was fine and would be leaving to head up to Santa Barbara in the morning with Roberto, if she was okay with that. She instructed him to call her friend, the art collector and trustee Mr. Charles Craig, at the Crocker National Bank down on State Street beside the Copper Coffee Pot when he got there.

"Mr. Craig will put everything in motion for the finances of Match Point," Irma said. "One more thing, Rene." She only used his true name when she was very serious and she wanted his full attention. "Take extra special care of Roberto. He has always been very special to me and H. A."

As Train's luck would have it, Roberto and his grandson, Pancho, were familiar with Match Point. They had worked for the Kersh family up in Santa Barbara four weeks every spring to do maintenance work at the tennis camp and manicure the gardens. As Train was leaving, Irma said they had both been so lucky that day that she would offer to pay for the super-intendent's stitches and give him a big raise, upon which they both erupted into uncontrollable and uproarious laughter.

Train offered his apologies to Irma's two young lady friends.

"Oh, we're very much okay with today's events," one of them said.

"It was all so exciting," the other said. "We have never been entertained so much in one day by one man."

"It was our pleasure," the first said.

Train's effort to make amends with Irma's two young lady friends couldn't have gone worse. Still all mixed up, he offered to make it all up to them and, without thinking, offered them private tennis lessons for two, all on him. This brought a smile to their faces.

"How soon, Train?" they both quickly answered.

Irma pulled Train close so she could deliver to him a private message. He bent over and the beautiful Irma Jean Boudreaux Kersh, formerly of New Iberia, Louisiana, perfectly expressed to him in a truly Louisiana fashion that he shouldn't even think about it, honey, because she would offer up his balls to the alligators on a silver platter. Only the fact that she addressed him as Train and not Rene did he feel as though he had escaped Irma's wrath and would be able to resume his manly pleasures, though at that moment he didn't think his pleasure racquet could have satisfied anything more than the size of a thimble. As he sheepishly walked away, he smiled at the two young ladies.

"On second thought, ladies," Train said, "better stick to golf."

This brought a half smile and a wink from Irma, his savior on that crazy day.

Train left Bel Air the next day and headed up the Pacific Coast Highway on his way to Santa Barbara. Luckily, this was not an express run. Roberto and Pancho had to pack and wouldn't be up for another week. Train figured there was no rush. He'd stop and hang out at his favorite beach restaurant and bar on the West Coast, The Hawaiian Surfer at Malibu Beach. He arrived around lunchtime, went into the Hang Ten Lounge overlooking the ocean, and ordered a couple of his favorites, the lomi lomi salmon and the ahi ahi fisherman's chowder, along with a nonalcoholic beer, Bundaberg Ginger Beer brewed in Australia.

The bartender Duke commented that just a few people ordered that drink and asked Train why he did.

"It's kinda sentimental to me," Train said playfully. "I won the Australian Open one year."

Duke smiled and said, "Yeah, dude, and I won the French Open that same year."

Train laughed.

Train changed into a bikini bathing suit, threw a towel over his shoulder, and sauntered on down to catch some golden rays on the beach and maybe uncover a "she shell" or two. As he was walking toward the ocean edge to spread out his towel, a woman tanning on the beach said hello.

"Excuse me, sweetheart," she said. "Can I ask a favor, please? My girlfriends are still up at the beach house. You wouldn't mind helping me with a little suntan oil, would you? I don't think my girlfriends will be down for a while, and I don't want to burn."

"Sure thing, darling," Train said. "We wouldn't want to put out any hot fires on the beach today, now would we?"

He used the whole bottle. Legs, arms, fingers, neck, shoulders, toes, both sides, French style, American style, all the techniques he learned while touring and living abroad.

"How 'bout that Malibu massage?" Train asked. "Didn't miss anything, did I, darling?"

He ended up staying for three nights with the three young women from Georgia in their rented four-bedroom Malibu beach house. When they offered him the extra bedroom, he didn't hesitate. He needed some Malibu time, especially with some pretty peaches on the beaches. He'd hang out with them for a while and maybe pick up a little Georgia accent.

He left on the fourth day after being surfed on by the three Georgia peaches. He was walkin' and talkin' with a slooow Southern drawl, y'all. With kisses and hugs, they wished him farewell and said they hoped for a few more rides on the waves with him one day. He drove on up the coast toward Santa Barbara with the top down, just humming along with Georgia on his mind and thinking how he loved that sweet Southern hospitality. Some mighty fine Georgia peaches, yes indeed.

When he pulled up to the Match Point Tennis Camp, he got out of the car and walked onto one of the tennis courts, looking around. It was in pretty sad shape. There were weeds, broken fences, peeling paint. It was dismal, broken down, locked away like his early childhood with Jacques. No one had paid it any attention in a while. His memories of his summer visit there years earlier helped to soften his sadness. He had seen the place in its glory days. He remembered Match Point as a once-vibrant camp. It was active, in motion, doing, helping, teaching, giving. Now the grand old camp in that earthly and heavenly setting seemed as though it had been wheeled to the empty back porch of an elderly rest home, an old person left to die alone.

Train closed his eyes. He saw the children running around, smiling and laughing all those long years ago. He wondered where they were then and how their lives had been influenced and enriched by their summers spent there. He knew how much all the children had meant to Irma, and he knew Match Point had more to give to them again. Standing there on the tennis court feeling sad made Train think of his mama. She had been like that before—left alone, broken, unappreciated, unloved, and abused by Jacques. Long after his death, she was reborn. She felt *joie de vivre* again.

Train looked up into the bright blue sky. A hawk soared down from the Santa Ynez mountain range and circled Match Point. This was his calling, that old, worn-out tennis camp. Score, Love-40. He knew Love-40. He had lived Love-40. His every waking childhood day started at Love-40 until Jacques died from those mysterious gunshots when he was twelve. It had remained a mystery to him to that day. The camp might be at Love-40, but he promised and vowed that Match Point, from that day forward, would be reborn and become a paradise of fun and learning for further generations.

He knelt down and kissed the court, sealing his oath, his commitment, giving his heart and soul. It would be his final championship trophy to earn, the rebirth of the Match Point Tennis Camp, Santa Barbara, California. There wasn't a sweeter, more rewarding, more cherished victory than a victory from down Love-40. How grand this win would be.

He unpacked all of his tennis gear in the cabin at the entrance to the camp, although it wasn't quite ready for sleeping in yet. It was around seven o'clock, and he was ready for a nice, quiet dinner. He went down to a little restaurant, Tiny's Mexican on Milpas Street, and ordered the number twenty-two, a chicken burrito, fish taco, and beef enchilada. He and Tiny would become good friends. Train even bussed a couple tables on busy nights. He told Tiny he was used to picking up silver and gold. Little did Tiny know the silver and gold Train meant was of the championship trophy kind.

After leaving Tiny's, Train checked into the Hotel Saint Barbara on State Street. He lay down in his hotel bed and felt the cool crisp air and the ocean breezes of the Santa Barbara harbor and the California night. A strange thought crossed his mind. Where would he have been without the thirteenth hole? What a crazy lucky number that brought him to Match Point and beautiful Santa Barbara. From then on he would forever walk up to the roulette wheel and bet on lucky thirteen.

The next morning Train walked up State Street to meet Irma's good friend, Charles Craig of Crocker Bank, at the Copper Coffee Pot. Mr. Craig gave Train all the plans for the resurrection of Match Point. Train stayed at the Hotel Saint Barbara until the main house at Match Point was remodeled. Irma provided temporary housing not far from Match Point for Roberto and Pancho until their living quarters were finished. Irma had an unlimited expense fund at the bank to resurrect Match Point at Train's discretion. Any supplies or equipment that Train or Roberto needed were to be ordered at Ott's Hardware. All fiduciary accounting and reports would be handled by Mr. Craig's assistant, Tamara Jones. She would be the go-to girl for any of Train's requests. Train and Roberto were to be responsible for overseeing all repair work to the grounds—the fences, grass, painting. Irma wanted their special touch on the project.

There was a pool on the property which Irma said could be repaired, though it wasn't necessary. She said they could decide. Her plan for the new tennis camp was to operate as a five-day-a-week day camp and not as an overnight camp the way it had been operated before. The camp was totally funded for all the day campers, no weekly fees. Irma even arranged for J. K. Frimples, with the fig tree in the middle of the restaurant down on State Street, to deliver catered lunches and an extra special treat, the famous J. K. Frimples's "rubble dubble cake," for the kids every day. Irma said it was important that Train become involved in the community while he worked at Match Point. Mr. Craig read Train a letter from Irma which was addressed "My Dear Rene," so Train knew she meant to be taken seriously.

One month from now you are to meet Mr. Craig's friend Jerry and my friends Robin, Esther, and Margaret at the Santa Barbara Museum for an exhibit of paintings featuring Diego Rivera and Rufino Tamayo. It is a black-tie event. Make sure to shave off your ever-present three-day scraggle. I want you looking like the museum piece you are.

Be there in all your smiling glory. Hope you understand this note clearly, Rene.

Train understood the letter very well. He would have a better chance wrestling two alligators than he would have disobeying a single Irma. Before leaving the meeting, Train asked Mr. Craig if he could borrow his razor before Irma used her razor on his two museum pieces.

Train left the bank and went directly out to Match Point. The carpenters, plumbers, electricians, and painters were there, ready to start working on the old tennis cabins. Train thought it might take two months to get it ready, but all the workers assured him they would have the place shined up and ready to go in six weeks or less.

"All right now," Train said. "Put the hammer down. The quicker the better."

He had been in California for five months working at the Palms and never knew how long he was going to stay or if he would even like the teaching job there, but he was hoping that in another month he would settle in at the tennis camp for a long time to come.

Roberto and Pancho showed up the next week around lunchtime. Train knew Roberto only briefly at the Palms, and they rarely ever crossed paths. Roberto was working mainly on the golf course but occasionally was sent to repair some fencing at the tennis courts, usually early in the morning. They drove up in an old pickup truck—Roberto, Pancho, and Pancho's goldendoodle named Stella. The dog bounded out and took off toward Train.

"She's a friendly dog," Pancho quickly hollered over.

Pancho asked Train if Stella could stay with them at the ranch. She wouldn't bite anybody.

"Sure thing, Pancho," Train said. He bragged on how pretty she was and made Pancho very happy when he officially announced that Stella, so pretty and white, was going to forever be the official mascot of the Match Point Tennis Camp. Train shook Roberto's hand and told him how much he appreciated him coming up to Match Point. Train explained he wanted the two of them to live permanently at the tennis camp.

"Any cabin you and Pancho prefer," Train said.

Roberto thanked him over and over for the wonderful opportunity he and Irma had given him and his twelve-year-old grandson. He said he was grateful for the chance to get away from Los Angeles. It wasn't the place he wanted to raise his grandson.

They all three went over behind one of the tennis courts to find some shade in a grove of avocado trees to have lunch. Train had earlier picked up some food down at Tiny's. They were in such a beautiful place, and Train asked Roberto if he knew the history of Irma's ranch.

"Yes, I know," Roberto said. He delighted in telling Train the entire history of this place. Match Point was once a one-hundred-and-fifty-acre avocado tree farm which earlier included the property where Irma's Santa Barbara estate and mansion were located. Irma bought the front fifty acres on a hillside plateau overlooking the Santa Barbara Harbor and built her mansion there.

Roberto's grandfather, who had lived not far from Santa Barbara, told him of the history of the ranch and the avocado farm on the property. His great-grandfather explained the word "avocado" came from the Aztecan word "ahuacatl," which also meant "testicles" because of the avocado's shape. His Mexican ancestors believed the avocado fruit granted sexual powers. They even hid away their virgins during the harvesting season, he told Roberto. It was a judge, Mr. R. B. Ord, who brought the avocados to Santa Barbara, Roberto's grandfather had explained. He carried three saplings with him in the 1870s.

Years after Irma had built her estate, the owners stopped working the farm and Irma bought the remaining one hundred acres primarily for the conservation of the majestic avocado trees, though she had no intention of becoming an avocado farmer. The property was adjacent to and just a short distance behind her Santa Barbara estate. Several years later, Irma's vision of a tennis camp for underprivileged and special children evolved and became a reality.

Since Irma was from Louisiana, she was unaware of the avocado's history. Many years earlier, when Roberto was in college and working summers for Irma on the estate, Irma asked him the same question about the avocados. Roberto told Irma avocados were also known as alligator pears because of their green color and their alligator like skin. Surprised, she felt right back at home in Louisiana.

Irma often told her lady friends at parties that when sitting out by the pool, she would feel herself falling into a very romantic mood. When her friends asked why and made guesses—the beautiful home or sitting on a hillside or lounging beside the pool and overlooking the Santa Barbara harbor—Irma, always one for a good laugh, replied, "No, none of those reasons, ladies. If you were sitting in the middle of hundreds of fruity testicle trees, you would feel a little romance too." Upon which they all broke out into uncontrollable and uproarious laughter.

It was perhaps the last place Train should live, a place with hundreds of testicle trees. He certainly had more than enough sexual prowess and enhanced fertility.

Train was curious about Roberto's background. He later found out from Irma that Roberto had actually been raised around tennis courts and learned the game from two of the greatest to ever play, Pancho Segura and Pancho Gonzales. His father had been the groundskeeper at some of the country clubs where they taught and often took Roberto to work with him. Roberto had seen some of the students learning and practicing a two-handed backhand. Roberto watched intently, liked what he saw, and started using the two-handed backhand at an early age. Tennis was the only sport he played. Roberto was given a tennis scholarship to the University of California at Santa Barbara and played number one for two years. A knee injury ended his career, and by the good graces of H. A. and Irma, he had been afforded a secure future at the Palms Country Club.

Roberto had taken custody of his grandson, Pancho, when Pancho was five years old. Roberto's daughter had died in a car wreck and the father was unknown. Roberto had been divorced for years and gladly accepted the role of taking care of Pancho.

"Lucky to do so by the grace of God," Roberto said.

They got busy early the next morning. Roberto handled all the landscaping, and Pancho helped Train with the fences, nets, and the court surfaces. After about six hours working at the camp each day, Pancho and Train played a little tennis together, and Roberto did a little instructing on Pancho's two-handed backhand stroke. Little Pancho had game, and Train recognized his talent.

Crazy Joe's Bar and Grill

Train went back to the Hotel Saint Barbara every afternoon about six o'clock, took a shower, lay around a little bit, and walked up State Street to his favorite bar, Crazy Joe's Bar and Grill, which had the greatest neon and lightbulb street sign he'd ever seen. He usually got there at seven o'clock and enjoyed his anonymity, at least for the time being. He knew he might get recognized eventually. Santa Barbara had always been an enthusiastic tennis town. Every day at Crazy Joe's was busy and fun, a carousel of characters and beautiful women. Train had a casual one- or two-nighter. He had one rule, though. Match Point was his steady girl. He always introduced himself as Rene to maintain his anonymity. One afternoon at Crazy Joe's, a guy took a barstool beside Train.

"Hey man, mind if I sit here?" the man asked. "How you doing? My name is Ferdinand, but just call me Freddie."

"My name is Rene," Train said.

Freddie was the sports editor over at the Santa Barbara newspaper, and the man said that "Rene" looked very familiar to him. Freddie mentioned the name Scratch from Lafayette to Train. Lafayette Scratch was the syndicated sportswriter from Lafayette and a longtime colleague of Freddie's. Train's anonymity was blown. Freddie had covered the New Orleans Open one year with Scratch, the year Train had won his last championship there.

"Do all these people around here know who you really are, Rene?" Freddie asked.

Train asked Freddie to promise to keep quiet.

"Just keep calling me Rene," Train said.

"Only if you tell me what you're doing out here in Santa Barbara," Freddie said. "Then I'll agree to keep your secret."

Train filled Freddie in on everything about the revival of the Match Point Tennis Camp. "Can you keep it a secret, Freddie?" Train asked before leaving Crazy Joe's.

"Of course I can," Freddie said.

Two days later on a Friday, Train walked into Crazy Joe's, and the place was packed, but Joe had saved Train's usual barstool. Train made his way through the crowd. It seemed like all eyes were on him. Cappy, the beautiful happy hour bartender, walked up and put Train's usual drink, a French lemonade, on the bar and handed him the sports page of that Friday morning's edition of the newspaper. She winked.

"Guess Freddie just blew your *Train* whistle," she said.

The headline read, "Australian and Spanish Open Tennis Champion to Reopen Match Point Tennis Camp in Santa Barbara." Underneath the headline was a photograph of Train captioned with his name. Freddie even wrote that Train regularly visited Crazy Joe's around seven o'clock.

It wasn't just a feeling. All eyes *were* on Train, and now he knew why. He guessed it was time to fully engage with all the friendly people and get some good press for Match Point. He answered questions, shook hands with the people excited about Match Point, and heard stories from people who stayed at Match Point as children. And, of course, he signed more than thirty copies of the underwear centerfold for some of Santa Barbara's finest beauties.

"Darling, you really want my autograph right there in that spot?" he'd ask.

"Oh, why, yes," they'd answer. "Where else?"

It was really great that Freddie spilled the secret about his reason for being in Santa Barbara. The events in the coming days would provide great benefit to Match Point. Freddie walked in about eight o'clock at the other end of the bar, saw Train, gave a limp wave and half grin, and walked slowly over. Train asked the girl beside him if he could borrow her stool for a moment.

"Anything for you, handsome," she said adoringly.

Freddie sat down, not knowing what Train might do or say. His article had really dropped the bomb on Train. Train wanted to buy his new trusting and secretive good friend Freddie a drink.

"Pour him a double arsenic garnished with a teaspoon of rat poison straight up," Train said to Cappy, who cracked up.

Freddie looked at Train and started laughing. Train slapped him on the back. Freddie was just doing his job and doing it like a champion. Lafayette Scratch would've been proud.

Freddie's article had the phone at Match Point ringing off the hook the following weekend. People from all over Santa Barbara County wanted to volunteer their time and services to help. Apparently, the camp had long ago been popular with many kids who grew up in the area. There were painters, landscapers, a fence company, and even a pool company offering their services. Train accepted all the help, and they were on track to open Match Point a week early. It was the best-kept secret that never got kept, thanks to Freddie's mouth and ink.

Roberto, Pancho, Train, and Stella moved into their Match Point cabins a month early. Roberto's cabin was at the rear of the property near the maintenance buildings, and Train lived close to the front gates in a two-story cabin near the pool.

Irma planned for everything. She wanted to delay the opening of Match Point for a month in order to let the Match Point board members, most of whom also sat on the Santa Barbara Museum board and led by Nan Dollinger, to select thirty children per week to invite to the camp. Train and Roberto, along with some volunteer tennis players from the high school and UC-Santa Barbara, would divide and rotate between the children, teaching different aspects of the game. A lifeguard was hired to supervise the newly refurbished pool, which was used by the kids in the afternoon after their tennis activities.

Mr. Craig called Train the Friday before the official opening of Match Point to remind him of the Rivera and Tamayo exhibit at the museum that Saturday night. Irma needed Train to pick up one of her late-arriving guests that Friday afternoon at the Santa Barbara airport. Irma and her other guests had decided to spend Friday night up in the little Dutch village of Solvang, a Danish village in the Santa Ynez Valley. The instructions from Irma's note were as follows: *Go to the airport. Hold a sign reading "Irma Party" and take her to the Santa Barbara mansion where she is to spend the night.* Mr. Craig didn't know the woman's name. Irma must have been in a hurry. She'd left the note for him that morning at the Copper Coffee Pot.

A Surprise Guest

Irma's Santa Barbara mansion sat on a hill. The rear of the mansion overlooked the Santa Barbara harbor. It had a pool, a guest house in the back, orange trees, a separate sauna building, a hot tub, and, of course, many avocado trees. The main entrance foyer of the mansion opened up into the large living room, and a huge painting of a sunflower by Rufino Tamayo graced the ceiling. After H. A.'s death and the closing of Match Point, Irma only made rare weekend visits to the mansion, driving up from Bel Air to host museum events or to visit friends for the weekend. A small staff was still, however, employed for the weekly upkeep of the house and grounds. Irma often offered the mansion to weekend guests.

Train got to the Santa Barbara airport early that Friday afternoon. He recognized the Kersh jet's lettering, "KOC 22," decaled on the side come over the mountain range. As it landed, Train walked into the airport lobby and held up the sign reading, "Irma Party." How ironic and funny. He used to be chauffeured everywhere, and now he was the chauffeur. His new reality cleared for landing, he knew. He turned his head away for a second, but then heard a woman's voice.

"Irma Party over here, please, driver," the voice said.

Train turned. He felt disbelief. He was overwhelmed with nervous excitement and all the other emotions that lead to premature cardiac arrest or fantasized ecstasy. It was Simone from Lafayette.

He laid the sign on a chair and walked to her. She put her bags on the floor. She was also visibly surprised and excited to see him. Irma had told neither of them the details. Train hadn't the slightest clue of why she was there, but Simone knew. She would be seeing him Saturday at the museum party. At least Irma had told her that much.

Leaving the airport on the way back to Santa Barbara, Simone explained the reason for her visit to California really had nothing to do with the museum party. Simone and her three amateur tennis team members, all of them single, were having cocktails at happy hour one afternoon about three months back and all agreed they needed some adventure and excitement in their lives. Simone remembered reading in one of her tennis magazines that a week-long public parks amateur tournament for ladies only would take place at a public park just outside of Los Angeles. After having another cosmopolitan and a round of "deep throats"—Baileys Irish Creams, Kahlua liqueur, and whipped cream on the top—their decision to enter was quick and unanimous.

Simone, who had long been friends with Irma before Irma moved to California, called with the news. Irma invited Simone and her friends to stay with her all week long during the tournament at her Bel Air home and asked Simone to come out the weekend before. She wanted her to be her guest at the Santa Barbara museum party and stay the weekend at the mansion.

Train was to take Simone up to the mansion that afternoon for her weekend stay. He told her that Irma and her friends had gone up to Solvang for the night and would be back Saturday around noon. It was around four o'clock when they finally left the airport. Rather than go straight to the mansion, Simone was ready for happy hour. She asked Train, if he wasn't busy the rest of the afternoon or in a hurry, if he'd like to join her.

Train was more than happy to accommodate her request. He took her to his favorite place, the perfect place to show her off, Crazy Joe's. He introduced Simone as Irma's friend from Lafayette, Louisiana. He explained she came out for a week-long tennis tournament down in LA and was staying the weekend up at Irma's mansion. Simone excused herself to freshen up in the ladies' room.

Simone had a couple glasses of her favorite wine, La Crema, and Train had his usual French lemonade. Simone met some more of Train's new friends before the two of them headed up to the mansion at about six thirty.

Simone wondered if anyone else was staying at the mansion. She figured it must be empty since they were all in Solvang. She asked Train if he had other plans because she would love to invite him to join her for dinner.

"Even if I had plans," Train said, "I'd cancel them in a skinny minute."

Train would return at eight o'clock to pick her up. He already had one of his favorite restaurants in mind.

Train picked her up at the door of the mansion sharply on the hour. He couldn't wait. If ever there was a woman of mansion quality, Simone was it. Since he'd moved out to the ranch, he hadn't spent a lot of time downtown. He was spending long days fixing up the camp. He had found another little jewel, a sexy restaurant closer to Match Point that wasn't quite as busy and had a little more privacy. There he wasn't so busy signing tennis magazines. Mr. Craig and his good friend Jerry had turned him on to the place, Café del Sol, tucked back in the corner of a little shopping complex in the heart of Montecito. It had killer margaritas, great food, and a beautiful ambiance.

Train made a reservation for the rear of the restaurant nestled in a garden setting across a little bridge. Nice and private. Very romantic.

Train and Simone talked a little about Claude and Betsy and not a word about Von. They talked about Simone's tennis game and all the goings-on back in Lafayette. After dinner they headed back up to the mansion. Simone invited him in. It was still early, and she wanted to go sit by the pool, look down at the lights and the harbor, relax, and enjoy the rest of the night. Once inside, she excused herself and went in to change into something a little more "pool-ish."

She came out barefoot in a silk, midnight-blue robe embroidered with gold stars that twinkled in the moonlight. She sat down, quietly gazing at the moon over the harbor, and sipped her wine. She brought him a glass of French lemonade. She went into the pool house and put on some music.

She came back out, sat down by Train, and put her hand on his knee.

The music was softly playing, and Simone's eyes were closed. She was smiling, quite alone in her own place. Train hoped she was remembering the last time she was with him. She stood up, the wine in her hand, and went to the pool's edge, moving her hips and body to the music. Her hand went to her robe, and it fell to the ground. The moonlight tickled her beautiful naked body. She slowly danced and hummed to the song. She gently glided down the steps into the pool. She swam around the pool with the gracefulness, beauty, and mystery of a mermaid.

She turned and smiled an inviting smile. Train rose up, slowly undressed, and swam to her. A moonlight serenade. They made love in the pool under the twinkling stars. They went into the bedroom of the pool house and made love all night long.

They woke up the next morning and shared some fruit juice, oranges, and avocados for breakfast by the pool. They took another refreshing skinny dip in the pool, then ended the morning before noon with a long, silky, lathery shower massage.

Train left around one o'clock. He went down the trail to Match Point. Irma and her friends returned to the mansion by one thirty. Irma called and thanked him for picking Simone up at the airport. She was impressed that he was such the gentleman to entertain her. Irma apologized for her last minute request and said she very much appreciated his hospitality and everything he did for Simone.

"You made Simone very happy," Irma said.

If only Irma had really known, Train thought. "I'd be more than happy, Irma, to uh, to uh, do it again," Train said.

Irma asked Train to be at the mansion by six thirty. He, Irma, her two young lady friends from Bel Air—appearing somewhat jealous that another woman, Simone, was along—took the limo down to the country club for cocktails before going to the Santa Barbara Museum for the Rivera and Tamayo exhibits.

Train wore a black-and-white tux with a purple bowtie and a red pocket square. As only he would, he sported a pair of Superman cufflinks. And he surely remembered to shave for Irma.

When he stepped out of the limo, all heads turned. He looked incredibly handsome. He went on the auction block that night as a favor to Irma.

While viewing the exhibit, he got into a conversation with the museum director, Nan Dollinger, about the works of Rufino Tamayo. He wasn't so artistically or culturally inclined, but as luck would have it, when he lived in Paris, Train lived next door to an art gallery which frequently exhibited Tamayo's works. Tamayo and his wife, Olga, moved from Mexico City and lived in Paris for ten years, and he'd met them briefly.

The auction went well, which isn't surprising considering that most of the wealthy elite of Santa Barbara were in attendance. Train was auctioned for ten thousand dollars for the tennis lessons and a night out. The bidder wanted no lessons and no dinner and wasn't a woman. It was a man, for Pete's sake, a local artist named Hans who wanted to do a chalk sketch of Train in the nude. Irma tried to console him with a little of her humor, telling him it could have been worse.

"Be thankful he doesn't want to do you in oil," Irma said laughingly.

Early the following Monday morning, Irma, her two young lady friends, and Simone headed back down to Bel Air for Simone and her teammates to begin their practice sessions for the week-long tournament. Irma had long been involved with the youth tennis programs in LA, sponsoring tennis lessons for underprivileged children in the area. She had befriended a young man named Andy whose band had played at a Bel Air guest event she'd hosted. She found out that not only was he a talented guitar player but also a skilled tennis player. Irma hired him to give tennis lessons to children during the day at the surrounding public parks.

Simone's tennis team did not qualify for the nationals but had a fun-filled week, shopping on Rodeo Drive, spending a day at Malibu Beach, hanging out around Hollywood, and even spotting a movie star or two. Irma invited them back in the future, offering to have the Kersh jet pick them up anytime on its way back from the Kersh oil operations in Louisiana.

Train wouldn't see Simone again for some time but he knew he could hop the jet to Lafayette whenever he was ready. And he would always be ready at a moment's invitation.

Match Point was ready and what a beautiful sight it turned out to be. It appeared as nice as it once was. The Chamber of Commerce did a ribbon cutting and the event was front page of the Santa Barbara newspaper. The front page headline, compliments of Freddie: "Match Point Tennis Camp Ready to Serve."

The Training Camp

Marcel told his mama he was headed to California for a couple months to work some studio sessions with some other musicians thinking of starting a band. She was happy he was continuing with his music. She assured him she would be just fine and told him to write or call her whenever he got the chance. Four days earlier Marlene's surgery to remove the brain tumor went as planned and was successful. Marcel struggled with leaving her, but Viola gave him a mother's reassuring hug. She told him to work hard and have fun and not to worry. She would check in on Marlene every day and call him to keep him updated on her condition when she began her chemo and radiation treatments. My father reassured Marcel that she would be closely monitored and that Marcel should go.

Marcel took off on Highway 10. He had never been west of Austin, Texas. It'd be an adventure and surely worth some good songs. Houston to San Antonio through Tucson and Phoenix and on to Santa Barbara, altogether a two-day trip with a one-night stay in Phoenix, a lucky stop. Just like Lafayette, the city of Phoenix had a Jefferson Street, and on Jefferson Street Marcel found a funky little music bar, Copper Alley, with a hot kickin' band named Allie Blue. The band even asked Marcel to sit in on the last set after they learned he was a guitar player. What a night.

Marcel left the next morning, admiring the beauty of the sunrise against Camelback Mountain. The "Valley of the Sun," as it was called, would inspire him to write an instrumental serenade entitled "A Camel Valley Sunset."

Marcel pulled into Santa Barbara and cruised down State Street across the railroad tracks and Highway 101. He drove onto Stearns Wharf and grabbed a cold beer and a crab cake sandwich for lunch. What a setting. He'd never seen anything like it before—the Santa Barbara Harbor, the sailboats and yachts, the beautiful mountain range, and the sandy beaches. He sure was happy to work on his tennis game here in Santa Barbara.

He arrived at Match Point right around two o'clock Saturday and parked by the tennis courts. There was no one around. A tennis ball suddenly rolled at his feet and a beautiful white dog ran toward him, followed by a child's voice.

"Stella!" the voice said. "Stella!"

A little boy approached, unafraid.

"Who are you, mister?" Pancho asked.

Marcel introduced himself.

"She won't bite. She's a goldendoodle," Pancho said, motioning toward Stella. "She likes chasing tennis balls."

"*Cómo estás, amigo?*" a man said and approached the two of them. "You must be Marcel." Roberto introduced himself. "We have been waiting for you. This is my grandson, Pancho. Train said you are going to be with us for a while?"

Marcel was looking around. Roberto said that Mr. Lacroix was over in his cabin and pointed in the direction where music was coming from.

"He's always playing music all the time," Roberto said. "He dances with all the pretty girls that take lessons on the weekends up here."

Marcel thanked them both and walked over to the cabin to check in with Train. He knocked, but no one came to the door. Marcel knocked again and hollered, "Train?" He heard laughing and giggling and a voice. Marcel opened the screen door and went into the living room. Train came walking around the corner out of the bedroom. He had on nothing but his tennis shorts. He was a little sweaty. He smiled and stuck his hand out.

"Welcome to paradise," Train said. "How was your trip?"

Marcel heard a girlish voice in the bedroom.

"Are we playing hide and seek?" the girl said. "Where did you hide my bra and panties?" She came around the corner completely nude. She screamed once she saw Marcel and ran back into the bedroom. Minutes later she came back out fully dressed and apologized to Marcel. Train smiled and told her it was all right.

"You've been blessed today, Michelle," Train said. "You've just royally and completely introduced yourself to this very handsome Cajun man, Mr. Marcel Jackson of Lafayette, Louisiana."

With a little bit of embarrassment, the girl smiled and said she might move to Louisiana if all the Cajun men were as handsome as Train and Marcel. She told Train to bring Marcel to the next museum fundraiser. She was sure he'd do quite well on the auction block. Train asked Michelle if she had intentions of bidding on young Marcel herself.

"Why, Train, honey," Michelle said, "it might be kinda fun to try a different Louisiana hot sauce."

Upon leaving Michelle reminded Train that she would be back for another lesson of hide and seek very soon. Train went into the bedroom to put on his shirt and shoes. When he returned, he and Marcel went out and sat down on the front porch. Train asked how sharp Marcel's game was then.

"Not too sharp," Marcel said. "Really very rusty, actually. I'd gotten away from it for about the last four months.

Been playing with a band at a bar outside of New Orleans and writing songs." Marcel explained he needed a break from tennis for a while after he finished his college career. Train understood.

"Everybody needs a break sometime," Train said. "Take a detour, step away for awhile, and refuel those jets."

Marcel filled Train in on what all had happened. Train said he was sorry to hear about Marcel's mama. Train assured Marcel he could improve those missing pieces in Marcel's tennis game. Marcel didn't think they would start practicing until Monday. He figured he could catch up on some down time from the drive over. When he asked Train what time he should be on the court Monday morning, he was more than surprised at Train's reply.

"That's two days away," Train said and handed Marcel the key to the cabin. "Unpack your stuff and be on court twelve in an hour."

Marcel said he had been traveling for the last seven and a half hours from Phoenix. "Shouldn't I take a break before getting started?" Marcel asked.

"No way, college boy. If you're ready to get your game on, then it's by my schedule. My time, my rules. If you don't like my rules, then you can put your keys back in that little red hot rod and take it on back to du bayous."

Train knew he only had a short amount of time to fix Marcel's game. No way was he going to treat Marcel with tender gloves during the next four months, Train explained, so if Marcel wanted to take the easy road, he might as well go back to the bar and keep on playing his music. But if Marcel stayed and worked with him, he'd be in better shape than he had ever been in before. He would be tougher than he had ever been, he would have all the shots, and he would definitely have a different mindset about how to play at a higher level of tennis. That is, if he didn't break down first. Train said he would be back at court twelve in one hour.

"If you show up, fine," Train said, "and if you don't, that'll be just as well. I'm not going to be doing any babysitting for the next four months."

I told Marcel from the beginning that Train would be intense, so it didn't take Marcel long to catch on. They met on court twelve at the very back of the ranch near the base of the Santa Ynez Mountains. Marcel wanted to know why they were working so far away at the back of the ranch.

The reason was simple. Marcel was going to be training six days a week from nine in the morning till five at night with Sundays off. They were training way out there because it was closer to that half-mile path going up the mountainside at a thirty-degree angle.

"Up and down that sweet thing eight times before practice and four times after practice," Train said. That added up to six miles a day. "No legs, no game," Train explained.

At least Marcel had a running buddy. Stella loved to run that path. After Marcel did the run, he and Train started the practice session. Train was anxious to see what he had to work with, to see if I'd told him the truth about Marcel's talent.

Roberto, Pancho, and Stella showed up a little later. They had never really seen Train play with anyone of Marcel's caliber before. The two were putting on a clinic. Train motioned for Roberto to see what he thought of Marcel's backhand, so Train kept hitting to his backhand. Train and Roberto quickly realized changing that backhand for Marcel would be a major part of transforming his game. Train was going to have Roberto work with him for many hours through the week on it.

They finished the session, a two-hour warm-up for the day just to see what Marcel had. Train and Roberto both agreed Marcel had the talent, but it would be a matter of time to put the puzzle together.

Marcel took a shower and relaxed for about an hour before he and Train headed downtown to Crazy Joe's for a little dinner and some getting to know each other. Marcel quickly realized what I had told him. On the court, Train was a terror. Off the court, he was the coolest guy you'd ever want to be around. They walked into Crazy Joe's about seven o'clock. Freddie the sportswriter was at the bar.

"Hey, Train," Freddie said, "what's up, man? How's everything out at Match Point?"

Train told him everything was great and the place was beautiful and that his article and all the volunteers had everything to do with getting Match Point ready. Train was about to introduce Marcel to Freddie when Freddie said he didn't need any introduction. He was already acquainted with Mr. Marcel Jackson, only the second tennis player from Acadiana to win the Oyster Bay Classic. Freddie had covered that tournament for about twenty years with Scratch, and Scratch told him everything about Marcel.

"I even covered it when that old grandpa here won it," Freddie said, pointing to Train. Freddie said he was honored to be meeting Marcel in person and more than honored to be sitting with two Oyster Bay champions.

Freddie was curious to know what brought Marcel out to paradise. Train told Marcel to keep his lips sealed because anything that rolled off his tongue could be front page news by the next day.

"Freddie ain't too good with secrets," Train said. "Actually, secrets are his business. The kid's just out having some fun tonight hanging loose, having a little dinner, and maybe even finding a little Santa Barbara cutie pie."

Cappy came up behind Train. "So who is your handsome young friend, Train?" she asked.

Freddie took over. "Why, don't you know, Cappy?" Freddie said. "This here is another Oyster Bay Classic champion and rising superstar tennis player. He's more hot sauce from down in the Cajun bayou country just like Train. Marcel be his name."

She thanked him for coming into Crazy Joe's and welcomed him to Santa Barbara. "If you keep hanging with Train and Freddie," she said, "consider yourself a local."

Train thought it might be dangerous at first but invited Freddie to have dinner with them, making Freddie promise that everything—and he meant everything—was off the record. The three of them grabbed a table for dinner at the rear of the restaurant where it was a little more private (fewer autograph signings for Train). A fork in one hand and a pen in the other got old fast.

During the course of the night, Train asked Freddie about his next tennis assignment. Freddie said he was going to cover the Pacific Palisades Open down in LA for amateurs in the country thinking about going pro.

"It's a big, big payday for the top three finishers," Freddie said. His pick for the finals was two guys, one guy in particular who plays out of the Palms Country Club named Harrison Price. "A great player," Freddie explained, "but a genuine silver-spooned, spoiled asshole of a kid. I'm hoping somebody will stomp his disrespectful, cocky ass."

Train told Freddie he knew Harrison all too well. His mother had signed him up for a lesson with Train when he was at the Palms. The truth was the mother was more interested in having a little thing with Train than a lesson for her son. The kid walked off the court only fifteen minutes into the lesson, telling Train his stuff was old school and that Train was just another washed-up old pro.

"A bona fide bastard of a kid, that Harrison," Train said.

Freddie had been watching Harrison since his junior days. Harrison won many tournaments.

"The other guy I'm watching is a pretty cool dude named Andy," Freddie said. This kid played over at the public courts at the Pacific Palisades. He'd always played pretty well, even against Harrison, and won the NCAA title that year. Marcel was about to speak up when Train kicked him under the table.

"Yeah, Marcel knows Andy," Train said, "but Marcel's out here working on his music. He's going to enter the band and songwriters contest down at Cozy's in LA."

Train and Marcel left Crazy Joe's and headed back to Match Point. Marcel wanted to know why Train kicked him under the table. "What's the deal if Freddie knows I'm going to play at the Pacific Palisades?" Marcel asked.

"It would be all over the paper by the weekend is why," Train said. "We need to keep you a secret, keep you under the radar." Train was sorry he had to kick him, but Marcel needed to keep his mouth shut.

Marcel agreed he'd keep his mouth shut in the future around Freddie. Marcel wanted to know if Train just made up that story about the songwriter contest down in LA or if it was actually going to happen.

"Yeah, it's going to happen," Train said. "My buddy Smilin' Jack, the owner at Cozy's, holds a band contest at his club once a year and all the music execs from the record companies show up looking for new talent."

The contest even paid a ten-thousand-dollar first prize, Train explained, and a two-year songwriter's contract to the winner. It began in about three months and took place over two weekends, all bands up the first weekend and then the final four bands the following weekend. Marcel asked Train if any bands played swamp pop or Zydeco music around there. Train didn't think so. But if somebody showed up with some original Zydeco or swamp pop songs, it could be the new sound record executives were looking for.

Marcel wanted Train to hook up with his buddy Smilin' Jack and get him in that contest. He'd written about twenty songs and had a kickass ensemble of great musicians back in Lafayette, and they sure could use some spending money and a chance to tour around the country. Train thought this the perfect mental getaway for Marcel during such a vigorous training schedule, perfect to take his mind off the game every so often. He didn't want Marcel to suffer paralysis by analysis, he explained. Train promised Marcel he could get him in. Train was giving Smilin' Jack's son and daughter tennis lessons. Marcel called his bayou bandmates to make sure everybody could come over. He knew Blind Willie's Bayou Boogaloo Band could sure enough sprinkle some smokin' hot sounds on Hollywood.

The first two months of running the six-mile mountain and the workouts with Train were grueling and a test of determination for Marcel. Marcel had never faced an opponent like Train. His tactics and maneuverings left Marcel scraped and bruised and flying into fences. Marcel was beginning to grow cold to Train but still listened to his teachings and studied his court strategy. After all, he had been a world-class tennis pro. There was a breaking point. Train knew he had to take Marcel to that point.

One night during a particularly hard session, Train had Roberto turn on the sprinklers on Marcel's side of the court to teach Marcel focus against anything. Marcel reacted just as Train thought.

"What in the holy fuck are you doing?" Marcel shouted. Marcel dropped his racquet. He was drenched. Train told him to pick up the racquet and keep up. Marcel could hardly see the ball coming across the net. Train called him a little baby and told him again to pick up the racquet. Marcel told Train to fuck off. He was done for the day. Marcel walked off the court and headed to his cabin, flipping the bird at Train with some blistering expletives. Train was relentless, calling Marcel a little bayou baby as he walked away. Train said he ought to just throw in the towel and head on back home.

"I'll even help you pack that little red hot rod right now," Train said.

Later that night around midnight, Train was in bed with one of his Santa Barbara honeys, listening to a little Zydeco, when the tennis court lights came on. Not a second later, his screen door flew open, and Marcel bounded into the bedroom. Marcel told Train to get his ass out of bed and get out on the court.

"This little bayou baby is gonna kick your ass."

Marcel stormed out of the house, slamming the screen door. Train rolled over and told his girl to put her clothes on and come watch the fireworks.

"Young Marcel is about to break mental serve," Train said, "and you might have to call 9-1-1 for him, or for me maybe."

Train slowly walked to the court. Marcel was standing with the sprinklers on. He wiped the water from his face and pounded balls back at Train, balls to the face, the midsection, and the feet. Marcel was at all-out war.

The noise woke Roberto. He walked out to courtside in disbelief. He had never seen Marcel act like that before. Train told Roberto to give him a little sprinkler action to even the match. Roberto turned on the sprinklers and drenched Train. Hard shots back and forth. Train lost his footing and fell at the service line. He looked up, and Marcel was at the net, his racquet raised.

The ball came down. Train was still on the ground. He turned and covered his head. The ball came down across the net, slamming into his butt.

Marcel stood at the net, the sprinklers still raining on them both.

"Having fun, you bayou bigshot?" Marcel taunted. Marcel couldn't wait until morning to get back at it if Train could still walk. Marcel told Roberto to help Train back to his cabin. Train stood up and limped off the court. He told Roberto he didn't need any help.

"Just turn off those damn sprinklers," Train said.

Roberto asked Train if he was okay.

"Yeah, I'm okay," Train answered. "But that was the most painful lesson I ever gave someone to take them to the next level." Train knew he had finally taken Marcel to that mental place where champions go.

The next morning Marcel, Pancho, and Stella came running down the mountain trail. Train stood at courtside, talking to Roberto. Train asked Marcel if he had a nice morning run.

"Great run, but I'm more interested to know how you're doing today after the little rain shower last night?"

They both laughed.

"Really very sore," Train said, looking at Roberto and winking. "Except that somebody took off half my ass last night."

Upon which they all three erupted into uncontrollable and uproarious laughter.

After the morning workout, Train, Marcel, and Roberto walked over under the avocado tree at the picnic table for lunch. Marcel knew he went to a new place during the sprinkler game the previous night, a place he'd never been before in his tennis life, a completely different mental zone. He was so full of anger and hate that he felt like destroying Train. He wasn't thinking of his form and shots like he usually did. He explained this to Train and Roberto. They told him it was the zone of a champion, a fierce competitor. It was just a matter of finding it or firing up that focus.

Marcel was ready to work on the final piece of his game, the last piece of the puzzle, which he knew would be the hardest part: changing his one-handed backhand to a two-handed backhand.

For the next four weeks, Marcel spent a lot of time with Roberto because Train used a one-handed backhand. Train commented that if he would have had Roberto's two-handed backhand on tour, he could have won twenty more tournaments. Roberto had Marcel hit backhands with little Pancho. Marcel could see a little of the mastery of the two-handed backhand in Pancho's swing. Pancho was going to be a top-shelf tennis player one day. Marcel was amazed that little Pancho could hit a backhand with such power and at so many different angles.

Roberto explained to Marcel that the top hand of the two hands on the racquet works three ways. The first was that it added force. The second was that it also added resistance to the ball which made for more velocity. The third advantage to the top hand was that it worked like a hinge to create different and greater angles at the moment of the shot which is deceptive to the opponent.

Marcel dived into the two-handed backhand, convinced and ready to change. He hit nothing but two-handed backhands from then on out, increasing his ball velocity by twenty miles per hour. He began to develop a complete command of ball shot angles and placements anywhere on the court. Marcel had worked long and hard with Roberto and had found a new weapon in his artillery of shots. The daily six-mile runs up and down the mountain had greatly increased his stamina and added to his lower body strength and improved his quickness and agility of footwork.

Roberto had worked a deal with the tennis coach at the University of California, Santa Barbara, his alma mater, for some of the college players to come down and play daily matches against Marcel, most all of which Marcel handily won. Unlike during his high school and college career, Marcel was now playing with a two-handed backhand. He had a particularly effective new winning shot down the line, known in the tennis vernacular as a *sledgehammer*. Roberto occasionally referred to Marcel as the "Santa Barbara Sledgehammer."

Everything was going as Train had planned. Everything in Marcel's game was complete. But what continued to worry Train was that Marcel played with an artistry and gentleman's approach to the game. He hoped that sometime in the heat of competition at the Pacific Palisades Open that the fire inside would ignite and the flame would burn hot enough for Marcel to want to destroy his opponent and go for the kill.

The Open was only six weeks away, and the training needed to heat up. It was time for Train to game up on Marcel.

Annie

Train got Blind Willie's Bayou Boogaloo Band into Cozy's contest. Cozy's was a very hip place down on Ventura Boulevard where the locals and celebrities hung out to hear up-and-coming musicians, singers, and songwriters, all trying to be spotted by record execs and agents. The band was something the left coast had never seen before: an accordion and a frottior occupying center stage. Marcel on lead guitar to the left, accompanied by a trumpet, saxophone, drums, and bass guitar. The place was packed and the bayou boys were rocking the house.

A couple notes into their fourth and final song, Marcel looked out into the audience, and about four rows back there she sat, a big smile on her face. It was the magical Annie that Marcel encountered at Papa Mojo's months ago before she rode off into the night in a limousine. She was at a table with four other girls and five guys. The band came offstage, and Marcel went out to the back patio for some air. Cozy's was hot, and Marcel was sweating. He stood off to the corner of the patio bar, gazing out, wondering what she was doing in California.

"This is a long way away from New Orleans," Marcel heard a voice say. He turned around and saw Annie standing behind him. He smiled and told her the same thing.

Annie asked Marcel his name. "The limo driver took off so fast that night I didn't get a chance to learn your name," she said.

"I remember," Marcel said. "Of course, I remember you very well. It's pretty hard to forget someone as beautiful as you." Marcel could be quite the charmer. He asked her what she had been doing down in New Orleans that weekend. He'd assumed she was from Louisiana and maybe going to school in New Orleans, but Annie explained that she and her girlfriends, all of whom were from California, were down in New Orleans for a bachelorette party.

Annie actually lived in Bel Air with her grandmother who, it turns out, and still unbeknownst to Marcel, was none other than Irma Jean Boudreaux Kersh. She placed her hand on Marcel's arm and thanked him again for saving her from that guy at Papa Mojo's.

Just then, a hand shot out of nowhere and pulled Annie's hand away from Marcel's arm. The guy grabbing Annie looked Marcel up and down.

"Get back to the table," he said, "and stop messing around with this bayou critter."

"You don't have to grab her like that," Marcel said.

Annie pushed his hand away.

"I'll be back when I'm ready," she said. "I was just going to the ladies' room, and I saw this nice musician here and I wanted to know the name of the song his band had just played."

When she returned from the restroom, she passed by Marcel. He asked her if that was her boyfriend.

"Yes, unfortunately that's my boyfriend," Annie said. "He's very jealous of me talking to other guys."

Before she walked away, Marcel told her to try and make it back the next weekend for the band competition finals.

He said he'd like to see her again. She smiled and said she hoped she could make it and gave him a kiss on the cheek. Marcel got hit with her magic dust again.

The band had to stay another week for the finals. They crashed in some of the cabins at Match Point, much to the delight of Train, who went over every night to listen to their rehearsals. They even let him join in on the frottior. Saturday night came around, and Blind Willie's Bayou Boogaloo Band was in rare form.

The audience at Cozy's was up out of their chairs and dancing, asking for more. When the night finished and the announcement made, Smilin' Jack declared Blind Willie's Bayou Boogaloo Band the winner. They were awarded a two-year concert schedule opening for some major acts. The big prize was a songwriting contract for Marcel if he chose to sign, but he couldn't make that decision yet. He still might take a shot on the pro tennis tour.

Smilin' Jack congratulated Marcel and gave him a piece of paper with a phone number and a name. Smilin' Jack said for Marcel to call the number on the paper if he was ready to sign. The piece of paper read "Clive" with the phone number underneath. Marcel had no idea who Clive was, but Smilin' Jack said Clive was ready to sign Marcel to his record label.

The band rolled out the next day and headed back to Louisiana with a ten-thousand-dollar check and a two-year touring schedule; not bad for two weeks of work. Marcel was on cloud nine. He had a possible two-year songwriting contract in hand, but there was something missing from that fairytale night at the finals—Annie. Where had Annie been that night? Why hadn't she come back to see him? Marcel figured she was partying somewhere else in Bel Air.

Four months had gone by then. All the training, practice, and playing put the polishing touches on Marcel's game. Train and Roberto both agreed the kid was ready. He had elevated his game to a level where he was winning some sets against Train. Both Train and Roberto agreed Marcel was ready if only he could capture that killer instinct in the tournament. That would be the difference.

Train and Marcel were finishing up a Friday afternoon session when Roberto came over to the court. He told Train that Miss Irma called and wanted Train and Marcel to come up to the mansion Saturday night. She was having a surprise birthday party for her granddaughter, Annie. She was bringing guests up from Bel Air and some of Irma's Santa Barbara museum friends were also coming over. She asked that Train and Marcel dress up real nice and wear jackets and that Train had better shave. Train called Irma and told her he and Marcel would be there in jackets and all shaved up with some pretty boy faces just for her.

Marcel didn't much care about the details of the party. The one thing that interested him was the subject of the party, Annie. Marcel was hesitant to go, anticipating an altercation with her boyfriend, but he had no excuse to bow out. Marcel wore a white shirt and a jacket, the only one he brought, a royal-blue stage jacket with a red alligator embroidered on the lapel. He also put on a pair of red alligator boots to match. Train told Marcel he looked like a million bucks and Irma would love the boots. She usually always wore a pair of her boots to parties and functions because it reminded her of Acadiana and her grandfather. It made her feel like she was back home as a Cajun girl, she'd confided in Train.

Train and Marcel decided to walk the half-mile trail from Match Point through the avocado orchard up to the mansion. They had become very close friends. They had a lot in common. They both grew up in southwest Louisiana, were fatherless, and raised by dedicated and loving mothers. They learned the game of tennis the hard way, underdogs without money, coaches, trainers, or the manicured courts of the country clubs. They got at it day by day, loving every minute of it.

They arrived at the mansion and Rosita, Irma's longtime housemaid and dear friend, greeted them. Irma's occasional habit of inviting Rosita to dine with her in the formal dining room often created a minor scandal among some of Irma's country club and museum friends. Everyone was poolside enjoying cocktails and hors d'oeuvres. Irma looked at Train and Marcel.

"Oh, my Cajun boys, looking so beautifully handsome tonight all dressed up," she said. "And look at Train's pretty shaven face." He had dared not ignore Irma's requests.

Both Train and Marcel had worn cowboy boots, much to her delight. She hiked up her dress just a smidge to show Train and Marcel that she was wearing her shiny pair of alligator boots. Irma told Marcel she was sure some of the young girls coming up from Bel Air that night would be interested to know if his red alligator on his jacket might bite.

Everyone was ushered inside to the dining room. The birthday girl and her friends were only ten minutes away. Train found himself in paradise. Irma seated him between her two young golfing lady friends from the Palms Country Club. They giggled that the private lessons Train had given them at Match Point were a kept secret from Irma.

Marcel had been honored with the seat right beside Irma. Rosita came into the room and announced the birthday girl and her friends were coming up the driveway. Rosita lowered the lights. The girls came in, greeted by Rosita in the foyer. She opened the door to the dining room, and everyone stood up.

"Surprise!" the crowd screamed, before breaking out into a raucous rendition of "Happy Birthday."

Annie stood among her friends like a jewel set in dull silver.

"Are you surprised, Annie?" Irma asked.

"Grandmother, you have no idea," Annie said, never taking her eyes from Marcel. "What a great surprise this is . . ."

Everyone sat down to a steak and lobster dinner and made their way out to the pool afterward to open presents and enjoy the red velvet cake presented with twenty-two sparkling candles. After all the presents were opened and the guests were enjoying the cake, Annie stepped away from her guests to find Marcel.

"What in the world are you doing here?" Annie asked. "I thought you'd surely be on your way back to Louisiana after winning the band competition."

Marcel said he had planned on telling her everything when she had come back to the band competition finals, but she never showed.

"I had a wedding shower that night," Annie said. "I was very sorry to miss you playing." She told Marcel that she heard his band had won.

Marcel gave her the full story about how her grandmother came to the rescue for him and his mama after his daddy died and about how they needed to move closer to Lafayette and how Irma moved them into one of the Kersh Oil Co. houses near Heyman Park when he was about six.

"Yeah, but that doesn't explain why you're here at Match Point," Annie said.

"I'm getting to that," Marcel said. "But first I have a question for you. Why isn't your boyfriend here at your birthday party?"

"He's in San Francisco playing in a tennis tournament," Annie said. "He's getting ready for a big tournament for college players planning to go pro. He's supposed to be one of the top seeds and a good bet to win the tournament."

"Tournament?" Marcel asked.

"He's playing in the Pacific Palisades Open."

Marcel was shocked. She wasn't going to believe the rest of his story. "Is this the same guy that grabbed your arm at the bar?" Marcel asked.

"Yes, it is."

"What's his name?"

"Harrison," Annie said with a quizzical look on her face. "Why?"

"Would that be Harrison Price *the third*?"

"Yeah, why?" Annie was curious how Marcel knew her boyfriend's name.

Marcel explained how Train and his friend Freddie had told him all about Harrison.

"Why would he be talking about Harrison?" Annie asked.

It was all too crazy for Marcel. "You've only seen me play guitar," Marcel summarized, "but I've been living right here at your grandmother's tennis ranch for the last three months, working with Train getting ready for," and there he paused for effect, "the Pacific Palisades Open, the same tournament your boyfriend will be playing in." Marcel explained he had been a nationally ranked college tennis player at Tulane and won the Oyster Bay Classic in New Orleans. He explained how he had to enter the tournament to try to win money for his mother's cancer operation, was training with Train and Roberto, and was living down in one of the cabins at Match Point.

Annie said she was sorry to hear about Marcel's mama, but she was in awe of Marcel's story. Annie took Marcel by the hand over to Irma's poolside table. She had a surprising story to tell her grandmother about Marcel. She told Irma how they met in New Orleans a while back.

"What lucky accidents," Irma said. "Count yourself lucky, Annie, to have been saved by one of southwest Louisiana's most handsome and talented tennis players."

The party ended and Irma's two young lady friends invited Train to go back down to LA and keep their party going. Annie's girlfriends headed back as well. Annie didn't want the moment or opportunity to slip by. She wanted more time with Marcel. She asked her grandmother if it would be okay for her to stay at the mansion.

"I don't want to go back down to LA tonight," Annie said. "I would rather stay here in Santa Barbara."

"It's your birthday, child," Irma said. "You can do anything you want. That's what birthdays are all about."

All of Irma's remaining guests stayed in the main house, so Annie had the pool house all to herself. Irma invited Marcel to stay for a while and entertain the birthday girl. Irma and her friends headed on to the house and called it a night.

"There are extra swimsuits in the guest house," Irma said, "for a dip in the pool if you wish. And the hot tub by the pool is the perfect temperature. Drink anything you want out of the fridge. There should still be plenty of wine from the party." Irma thanked Marcel for joining Annie's surprise birthday party. "Way too cool in those cowboy boots and that dashing blue jacket with the red alligator on the lapel," Irma said. She wished Annie happy birthday, kissed her on the forehead, and told them to have fun and warned, "Beware of Marcel's red alligator. It may bite if you get too close."

They all laughed. Marcel and Annie changed into swimsuits, grabbed a couple of towels, and slipped into the hot tub with two glasses of wine and some chocolate-covered cherries. They sat and talked in the hot tub, enjoying a beautiful, crisp Santa Barbara night and looking down toward the harbor, Stearns Wharf, the lights, and the clear sky, brightly lit by millions of twinkling stars. They floated around in the heated pool for a while and sat in the lounge chairs until three o'clock in the morning, listening to each other's stories.

Annie had been living with her grandmother Irma since the eighth grade. Irma's only daughter, a real wild child, grew up and left college after two years to become a band groupie. Annie was born out of wedlock, sperm-donored by some musician at a San Francisco music festival, conceived during one of her mother's frequent drunk and drug-induced one-night stands. Irma stepped up and took control to provide some normalcy to Annie's young life. She moved Annie in with her and H. A. at their Bel Air home. Annie grew up participating in all of Irma's charities.

She learned many valuable lessons and absorbed Irma's unselfish and kind sensibilities. She earned good grades in high school and college and became involved in all kinds of social and civic groups.

Marcel wondered how in the hell she ever ended up with a jerk like Harrison. It was crazy. Was it arranged? Some weird attraction? But Marcel figured it certainly wasn't the time to include Annie's boyfriend in the conversation. Marcel thought it best to leave once it was around four in the morning.

"Are you sure?" Annie asked.

He wanted to stay all night with Annie, but he didn't want to cross Irma. And he didn't want to move that quickly with Annie, not yet, not right then anyway. He gave her a big hug, and she gave him a long kiss and said it would be nice for them to see each other again. He was under her magic spell. They kissed again. He wished her happy birthday and thanked her for such a special night. She invited him to come down to Bel Air sometime before the tournament. She would show him around. He appreciated her invitation. He said he might just surprise her one day, and she said she would like that surprise very much.

Marcel walked back down the half-mile trail to his Match Point cabin. He stopped halfway and turned around, desperately wanting to go back to the pool house and spend the night with her. He could show her real love, real passion. But maybe not then. If it was to be, it had to be the right moment. That wasn't the time to go for the winning point. If he missed, he would surely add out.

Marcel turned and walked down to the ranch to his cabin and got his guitar. He sat on the front porch and quietly played song after song late into the night. He was still asleep at noon the next day.

I called Marcel up around that time. I could tell he was groggy, so I told him it was me.

"Sorry, Louie," he said. He told me he'd been up late the previous night and was sleeping in. He asked me the time, and I told him I just finished a late afternoon lunch.

"Must have been a long night for you, Marcel," I said. I told him I'd call him back in about thirty minutes to give him some time to wake up and maybe grab a shower. When I called back, he explained how his tennis game had greatly improved. He wished he'd have met Train years ago. He told me I was right. Train had taken him to another level of tennis that he never imagined. He said his work with Roberto adopting the two-handed backhand had given him a new arsenal of shots. He asked if I knew Irma had a granddaughter named Annie.

"Oh yeah," I said. "Annie, of course. I haven't seen her in years."

He told me how beautiful she was. He thought Cupid's arrow had pierced his heart. I finally got around to my reason for calling. I wanted to give him some news about his mama's condition. She was having some problems with the treatments. Things weren't going as planned. I strongly suggested to him that he should take a break from his training and come back for a couple of days to visit with her until things were a little more stable. I assured him there was no cause for alarm. There was nothing life-threatening, but I thought it would help lift her spirits if he made the trip back home as soon as he could.

Marcel had been thinking about her every day. He missed her very much and worried about her all the time. He was going to leave later Sunday afternoon and be back home by Tuesday.

He asked me to keep his trip back a secret from her. He wanted to make his visit a surprise. I asked him to call me when he got into town and we could go see her together.

The Invitation

Marcel was packing up a couple things for his visit back to Lafayette and he couldn't get Annie off his mind. So what if Harrison was her boyfriend, he thought. She wasn't married to him.

Annie and Irma were still up at the mansion that Sunday morning. Marcel decided to walk up to the house and give it a shot. He had no idea what Irma or Annie's reaction to his question would be. He told Annie about my phone call. He was driving back later that afternoon to Lafayette to see his mama. He was very nervous.

"Anyway," Marcel said, stuttering a bit while trying to get his words out, "you, um, maybe interested in driving back to Lafayette with me?" Marcel said. But he quickly added, "Just consider it a road trip. Nothing serious."

Annie was surprised and didn't answer at first.

"If it's not cool with you and your boyfriend, I understand," Marcel said. "It'd be all right."

"It's not my boyfriend's decision," Annie said, breaking her silence. She said he was up in San Francisco for the tennis tournament and wouldn't be back until next Sunday. "Harrison is all about Harrison, always. He doesn't even call me for three or four days when he goes off."

She and Harrison were always arguing and having problems. At the moment they were not getting along very well at all. A little adventure was just what she needed. She went to talk to Irma to make sure it would be all right with her. Irma's house guests had left the mansion after lunch, and she and Annie were getting ready to drive back to Bel Air. Annie told her of Marcel's invitation. Irma was aware of Marlene's situation because I had been keeping her updated. Irma thought it was a very interesting and exciting invitation. A couple days around Lafayette and Acadiana was always a lot of fun.

"Have you told Marcel that you're engaged?" Irma asked Annie.

"No," Annie said. "I don't see any reason to tell him that." Harrison still hadn't committed to a wedding date and became very angry when the conversation arose.

Irma asked Annie if she had feelings for Marcel.

"I do," Annie answered. "It's all very confusing."

Irma's opinion was that it was a great time for Annie to do a little soul-searching, go on an adventure. Maybe Annie could figure out if that ring of Harrison's was going to fit on her finger and in her life. Annie didn't think it would be a good idea to tell Marcel that she was engaged. It might make things far too uncomfortable for him. He wouldn't be his normal self around her.

If anyone wanted to know why Annie had gone to Lafayette, Irma said she'd explain that she sent Annie over to conduct interviews for several Kersh scholarships at the University of Louisiana, Lafayette.

Annie always had an extra closet of clothes and shoes at the Santa Barbara mansion. There wasn't any need to go back down to Bel Air. She could leave with Marcel as soon as he was ready. She quickly packed and told Marcel she had Irma's blessing. Marcel said he'd return for her shortly. He had to go back to the cabin and tell Roberto of his plan.

Roberto could tell Train who was most likely giving Sunday afternoon doubles lessons to Irma's two young lady friends.

Marcel picked up Annie at the mansion. They would spend one night in Austin, Texas, to break up the trip and check out some music halls. He vowed to Irma he would be a gentleman.

They stayed in separate hotel rooms.

Marcel and Annie got into Lafayette at about lunchtime on Tuesday. Marcel had a craving for some hot, fresh boudin at Johnson's Boucaniere. She asked if she should peel off the casing or leave it on. She tried it both ways. She liked it with the casing off.

After lunch they headed straight over to the hospital to see Marlene. Marcel had called me, and I was going to meet them there, but I got held up and couldn't make it. No one knew Marcel had a beautiful young girl in tow, much less Irma's granddaughter.

At the hospital, Marlene was asleep in the bed and Viola was sitting in a chair reading her Bible when Marcel and Annie walked in. Viola stood up and hugged Marcel.

"Who's this beautiful young lady?" Viola whispered in Marcel's ear.

He told her she was Annie, Irma Kersh's granddaughter. Viola knew Annie but hadn't seen her for probably fifteen years. She had been about seven back then and came to Lafayette with Irma and H. A. in the fall of that year for the Acadiens et Creoles Festival. Viola smiled and hugged Annie.

"I haven't seen you since you was knee high to a grasshopper," Viola said. "What a beautiful young lady you turned out to be."

Irma had told Annie to give Viola a big hug for her. Viola wanted to know why Irma hadn't come with them.

Marcel laughed. "My little Benz was only built for two," Marcel said.

Viola wanted to know how everything was going out in California. He told her his tennis game has gotten better thanks to Train and Roberto. About that time, Marlene rolled over and opened her eyes. A big smile came across her face.

Marlene was oh-so-happy to see her son. "Why didn't someone tell me he was coming home?" she said. "And such a long drive over from California. Oh, you're so sweet."

Driving from California was very nice, he told her. "A special friend has come with me, Mama," Marcel said. "Irma's granddaughter, Annie. She wanted some crawfish and jambalaya this week, so she just jumped right on in for the ride."

They all laughed. Marlene, like Viola, hadn't seen Annie since she was a little girl. Marlene thanked Annie for taking good care of her baby boy on the long trip and getting him home safely.

"It was my pleasure," Annie said. "I've never ridden through the state. I really enjoyed the beauty of the bayous and swamps. Louisiana is such a beautiful place."

Marlene said she was fine and that the doctors were making a fuss over nothing. She was just a little tired, that was all. They needed to hurry up because she was ready to go home.

I didn't get to the hospital that day because I had a recruiting interview. Marcel and Annie stayed for a couple of hours. The medication made Marlene tired, so Marcel said they'd be back after dinner. Viola walked them to the door. Marlene had gotten much weaker over the past few weeks, she explained. The doctors were concerned that the treatments were affecting her immune system. Pneumonia was always a threat in these circumstances, but they were still hopeful. She had lost about fifteen pounds since the treatments began. Viola reassured Marcel that my father was monitoring her situation very closely.

Viola had been staying overnight at the hospital with Marlene. Marcel used to have his own room over at Viola's house, and she offered the room to him if he chose. That's where he decided to stay. His old guest room looked out over the Petite Bayou, and Annie could listen to the sounds of the night critters.

After dinner, Marcel and Annie went back to the hospital around eight o'clock. Viola was still there and Marlene was asleep. Viola told them Marlene was very tired and ate only a little of her dinner and went back to sleep.

"She probably won't wake back up tonight," Viola said. "Better come back tomorrow morning when she has a little more energy."

Marcel and Annie went to Viola's house. Marcel couldn't wait to take Annie for a ride in Blind Willie's piroque down the Bayou Vermilion beneath the bright yellow moon and through the bald cypress trees, so serene and quiet. Marcel shared with Annie all his boyhood adventures down on the bayou with Blind Willie.

When they got back to the house, Marcel went in and got his guitar while Annie sat on the back porch, still enjoying the stillness and beauty of the night. Marcel strummed his guitar and Annie enjoyed the simplicity and romance of the moment, just her and Marcel alone together.

With a hug and a goodnight kiss, they went to their rooms. She thanked him for the invitation.

The next morning, Marcel took Annie for breakfast and then onto the hospital. Marlene was wide awake, smiling and sitting in a wheelchair beside Viola.

She'd already had breakfast and been on her morning ride around the hospital. Marcel and Annie stayed a couple hours until noon. Viola had gone home for a break. Marlene told Annie stories about Irma and all the good times they'd had together. Annie heard how special her grandmother truly was.

Viola returned from running her errands and urged Marcel to show Annie around town for the afternoon and take her to lunch at Dwyer's Café for their famous meat and three specials.

"Dwyer's is always packed at lunchtime and I'm sure you'll see a lot of your friends," Viola told Marcel. "You need to show this pretty girl off to all your friends."

The Paul Breaux Middle School chorus was presenting a concert in Heyman Park that afternoon. Many of the children had been taught by Marlene, and Marcel knew most of the teachers there.

Marcel chose a special place for them to sit, right beside the old tennis wall where he had hit thousands of tennis balls when he was a young boy. The chalk writings of his make-believe wins were still scribbled on the wall, though faded with time: "Marcel Jackson Wimbledon Champion 1975," "Marcel Jackson French Open Champion 1972, 1973," "Marcel Jackson US Open Champion 1975, 1976." Only then did Annie understand his passion and true love for the game.

After the picnic and the concert, Annie dropped Marcel off at the Beaver Park Tennis Center for a couple hours of tennis practice with Mr. Cristola. She headed over to the University of Louisiana at Lafayette to interview applicants with Mr. Coteau for the Kersh Trust Fund scholarships.

They had dinner that night at a restaurant up in Carencro with my mother and father. One of the cooks came out of the kitchen to tell Marcel that he worked with his father, Mel, years ago before he took the oil rig job. The cook said his father was a fine man.

At dinner, Marcel learned a little more information about his mother's condition. My father said the treatments had taken a toll on Marlene, but they were cautiously optimistic.

Later in the night, my mother told my father to hush when he suggested that Marcel ought to go ahead and marry Annie right after dinner; the justice of the peace was sitting just three tables over.

"I'm sure you'd make some beautiful babies," he said.

Marcel's face turned the color of a red pepper. Annie winked and patted him on the knee.

They visited Marlene the following mornings and early evenings on that Friday and Saturday. Marlene was showing signs of continued weakness from the treatments. She would regain some strength during the coming month's departure from the treatments, my father assured Marcel.

Early Saturday afternoon Marcel decided to take Annie down to Avery Island to Jungle Gardens to visit the Buddha temple and have another picnic on the banks of magical Bird City, the spring migratory home to thousands of snowy white egrets and species of plants, flowers, and trees. Their hearts were beginning to beat to the same song. The kisses and touches became more frequent. The moments in the gardens were heavenly.

Being Irma's granddaughter granted her a Cajun heritage and lineage. Marcel decided to introduce her all night long on Saturday night as his California Cajun queen. She was most worthy of the crown in his eyes.

After an early evening visit to the hospital, Marcel took Annie to the original Don's Seafood and Steakhouse on Vermilion Street, open since 1934. He was craving one of their original creations, and he knew Annie had never had anything like Don's jacked-up shrimp: shrimp with bacon, jalapeño peppers, and pepper jack cheese—baked—and the main dish ordered for the two of them, Don's crab dinner. A lot of people came by the table to talk to Marcel and inquire of his beautiful dinner date and ask how his mama was doing. Many were surprised to find out that Annie was Irma's granddaughter. Annie excused herself to the restroom, and on her way back to the table, she spotted someone she knew. It was none other than Train's mother, Joline, and her husband, Russell. Annie met them in Bel Air when they came to visit Train when he first started teaching at the Palms Country Club.

"Annie, what a great surprise to see you in Lafayette," Joline said. Marcel told them Train loved being at Match Point; he was much happier there than teaching at the Palms Country Club and was charming everyone in Santa Barbara.

"He's quite the celebrity," Marcel said. Marcel invited them to join him and Annie to a little fais do-do that night at the Blue Moon Saloon. Joline stuck her red-and-gold cowgirl boots out from underneath the table and looked at Annie.

"Sounds like a great night," Joline said. "Annie, I sure do hope you have some cowgirl boots, honey."

Annie smiled. Marcel had surprised her that afternoon with a pair of boots and wrapped them up as a gift along with a cowgirl hat. With that, she stuck her boots up in the air.

"I don't know if I'm going to fit in with all this," Annie said.

"You fit in anywhere on earth," Marcel said.

Annie kissed him on the cheek, and they all four took off for the fais do-do. They danced the two step and the waltz and saw all their friends. Marcel joined the band on stage for a couple of songs.

It was after midnight when Marcel and Annie took Joline and Russell back to their car at the restaurant. They said their goodbyes.

There were still some more dance clubs open, Marcel explained, but Annie didn't want to share Marcel with anyone else the rest of the night. She wanted to go back to Viola's house by the Petite Bayou and be alone with him.

And that's what Marcel wanted too.

They went back and sat on the porch, talking and kissing. Annie headed to bed because she had to catch the Kersh charter at ten o'clock the next morning. They went to their separate rooms. Fifteen minutes later Annie opened the door to Marcel's bedroom. She pulled back the covers and lay down beside him. She had startled him. She wanted to be with him. She wanted to sleep with him. She wanted him to make love to her. She wanted to be all his. She had waited long enough.

They spent a sleepless night together. The night was too short for them both, way too short.

Marcel and Annie had about an hour before the Kersh jet was to pick her up at the Lafayette Airport at noon. Marcel decided to take her for a little stroll over in Girard Park. Marcel told Annie this week with her was like something out of a movie for him. She touched his soul, he confessed. He'd thought of her often since the first time he had seen her on the dance floor at Papa Mojo's. He never forgot her face. He said he should have sent that guy Jasper a thank-you card because if not for him, who knows what would have happened. Then his mama gets sick and he goes to California and sees her again. It was in the stars, he thought.

But he didn't know if the romantic time they had last night was right. He didn't want to be responsible for causing problems with her and her boyfriend. Marcel didn't know anything about her situation back in California with her boyfriend. He told her his hesitations. Annie explained that it was precisely because of her boyfriend situation that she decided to go to Lafayette with him. She didn't tag along just for a sightseeing trip to Louisiana. She went along to explore and search her feelings. The week with him had been one of the happiest times in her life. She had no regrets about any of it. He made her smile. He made her happy. He made her feel loved. She could see he touched all the people around him in a very special way. They loved him. She had come to know the kind of person he was. She wouldn't change anything they had shared together.

She wanted to see him the following weekend at Irma's mansion in Santa Barbara. There were things she needed and wanted to tell him. She hugged him and kissed him. Her journey with Marcel to southwest Louisiana had been heavenly.

"You better watch it when you get back to Bel Air," Marcel said. "Irma might steal those pretty new boots, Annie."

Annie said her grandmother would have an easier time taking her boots off a Louisiana gator than her. Annie went up the Kersh jet steps. She turned around and, with a smile and a wink, blew Marcel a kiss.

Marcel watched as the jet flew away. He turned and walked away with a big smile on his face and a new bounce in his step.

Break Point

Annie was the only passenger that morning on the flight back to California in the Kersh Oil company jet. Annie went straight to Irma's Bel Air home for her mother's birthday party that afternoon. Annie hadn't seen her mother—away in France or Monte Carlo or who knew where—in months.

Annie saw her mother standing by the pool. She walked over and wished her mother a happy birthday and gave her a small hug. They had never been very close. She told Annie she had been in Spain for a while and introduced her to her new friend, Count Raimondo. The Count, as all counts do, Annie supposed, bowed and kissed her hand.

"Just as beautiful as your mother," he said in a thick accent.

Annie's mother asked how that handsome beau of Annie's was doing. "I know Harrison is perfect for you," her mother said. "When is the wedding? I'll have to make sure I'm in town."

"There's not a date yet," Annie replied and excused herself. She said she needed to say hello to Irma and let her know she was back.

An hour later, Harrison and two of his friends arrived, and Harrison found Annie.

"How's my sugar baby?" Harrison asked. "Did you miss me all over?"

His friends laughed. He stepped forward to kiss her, and she turned her cheek.

"What are you doing back from San Francisco so soon?" Annie asked. "Who invited you and your friends to my mother's party?"

"There was no invitation," Harrison said. "I thought we'd just crash." He told Annie he came by to see how many guys her mother showed up with.

Annie asked him to leave.

"Come on, Annie," he said. "I haven't seen you in ten days. Let's leave this old folks party. My parents are down in Cabo San Lucas. Let's go back to the house and let me show you how much I've missed you."

His friends laughed again. Annie demanded he leave. Before leaving he told her it was too bad she wasn't more like her mother.

"*She* would never ever turn down a night of sex from anyone," he said. "You need to take some lessons from her. Get better at it."

Annie went into the bathroom and slammed her hand on the counter. Irma came in behind her and asked her to calm down.

"What in the world is wrong?" Irma asked.

"He's a spoiled bastard," Annie said. "I'm only part of his collection. I'd be nothing more than a trophy wife to him."

Irma told her not to let him spoil the birthday party for her. She gave Annie a hug and a kiss, and they went back out by the pool for the birthday cake and to watch her mother blow out the candles. Annie thought of Harrison's comments and looked at her mother with disgust. Her mind raced. No, she wouldn't let Harrison spoil that day or any other day for her. The trip to Lafayette with Marcel had given her a new perspective of who she was and how she wanted to be treated. She had changed. She could feel it, and it felt good.

The next morning Annie woke up late and went out into the back garden. Irma was sitting alone having a beignet and cup of coffee and looking out over the par four fifteenth hole at her Bellagio road home. Her neighbor was a famous, eccentric director who made movies about birds and a psycho killer.

"Good morning, my beautiful Annie," Irma said.

Annie bent over to kiss her. Irma wanted to talk about Harrison. Annie asked where her mother was.

"She's taken off early with the Count," Irma said. "She told me to give you a kiss and tell you she'd be back in a month or two."

Annie looked up toward the sky with a frown on her face. Irma touched her arm.

"She's not going to change, Annie," Irma said, "but please try and find a way to love her just a little. We aren't all born to be caring mothers."

Annie changed the subject and began to tell Irma all about her trip to Lafayette.

"It was like a wonderland," Annie said, "a fantasy. I wanted to stay for another week or two." She excitedly told Irma everything, about how she and Marcel talked and laughed and ate boudin and jambalaya and all kinds of great Cajun and Creole foods and about how they danced to Zydeco and how she learned some waltzes, how they went for piroque rides in the bayous. Annie loved Marcel's mother. His mother was so wonderful and loved him so much, and Viola was just as great. Annie said that they all love each other so much. Irma was excited when Annie told her that Marcel took her down to Irma's favorite place, Avery Island and Jungle Gardens, and about the picnic they had at Bird City with the thousands of snowy white egrets.

Irma was very excited for Annie. She noticed that Annie was not wearing her engagement ring. She suspected she hadn't told Marcel while she was with him in Louisiana that she was engaged. When Irma asked, Annie confessed that Irma's suspicions were correct. She didn't tell Marcel.

"I wanted him to be himself," Annie said, "and I wanted to find out my true feelings for him." After the trip she realized she had never really been happy with Harrison and never would be. Her time with Marcel in Lafayette away from Bel Air gave her the time to explore the things that made her really happy. Everything was beginning to make sense to her during the trip, but the plane ride back was the turning point. While sitting on the plane and ruminating on her trip, she realized she wanted that kind of happiness she felt in Lafayette with Marcel. When they were about an hour away from landing, she closed her eyes. It was surreal. She could see herself down below in Bel Air as a little girl. She could see herself as Harrison's girlfriend since the tenth grade and she could see that girl in college, still Harrison's girlfriend.

And she saw herself in the future. She had three children with Harrison. She had a chain on her leg, and she was running and running and running with her children, trying to get away from him, and he was holding the chain, laughing. She couldn't get away. She was chained to him forever. That's the way it always was with him. He would want to control her life. She would do what he wanted or else. She opened her eyes. She could see the ocean and the palm trees coming closer and closer and as she got closer, she felt she was moving farther and farther away from the life she had known before. A warm and peaceful feeling filled her body. A smile came across her face.

She knew in that moment that she had escaped her past and her future.

Annie decided that when it came to her decision with Harrison, the sooner the better. She met Harrison on Tuesday at the country club outside at the patio bar to talk. He was having a frat party over at the fraternity house that night, so he didn't have time for some—as he put it—long, girly rap session with her.

He was in luck. She wasn't going to have a long, girly rap session with him. She wasn't going to have any more time with him. She was getting ready to put him in her past. She told him the engagement was over. She was done with him. A shocked look came across his face. It was a look Annie didn't recognize because, she assumed, rejection was something that had never happened to him before. She was almost certain no one had ever turned him down.

"You can't do this," he said. "You'll ruin my mother's plans for the engagement party after the tournament." He said canceling the party would embarrass the hell out of his mother and father and all their friends. "You can't do this," he repeated.

She was amazed but not surprised that he thought about his mother's party instead of their relationship. He had no concern for her feelings. He never did. It had always been all about him. She was done with all his disrespect and the shameful moments she had endured in the past with him. Again, he told her she couldn't do this. She was screwing up everything.

Annie handed him the ring. "Yeah, you are one hundred percent right about that, Harrison," she said.

He grabbed the ring and called her a crazy fucking bitch and a slut. He said he'd give the ring to some chick that would know how to treat him right. Annie told him he would need a whole lot of luck with finding that girl. He sent his beer glass crashing into the patio fireplace, walked away, then turned and said, "Go to hell, bitch."

Annie had some of Irma's sassiness about her. She had to take the last shot, hit him where it hurt, a *brutalizer*, something he understood.

"Harrison," she said. He turned back to look at her.

"What is it, bitch?" he said.

She smiled at him and winked. "Break point, asshole. Game over."

He was gone. He was out of her life forever. Sort of.

Irma and Annie had just finished a round of golf the next day on Wednesday at the club. They were headed back to the clubhouse when Harrison's mother, Eloise, left the patio and stepped in front of their golf cart. She called Annie a little bitch and asked Annie what in the world she thought she was doing, ruining the engagement party and calling off the wedding?

Irma told Annie to take the cart on around to the clubhouse. She stepped out of the cart and told Mrs. Price she needed to step out of the way or she would soon be nothing more than Bel Air roadkill. Annie drove away and in her rearview saw Irma approach Eloise. Irma could play some serious hardball when it came to the well-being of Annie. She wasn't going to let anyone disrespect or run over her granddaughter, certainly not a mindless, pampered trophy wife.

Annie came around the corner, and Mrs. Price was there to apologize. She said she understood that some relationships didn't always work out and wished Annie all the best in her future. Annie wondered what in the world her grandmother had said to Eloise.

Annie never heard another word from Eloise, and she never asked her grandmother what she said to Eloise that day, but she came to find out later from some gossiping friends of Irma's that Irma knew a secret of Eloise's. As long as Eloise was respectful of Annie, Irma offered silence about what she knew about Eloise, which was that Eloise's husband, Mr. Price, was always complaining about the club golf pro, Rich. Mr. Price had been paying for Eloise's golf lessons over the last year, and her game hadn't improved one damn bit, and every time she came home from a lesson, she was very tired and went to bed early.

When the Goldfinches left for Denmark for a year, they asked Rich to ride by their house on the fifteenth hole every week to check on things and make sure no break-ins or problems occurred. They had asked Irma, their neighbor, to change the video monitoring tapes in the house every month. Those tapes proved quite telling and entertaining to Irma. She thought it might be fun to make some copies before she erased them and put in the new blank tapes. To add more fear to Eloise's predicament, Irma told her she had shown the tapes to a porn video editor friend of hers who offered to edit and voice over the twelve-month series and entitle the tapes "Fantasies on the Fifteenth Hole," then distribute and split the profits with Irma. They could make a fortune, he'd told Irma.

The Museum Auction

It was Wednesday night in Lafayette. Marcel had been there over a week. He would be leaving tomorrow to go back to Santa Barbara and Match Point and continue training and practicing for the upcoming tournament. His mother was pretty stable and my father told Marcel he shouldn't worry about about Marlene. She was in good hands. "Go back to California and show 'em what you got, kid," my father told him.

Marcel and I went for dinner about eight o'clock. He was craving a special Mexican dish, the crawfish enchiladas, at one of his favorite restaurants, Randol's over on Kaliste Saloom Road in Lafayette. It was one of my favorites too. They shipped seafood in fresh daily from the Gulf of Mexico. Randol's had bands playing nightly, so we invited Viola to join us. We needed a dance partner other than each other.

Marcel told us of his plans for when he got back to Santa Barbara. After the fundraiser for the museum, he was going to totally focus on the Pacific Palisades Open, focusing every waking hour of the day on his tennis game, preparing the next three weeks before the tournament. He had to win or finish second in this tournament. He never talked about any future plans to join the tour. He was taking it one day at a time. His only concern at this time in his life was the health and care of his mama and the tournament in California.

Nothing else mattered at this point in time, except Annie, I knew.

He still had a lot of interest in his music and songwriting, especially after winning the band and songwriting contest down in LA and with a record contract in hand. There was always a music career to pursue if he decided not to join the tour. But at this very moment in his life, his entire focus was on his tennis game. Train and Roberto had spent a lot of time with him and taken him to a different level.

Marcel got back to Match Point on a Friday evening, unloaded his little red Mercedes, and headed down to State Street to meet Train around seven o'clock for dinner at Crazy Joe's. The valet parking guys always put Train's red 1954 Mercedes-Benz Gullwing right out front. He won the German Open years earlier and the Gullwing was part of the winner's prizes. The eligible — and some not-so-eligible — ladies of Santa Barbara always recognized Train's unmistakable chariot out front and decided to drop in for a drink or two. Add Marcel's little red Benz roadster right next to the Gullwing, and Crazy Joe's would turn into the busiest ladies' night in Santa Barbara, "cha ching."

The buzz was all over town thanks to Freddie's article in the Santa Barbara newspaper that Train and Marcel both would be on the auction block for the museum fundraiser over at the country club Saturday night. Annie called Marcel to ask him to escort her to the fundraiser, and he quickly obliged. He was curious, though. Harrison must have been out of town again.

Annie's reason, he found out, was not just for an escort but to have time before the fundraiser up at Irma's mansion to tell him the truth about her engagement and breakup with Harrison. Once she told him, he was shocked. He would never have asked her to go to Lafayette had he known she was engaged. He just thought Harrison was a jerk boyfriend. He didn't think it was possible she would be engaged to a guy like that.

"Did Harrison know about your trip to Lafayette with me?" Marcel asked.

"Harrison never cared where I was or what I was doing when he was out of town with his guy friends or at a tennis tournament," she replied. "He never asked me where I was. He just knew I was out of town."

When she told him they were through, he accused her of sleeping with an old boyfriend that week, a musician who was in a band when they were both in school at UCLA, a guy named Kenny who was a professional musician living in Santa Barbara. Harrison had no idea she had been with Marcel all week. Marcel and the people of Lafayette gave her the feeling of what living and true feelings were all about. She didn't know where she and Marcel would go from here, but she didn't want him to feel any extra pressure with so much going on right now, his mother and the tournament only three weeks away. She had planned on waiting until after the tournament to tell him, but she couldn't wait any longer.

Marcel got up out of his chair and moved over onto the couch beside her. He put his arm around her and held her hand. There was no pressure, he explained. Quite the opposite. He assured her he was relieved and happy now. He had been struggling with his feelings for her for a long time now. He felt as though his time in Lafayette with her might have been just a fleeting moment and that would be the end of their time together. He didn't think he could ever fit into her world. He had slowly been falling in love with her but didn't think he would ever have a chance to let her know.

"You do fit into my world," she said. "I want you in my world. You have changed my world forever, and I want to be in your world." Annie leaned over. "Please kiss me, Marcel."

The door to the parlor opened. It was Irma. Marcel quickly moved away. He stuttered and started to apologize.

She told him to just hush up and be quiet. She laughed and asked Annie if she thought Marcel's kisses would bring a high price at the auction tonight. Annie brushed a tear from her eye and with a little giggle said, "Yes, Grandmother, probably enough to buy a couple of Warhols and Picassos."

Irma turned around and closed the parlor door, peeked back in, and told them to keep practicing but not to miss the auction, laughing all the way down the hallway. Irma, I suspect, was even happier than her granddaughter that her little Annie was falling in love with a Cajun boy from the land that she grew up in.

Marcel headed back down to Match Point to get ready for the auction. They all needed to be at the country club by six o'clock. Irma called the ranch a little later. Marcel answered the phone.

"Is your fellow Ragin' Cajun, Train, ready yet?" she asked.

"No," replied Marcel. Train was still shaving off all his scraggly facial hair. Marcel told Irma he was putting on his movie star face, getting all pretty for the bidding ladies. "We'll be at the country club in fifteen minutes, six o'clock sharp," Marcel said.

"Don't you and Rene dare be late," Irma reminded him.

"She called you 'Rene,' Train," Marcel said.

"Uh-oh. Irma's very serious, Marcel. Better get going," Train said and chuckled.

The fundraiser for the museum set records for attendance and funds raised. Both records were attributable to the preview of the newly renovated country club and the presence of two celebrities, Marcel Jackson and Mr. Rene Pierre Lacroix, who was certainly the most handsome, most eligible, most desirable, and most prized auction piece of the night. Many women tried to pay handsomely for tennis lessons, dinner, dancing, and even a little Train ride. Train was the centerfold of the night, wearing a cobalt-blue, sequined-lapelled tuxedo jacket. He was the image of a Spanish conquistador and had the swagger of a Spanish matador. The club manager should have turned the air conditioners on high because of all the heat the women were putting off.

Train's first greeting as he royally entered the ballroom was to Irma. His gesture was a greeting fit for a queen. Train reached out for Irma's hand and knelt to give it a kiss. The other patrons and guests one by one thanked Marcel and Train for so kindly giving their time to this big event of the year.

It didn't take very long before Train brought his sense of humor quickly to the top. As a group of women from a local lawn tennis club stood around him, making small talk and asking all about Match Point, Train interrupted them and motioned for them to move in closer. He whispered that he was so happy to be here with all the lovely ladies tonight but was even happier to learn that the local artist Hans, who won a bid several months ago, was in Europe this time. Train just hoped that Hans hadn't placed a silent bid this year. It took four days, Train told the ladies, for him to pose in the nude for Hans's chalk sketches.

One of the ladies' lawn tennis members then asked, "Why, Train honey, why did it take Hans so very long?"

"When Hans got to sketching my private parts, he kept running outta chalk," Train answered.

All the ladies began laughing hysterically. Irma looked over and could only wonder what Train had said to pull those beautiful women into his charming web so quickly.

The bidding started for Marcel and rose rapidly. Irma and Annie smiled and watched as the bids for Marcel got higher.

"Going once, five thousand, going twice, five thousand," the auctioneer said before suddenly a new bid from the back of the room was called out.

"Six thousand dollars!"

"I have six thousand," the auctioneer continued. "Do I hear seven? Yes, seven, we have, we have seven thousand dollars. The final bid for Marcel, seven thousand, going once, going twice—"

The auctioneer was interrupted by an assistant with an envelope.

"Hold everything, ladies and gentlemen," the auctioneer said. "We have a final bid, a sealed envelope, ladies and gentlemen. Ten thousand dollars, going once, going twice, all in, sold! Congratulations to the anonymous bidder."

The guests applauded and cheered. Who was the anonymous lucky bidder, the quietly jealous Annie wondered.

Train went for the record price of twelve thousand dollars. Four members of the Ladies Lawn Tennis Club won the bid and promised him they would bring boxes of chalk. Train smiled and motioned them closer. The women huddled around him.

"Not so fast, girls," he said.

Train, always one to be quick of mind, whispered to them that he preferred to be done in oil this year.

"You'll need gallons," he said.

They all laughed and squealed with delight. Irma again could only wonder again what passed through those beautiful lips of his.

As everyone was leaving the ballroom, Irma and Annie went into the ladies' powder room. When they came out, the auctioneer was there waiting. He smiled and handed Annie an envelope. She opened it and read the contents. It was an auction certificate for an overnight weekend dinner cruise to the Catalina Islands and a month of tennis lessons at the Match Point Tennis Camp with Mr. Marcel Jackson. Annie gasped and put her hand to her mouth, looking at Irma in disbelief.

"It's about time for you to start learning the game of tennis," Irma said.

"Oh, Grandmother, I love you so very much," Annie said.

The Semifinals

Early Monday morning back at Match Point, Marcel was getting ready to start practicing at the rear tennis court. The next three weeks would be intense preparing for the tournament. He had just finished his morning mountain run with Stella when he felt a pat on the back and heard laughter. It was Train. He told Marcel he couldn't believe someone paid all that money for an overnight dinner cruise and tennis lessons with him.

"I guess there must be two prized Cajun gators in this California swamp now," Marcel said.

The next three weeks were the most grueling workouts and training of Marcel's tennis life. His daily mountain runs had strengthened his legs and increased his stamina. He could endure long sets against Train and the college players from the University of California at Santa Barbara. He was working out six hours a day and wanted more, but Train insisted on rest and muscle recovery time. The biggest improvement in his game was the many hours he spent with Roberto fine-tuning his two-handed backhand. The velocity of his backhand shots was now very powerful, and he was scoring many points with his sledgehammer, his backhand shot down the line.

Roberto knew Marcel's two-handed backhand was ready, and Train knew Marcel was ready for the tournament, having survived some very tough physical and mental exercises over the last four months, but Train wasn't sure if Marcel had developed the one thing that separates true champions from the rest: killer instinct.

The Pacific Palisades Open began with sixty-four of the top college players in the country. All preliminary matches were to be played at different tennis centers around Los Angeles. The semifinals and finals would be played at the Palms Country Club in Bel Air.

The players had to win four matches to proceed to the semifinals. Win five and they were in the finals. Six and pay dirt, two hundred thousand dollars, the championship, and four sponsor exemptions on the pro tour. Second place paid one hundred thousand dollars and third place awarded fifty thousand. Only the top three finishers were paid. Marcel played victoriously through his first four matches. His new two-handed backhand won him many points. His game was at another level. Marcel and little Pancho drove down to the Palms Country Club on Friday for his semifinal match against an all-American from Florida State University. If Southern California was christened the "vineyard of tennis," equally so Florida could be christened the "grove of tennis."

Roberto had to stay at Match Point that Friday for the kids' camp, but Train was already in Bel Air for some pregame strategy. The second semifinals match would pit Andy, the current NCAA champion, against none other than Harrison Jennings Price III, a.k.a. "Houdini," a nickname given to him for hitting some magical shots in big tournaments. Andy had beaten Harrison some weeks earlier up in San Francisco, while Marcel was in Lafayette charming Harrison's fiancée, a double match loss for "Houdini." Marcel and Harrison had never been in the same bracket or even seen each other during the preliminaries. Harrison would be very surprised when he bumped into him unexpectedly at the semifinals at the Palms that Friday. Harrison had no idea that the name in the semifinal bracket, Marcel Jackson from Tulane, was none other than the guitar-playing swamp critter from Cozy's band contest, the same guy he caught Annie talking to that night out at the back patio bar.

Marcel walked into the clubhouse to sign in. Pancho waited outside the door with Marcel's bags and tennis racquets. As Marcel came out of the clubhouse, he heard a commotion. Harrison was giving little Pancho a hard time. Harrison knew Pancho from when Roberto worked on the grounds crew at the Palms. Harrison never respected them or treated them kindly.

"What are you doing back here? I thought you and your old burrito grandpa got kicked outta here and we wouldn't be seeing you around anymore. You better scram before I go get security."

Marcel walked through the door and pushed Harrison against the wall. He told Harrison to back off. Train would have appreciated this display of killer instinct peeking through.

Harrison stepped back, surprised and speechless that the swamp critter from Cozy's was all dressed up in tennis clothes.

"Man, you need to take your little boy and go somewhere else," Harrison said. "There's a big tournament here today. You gotta be a member to play here, and I'm positive you're not one."

Marcel said he thought he'd hang around for a while and watch the tournament.

"Are you in the tournament?" Marcel asked, playing dumb.

"You fucking bet I am," Harrison said. "I'll probably win the whole goddamn thing."

Marcel sensed a perfect moment for a punch in the gut. He asked Harrison if the girl he was with at Cozy's that night was here to watch him play in the tournament.

"I dumped that stupid bitch," Harrison said. "It's none of your business, anyway." He turned to walk away and heard Marcel say maybe they could play a set or two one day.

"In your dreams, motherfucker," Harrison said, turning around. "Now get back to the swamps where you belong."

Marcel watched through the window of the pro shop as Harrison signed in and headed down to the dining room for lunch. Marcel waited until Harrison was down the steps and around the corner before going to sign in.

A couple of hours later, Harrison headed down to the locker room to get ready for his match with Andy. They had played each other many times in tournaments since their junior days in California and were pretty evenly matched. They both usually ranked either first or second. Marcel and the kid from Florida, the fourth seed, played the first semifinal round match.

Marcel was already up two sets on the guy from Florida and at 3-1 in the third. In the locker room, Andy told Harrison that the kid from Tulane was a hell of a player. Andy said he barely beat him earlier in the year in an NCAA match but was able to win because he noticed the guy had a weak backhand. Andy heard he had been working with Train up in Santa Barbara for a couple of months, preparing for the tournament.

"Lotta good that's gonna do, working with that old washed-up pro," Harrison said. "I spent fifteen minutes with that old jackass and walked off the court. I told my mama to get her money back, or she could take the lessons herself."

Harrison decided to go up and watch the rest of the match. He wanted to see this Tulane kid's stuff. Marcel was seated during the court change when he saw Harrison walking toward the court. He saw Harrison look up to see Annie and Irma in the stands. Marcel could tell he was confused to see them there. Harrison continued down the walkway when he saw Pancho race across the net at center court, wondering what that kid was doing on the court. Marcel went to the baseline, ready to serve. Harrison looked back at him, not believing his eyes.

"You gotta be shittin' me," Harrison mumbled to himself. "There's no fucking way."

Marcel won the third set, 6-3, and stayed away from using his two-handed backhand too often. He wanted to save his new weapon for the finals.

He won the semifinal match and was lined up to play for the Pacific Palisades Open Championship on Sunday at one o'clock. As Marcel left the court, Andy congratulated him on his victory. Marcel wished Andy good luck, but his real wish was for Andy to lose so that he could play Harrison in the finals. Harrison walked by and Marcel winked at him. Marcel wished Harrison all the luck in the world today.

"If I could," Marcel said, "I'd even pay for you to win today."

"Fuck off," Harrison said.

"Save it for Sunday. Make sure to bring all your magic tricks, Houdini."

Harrison slammed his hand into the fence.

Train had been standing at the fence and heard the whole exchange. Train had never heard Marcel talk that way, but figured he must be tapping into that killer instinct. He met Marcel in the locker room while Pancho was putting the bags and tennis racquets in the Benz.

"Hell of a match today, Marcel," Train said. "I kinda think you tanked around a little bit, huh?"

"I didn't want to give too much away," Marcel said. "I have to save it all for the finals." Marcel told Train he played at a level of tennis today that he never thought possible. He knew he could put his opponent away at any time during the match. Train said that if Marcel met Harrison on Sunday, he'd better go on and finish it and not just think about it.

"You need to knock him out when you have the chance," Train said. "Sunday isn't just any other match."

Train asked Marcel if he had seen Harrison play during the tournament.

"Yeah, I paid a groundskeeper over at another country club twenty bucks to borrow his uniform and hat," Marcel said. "Harrison never saw me, even though I was only twenty feet away from the court with a broom in my hand. I got a good look at his game and his hot temper. I've got his weak points all figured out."

Marcel wanted to work out all day on Saturday back at Match Point. He asked Train to meet him at nine in the morning. Marcel and Pancho headed back up to Match Point as soon as he said goodbye to Annie and Irma. Marcel walked up to Train in the parking lot and asked him for a favor.

"Anything for you, Marcel," Train said.

"No late doubles matches tonight," Marcel said, and Train knew what he meant.

It being Friday night and things hopping and hot in Bel Air, Train figured he'd better stay in shape. "No worries," Train said. "A little fun tonight for sure, but I'll be at Match Point at nine o'clock in the morning with enough energy to wrestle three gators with one arm tied behind my back."

Marcel and Pancho got back to Match Point right around six o'clock. As soon as the car stopped, Pancho got out and raced quickly toward Roberto's cabin. He was so excited to tell him that they won the semifinals and would be in the championship on Sunday. He would be a ball boy in a championship at the Palms Country Club. Roberto was just as excited. He knew all the hard work had paid off and was proud. He'd had a lot to do with Marcel's improvement. He congratulated and hugged Marcel.

Marcel reported to Roberto that Pancho worked hard today and said he couldn't have won without him. This brought a big smile to Pancho's face. Marcel decided they should all drive down into Santa Barbara and celebrate with a victory fiesta at Tiny's Mexican Restaurant.

Marcel woke up early Saturday morning for his daily mountain run. He was 100 percent in his mind's eye. He could see everything unfolding and happening, just like Blind Willie had said.

As Marcel ran back down the mountain, he saw the red Mercedes Gullwing travelling up the 101 coastal highway. Train had kept his promise. He was on the court at eight forty-five. They went through all the drills: hard serves, flat serves, spin serves, lob volleys, cross courts, drop shots, moon balls, jammers, backhand slices. Marcel commanded them all. And his most important weapon, the sledgehammer, the two-handed backhand down the line so powerfully and deceptively, was now his favorite shot. The only question remaining was whether or not Marcel could execute his shots at the right moment. Train's last shot at Marcel that morning was right at him. Marcel had to dive to the ground to avoid getting hit. Marcel got up, furious.

"What the hell are you doing?" Marcel asked.

"It's my final lesson," Train said. "Don't ever let up. Keep going for the kill until it's over. And even then . . ." Train told him to remember that last shot when he played Sunday. Train was going to head back down to Bel Air on Saturday night. He would meet Marcel Sunday morning at sign-in for the finals at twelve o'clock. "Harrison is nothing but a silver-spoon-fed brat," Train said. "You need to destroy him. Go at him with everything you got, or he will beat you, guaranteed. He plays the game well and ferociously. Remember that."

Marcel went back to the cabin and took a long shower. He was mentally and physically drained. He lay on the bed, his thoughts bouncing from the finals to Annie to Train and to his mama. He wondered how she was doing, so he called down to Lafayette. Viola answered the phone. He told her about advancing to the finals and asked about his mama.

Viola told him not to worry. His mama was a little weak, but she was doing all right. Viola told Marlene about the tournament. Marlene asked for the phone. Marlene told Marcel not to worry and to come see her after the tournament. She said she missed him very much and wished him luck in the tournament. He told her he wanted to win for everyone— Viola, Blind Willie, Bones, Dr. and Mrs. Mouton, and especially for her and his daddy that he missed so much.

He told Marlene that he'd booked a flight home right after the tournament and said he'd be there Sunday night. This news excited Marlene. She couldn't wait to see him. She asked him if he was still seeing Annie. He told her he had a lot to tell her about Annie when he got there Sunday night, a lot of things that would make her happy.

Marcel hung up the phone. He felt homesick. He didn't think his mama sounded good. He got dressed and put the top down on the Benz. He wanted a quiet night. He drove out of Match Point. The sun began to set and the view down and over the Santa Barbara harbor was worthy of a Monet painting. There was one place in Santa Barbara that could satisfy his homesick blues and remind him of Acadiana. After a long walk out onto Stearns Wharf, reflecting on life, he drove up State Street. Marcel pulled up to the valet in front of Crazy Joe's. They congratulated him on his victory and wished him good luck in the finals.

"Seeing some people at Joe's tonight, Marcel?" they asked. "A victory celebration maybe?"

"No, I'm going solo tonight," Marcel said. "I just need a little taste of the bayou to make everything all right."

They parked Marcel's car out front, and he walked a couple blocks down State Street to the Bayou Palace. The Bayou Palace was a true Cajun and Creole restaurant right in the middle of Santa Barbara. Marcel felt at home with the music, the wait staff, and the food: andouille sausage gumbo yaya, creole crawfish, crab cakes, jambalaya piquant, po' boys, red beans and rice, and, of course, bread pudding soufflé. He washed it all down with a little liquid refreshment from Louisiana: Abita and Dixie beer. Marcel was truly at home, sitting at a corner table under the glow of the diamond-shaped, red-and-green neon TABASCO sign.

Marcel returned to Match Point by nine o'clock and re-laxed on the porch in the cool Santa Barbara air, strumming his guitar to some of his favorite songs. He fell quietly to sleep singing an old Cajun song about Mother's Day, thinking about his mama. Now every day was Mother's Day to him.

The Championship

Marcel woke up and did a half mountain run. The day had come. Sign-in was at twelve o'clock at the Palms Country Club. A minute late and he'd be disqualified. The drive down to the Palms from Santa Barbara with very little traffic would take about an hour and a half. Pancho came running up to Marcel's cabin, dressed for the championship in a white Lacoste tennis shirt to match the outfit always worn by Marcel. They were big buddies now. Little Pancho wanted to be just like Marcel.

The time was nine o'clock. Marcel was going early to talk strategy with Train. Pancho ran into the cabin to get Marcel's bags and tennis racquets. Before Match Point, Marcel always carried two Wilson T2000 racquets into tournaments. Early on, Train added another two T2000 racquets to Marcel's bag because of something Train had discovered years ago by accident in the Australian Open. During the middle of a match, some strings broke loose in his racquet, and the whole racquet became loose as a result. As he continued on with play, he noticed that the ball was flying off the racquet. After that, Train always carried extra racquets with looser or tighter tensions. He used one or the other depending on the desired effect of shots he wanted during certain points in the match. The result of the loose strings created a higher-velocity shot. Train explained to Marcel that changing racquets in a match left the opponent perplexed as to the changing speeds of the balls, like a baseball pitcher throwing fastballs and changeups. Pancho put the racquets in the little red Benz roadster.

As they were driving toward the front gate, there was a sudden loud noise and the car shuddered. They got out to see what had happened. The front left tire had blown out. Marcel quickly went for the spare, but it had gone flat too. He told Pancho to go get his grandfather. Roberto would have to drive them to the Palms. Nobody was staying at the mansion this weekend, so there were no cars up there. They only had one chance to get to the Palms on time.

Roberto was up at Irma's mansion taking care of the swimming pool. He had planned to ride down to the tournament later that morning with some other friends. Pancho ran as fast as he could. He ran to Roberto and told him to hurry down because Marcel needed help. The boy and his grandfather came running back down the trail from the mansion. Roberto was still in good shape for a sixty-one-year-old man. Marcel explained the problem to Roberto. They'd have to take his pickup truck to the Palms but Roberto's truck was in the shop.

At the back of the tennis ranch in an old maintenance barn sat their only hope, an old 1949 Studebaker pickup truck that they used to haul things around at Match Point in the glory days. Roberto didn't know if it even still ran or not. He raced to the barn and flung open the door, and there, like magic, was the key, still in the ignition. He reached in the truck and turned it. Nothing. No sound, no spark. It was dead.

"Pancho, run fast and bring the battery charger off the back porch," Roberto said. *"Rapido, muy rapido."*

Marcel told him they needed to leave in fifteen minutes to make it to sign-in on time.

Roberto told him to cross his fingers and pray that the old truck would take a charge. Roberto scraped the battery posts and attached the cables.

"*Por favor, por favor,*" Roberto pleaded before he turned the key.

The trusty old Studebaker started, and even with the faded paint and the worn out Match Point logos on the doors, Marcel said he would pay a million dollars for that beautiful truck.

The three of them sped out of the driveway. It was now about ten thirty, and Roberto had to drive down the 101 at about seventy miles an hour to make it to the Palms on time. Marcel asked if the old truck could make it. Roberto said they would make it all right because the "old Stude" had a strong engine. The problem was not the old truck, Roberto said, but the license plate on the old truck. It was five years out of date, and if they got pulled over by California's finest, they would never make it. They got into LA on Sunset Boulevard and headed over to the Palms.

By the time they got to the guard gate at the country club, it was eleven forty-five, sixteen minutes away from a disqualification. The young gate attendant, a member's son, approached the pickup truck and peered into the driver's side window. When he saw Roberto, he said, "Sorry, but maintenance workers are not allowed entrance through the main gate and there is no work on Sundays."

Marcel leaned over Pancho and began to explain they were not maintenance workers but going to the tournament, but the kid wasn't listening and interrupted Marcel.

"I'm sorry, but it's absolutely against the rules."

Marcel started to get frustrated. He didn't have time to deal with some kid. He got out of the truck, walked around to the kid, and got only a couple inches from the kid's face. The kid put his hand on Marcel's chest, and Marcel shoved him against the guard shack. He told the brat he was Marcel Jackson from Lafayette, Louisiana, and he was in the championship match today and he only had five minutes to get in there and sign in to play. The kid opened the gate.

Marcel walked into the clubhouse, official time eleven-fifty-seven. Train was there with his arms crossed and visibly irritated.

"Where in the hell have you been?" Train asked.

Marcel told him to calm down and explained the situation. Train told Marcel his lucky "gris-gris" was working today.

"What's a 'gris-gris'?" Pancho asked.

"It's a voodoo object to ward off evil spirits or bring good luck," Train explained. "Blind Willie gave Marcel one for his birthday years ago and apparently it worked today."

Marcel wanted to know if Train had seen Annie anywhere. Train said she was at the club earlier, eating breakfast with Irma. She left for a bridesmaids' luncheon and would be back early that afternoon in time for the championship match.

"Does Harrison know you've been seeing his ex-fiancée?" Train asked.

"No," Marcel said. "Harrison thought she was seeing some old college flame up in Santa Barbara. He doesn't know nothing about us."

Train started right in on Marcel about the match. "Don't let up today. Attack," Train said. "Volley and serve. In the second set, start to run him more. He's not in the best shape. He never works out. Your stamina and strength will be a big advantage to you today. He should start to wear down in the third set."

Marcel began to feel nervous, but he listened to Train's voice.

"Like we talked about," Train continued, "don't use too many of your two-handed backhand shots until the third set. You can turn it loose after that. Don't give away all the shots too early. Build up his false confidence and run him a lot. His real weakness is his ego and cockiness. You gotta find a way to break down his psyche. Depending on how you're doing in the third set, slam a steady barrage of sledge-hammers by him. That will rattle his confidence. The icing on the cake is to set yourself up at Love-40 if you're up a couple games in the last set."

Marcel nodded along, trying to visualize the match.

"We've practiced this over and over. If you can make it happen, then he's done," Train said. "Go for his blood, Marcel. Destroy him and go for the kill."

To fuel the fire even more, Train reminded Marcel of all the things Harrison had called him in the past: swamp critter, gator shit, gumbo garbage. He also reminded Marcel of the way Harrison had mistreated Annie.

Marcel told Train he would try his best, and Train went ballistic.

"Try, my ass," Train screamed. "When you walk out on that court, you better give that spoiled son of a bitch a Louisiana ass-kicking. Roberto, Pancho, and me worked hard for this, real hard. We spent four months of blood, sweat, and tears on this. This ain't just another college trophy game you're in today. This is a money game. Everybody's hopes are riding on you. You gotta play this match like a warrior, Marcel." Train walked to the locker room door and turned with a smile on his face. "Good luck today, young man. I'm proud of you. *Laissez les bons temps rouler.*"

One of the officials came into the locker room. "Courtside in ten minutes for warm up and announcements please," he said to Marcel.

"Yes sir," Marcel said. "Thank you."

The official walked around the corner to the other side of the locker room and Marcel listened to the conversation, though he couldn't see it.

"Mr. Price, courtside in—"

"I know what time I'm supposed to be out there," Marcel heard Harrison say. "Leave me alone, man. I'm busy. Get outta here."

As Marcel left the locker room to head to the court, he passed by a legion of Harrison's fraternity brothers. There was going to be some serious home court advantage today, Marcel thought. He heard taunts when he passed by the large Houdini gallery. He smiled up toward them. If only they knew he was the magical reason why the beautiful Annie had disappeared from the great Houdini's life.

Harrison was already at courtside when Marcel and Pancho walked by Harrison's chair. Irma, Train, and Roberto were sitting in the stands on the side behind Marcel's court chair. Mr. Price and his wife, Eloise, walked by Irma to take a seat behind Harrison's side of the court.

"Hello, Harrison," Irma said. "And hello, Eloise. How are your golf lessons going? Or maybe I should say, 'How are they coming?' I hear there are some new golf videos that may be coming out soon that could greatly improve your game."

Eloise quickened her pace.

The match began, and the stands were packed, standing room only.

Freddie had written an article about the championship match he titled "Gumbo Versus Caviar" which appeared in the LA and Santa Barbara newspapers.

"Ladies and gentlemen," an announcer started, "playing for the championship in the Pacific Palisades Open from Los Angeles, California, Mr. Harrison Jennings Price III." The announcer paused to let the loud applause and whistles subside. Many spectators in the stands were on their feet, cheering. "And playing for the championship from Lafayette, Louisiana, Mr. Marcel Jackson." This time when the announcer paused for the audience, there was only scattered applause and a few catcalls.

Marcel lost game one, and Harrison broke serve in game two. Marcel took him to deuce in game three, but Harrison prevailed, blowing two aces right by Marcel. The score right out of the box was 3-0, Harrison. Marcel's mind was racing and cluttered. He was thinking about his mother, Annie, his music. He couldn't focus.

He won his serve, 3-1. Harrison won his serve and broke serve on Marcel again. It was now 5-1. In game seven, Harrison aced Marcel twice again.

"First set, ladies and gentlemen, goes to Harrison Price, 6-1," the announcer said in a low voice.

Train was bewildered. Marcel just lost a breadstick in the first set. He knew that Marcel wasn't focused and wasn't trying to tank. Train had an idea. He motioned for Pancho between sets to tell Marcel that his mama just called and wished him to victory. Pancho delivered the message.

Marcel served first in the next set, game Love. Marcel broke serve in game two and won his serve in game three. Marcel was at 3-0. His mind was clear, and all of his focus was on tennis and Harrison now. Harrison came back with three aces and an unreachable overhead lob behind Marcel. The second set was now at 3-1. Marcel punched back three aces and a crosscourt winner, sending Harrison crashing into the fence. 4-1. Harrison won game six. 4-2. They played a long game seven, and Marcel unbelievably won the game on a "tweener" shot hit backward between the legs. Harrison slammed his racquet onto the court. 5-2, Marcel. Marcel broke serve in game eight, and it was 6-2.

"Second set, ladies and gentlemen, Marcel Jackson," the announcer said.

The third set was evenly played, but Harrison won a hard-fought battle, 7-5. Train again motioned for Pancho.

"Tell Marcel he's got to rattle Harrison somehow," Train said. "Tell him to do anything he can think of."

Pancho relayed the message to Marcel, but Marcel couldn't think of what to do. He turned to Train and shrugged. As Marcel and Harrison got out of their chairs and were walking toward each other to their respective sides of the court, it came to Marcel. He paused and told Harrison Annie wasn't up in Santa Barbara that week with Kenny.

"She was with me at Irma's mansion in Santa Barbara," Marcel said. "While you were getting your ass kicked by Andy in San Francisco, guess where Annie was spending her time?"

Harrison turned red, clenched his fists, and slammed his racquet on the court. "You—"

Harrison was interrupted by the chair umpire telling the two players to take the court. Marcel walked slowly to the baseline, turned to Train, and smiled. Harrison lost control: double fault, double fault, wide, long. Marcel was up quickly, 1-0. Marcel, serving game two, had four straight aces, and the set was quickly 2-0. Marcel broke serve, and it was 3-0. Marcel won serve. It was 4-0, Marcel, but Harrison was no quitter. He blew three aces by Marcel and then a crosscourt winner to make it 4-1.

Harrison's play had been fast-paced all day, so Marcel decided to knock him out of his rhythm. Marcel went crocodile style. He hit shots deep and wide, side to side. He had Harrison running all over the court. Harrison was tiring and becoming frustrated. Before game six, Pancho got the sign from Train and showed Marcel four fingers. Marcel understood to tank to Love-40. With a commanding lead, he could really blow Harrison's confidence if he pulled it off, so Marcel went to Love-40. As expected, Harrison was fist pumping and pointing at Marcel as if the match had suddenly turned upside down.

Marcel upped the speed on his serve by about ten miles per hour and blew four unreturnable aces by Harrison, who looked drained. His shoulders were slumping. Marcel was now up 5-1 in the set. Harrison won his serve, and it was 5-2. Marcel, serving in game eight, changed strategy again. He went back to serve and volley, running up to the net after every serve. On the last point Harrison went crashing down onto the court and bloodied his knee. Marcel, 6-2.

"All tied at two sets apiece, ladies and gentlemen," the announcer said.

"Mr. Price, your serve," the umpire said.

Harrison blew two aces by Marcel and won the first game. Marcel decided to tank again to Love-40. He had practiced this for months. The score went to deuce and add out. Harrison returned a crosscourt fastball, and Marcel slipped and fell, a mistake at such a crucial time, Marcel thought. Harrison was up 2-0. Harrison won his serve to go to 3-0. Marcel shook his head. Why didn't he just put Harrison away in game two? Where was his killer instinct, he wondered.

Train motioned to Pancho to pull the third racquet out of the bag. It was time for a little loose string play. Marcel's first serve blew by Harrison like it was shot out of a cannon. Even the home court crowd applauded. He shot three more aces that Harrison couldn't touch. Game four, Marcel.

Marcel was baiting Harrison to play to his backhand. It was time to deliver a two-fisted punch. Harrison took the bait, and Marcel began blowing two-handers by him at will. Marcel broke serve. It was now Harrison, 3-2. Marcel was on an aces run. He couldn't miss, and every serve was at around 130 miles per hour. His crushing two-handed backhand was everything he had hoped for. The hard work with Roberto was paying off handsomely. Marcel wished he would have played two-handed earlier in his career. How many more tournaments could he have won, he wondered. Game, Marcel. It was tied, 3-3.

Marcel broke Harrison's serve in game seven. Marcel was up 4-3. He was hoping for his killer instinct to appear, but it just wasn't there yet.

As Marcel was toweling off, Pancho tapped him on the shoulder and pointed up in the stands. Marcel turned to look. She had finally arrived from the bridesmaids' luncheon. Annie was sitting between Train and Irma. Annie was wearing sunglasses, and when she took them off, Marcel could see she had a black eye. Marcel looked at Train and shrugged his shoulders as if to ask what had happened. Train motioned toward Harrison, who was standing and waiting for game seven on the other side of the court. Marcel knew that Annie had seen Harrison at an engagement party the night before. He'd heard there had been an argument, but he didn't know he'd hit her.

Marcel looked across the net at Harrison, who was stoically waiting for the next game to start. Marcel was on fire inside. He was overcome with a desire to destroy Harrison. His mind was not on a victory. He wanted to blow Harrison away and crucify him with everything he had.

"Your serve, Mr. Jackson," the umpire said.

Marcel hit two aces and a two-handed backhand down the line to make it 40-Love. The velocity on his shots was now too powerful for Harrison to return with any success. Marcel was in a mental place he had never been in before. Marcel hit a high lob back to the baseline, a moonball. Harrison was predictable. Marcel knew he would return it deep and ghost into the net. Marcel had learned this shot from Train, who called it "alligator balls." Predictably, Harrison rushed the net, and Marcel delivered his most powerful overhand yet which winged Harrison's side as he dove out of the way.

"Game, Mr. Jackson. 5-3 in set," the announcer said.

"Mr. Price, your serve please," the umpire said.

Unbelievably, Harrison fought with everything he had and won game nine. Marcel was only up 5-4 now.

As they passed at court change, Harrison said, "I'll take the trophy, and you can take the slut."

Marcel clenched his racquet. He went to the baseline to serve. He stood still and thought he'd play this final game for Train. He looked up into the stands at Train and held up four fingers. Train smiled back and held up four fingers too, their sign for Love-40. As Marcel was about to serve, everything was in his mind's eye, just as Blind Willie had said it would be. Marcel purposefully meant to lose the first three points to Harrison. It was only fitting to win match point in the Pacific Palisades Open Championship being down Love-40, the mark of a true champion, a champion like Train.

Marcel won the next three points. The next point was an exploding two-handed backhand that Harrison, now limping, could only watch go by.

"Add in, Mr. Jackson," the umpire said.

Marcel didn't want this to end, but it was time. He would set Harrison up for the final winning point, a hard jammer straight at Harrison.

As Train sat in the stands, watching the end, he thought of my father, wishing he were there to savor the moment at hand.

"Time for the matador to silence the bull," Train uttered to himself.

The time had come. The championship was Marcel's. All those yeears, all the training, all the hard work at Match Point over the last four months with Train and Roberto—it was worth it all.

Harrison returned the serve. Marcel was in a zone he had never been in before. He didn't have the desire to win but a desire to eliminate and destroy. It was time for the final setup. Marcel would return to the baseline, and Harrison would come to the net. Harrison was exhausted.

Harrison drifted back up to the service line and stopped. Marcel was ready and poised to win it with a powerful overhand right to the body. As his racquet came forward, he thought of his mother. All the hatred drained from his body. At the last minute, as the ball came downward, Marcel lowered his racquet and placed a perfect drop shot just across the net. Harrison, helpless, slung his racquet at the ball and fell face first.

"Game, set, match," the announcer said. "Mr. Marcel Jackson of Lafayette, Louisiana, is the new Pacific Palisades Open champion."

Everyone was at courtside to celebrate his victory—Irma, Train, Roberto, Cappy, Joe, Tiny, and Freddie. Annie ran up and hugged Marcel and gave him a big kiss in front of the country club crowd. Marcel looked at her eye and asked her why Harrison hit her.

"What made you think that?" Annie asked. "Harrison didn't hit me. I hit my face into a car door last night."

"Well, I thought . . ." Marcel said but couldn't finish his thought. He looked over at Train who gave a shrug and smiled.

"It's all about the killer instinct, Marcel," Train said. "Whatever it takes, awright now, killer?"

> *"The killer instinct, the single-mindedness, playing*
> *like a machine, boy, that's what made me a champion."*
> —Chris Evert

Part Four

Mama

Everyone met at Irma's house on the fifteenth hole after the match.

"Better to celebrate victory at my house," Irma explained, "and not down at the club since a Louisiana Cajun pirate just stole away the prized trophy from one of the favored sons of the Palms Country Club."

The celebration only lasted a few hours. Marcel had to catch his plane back to Louisiana at seven o'clock out of LAX. He was anxious to see how his mama was doing. As Train, Roberto, and Pancho were leaving, Marcel said, "Pancho, you're forgetting something."

Pancho looked confused.

"I couldn't have won this trophy without you," Marcel said. "I want you to take this trophy back to Match Point to be the first trophy put into the new trophy case that Roberto is building. It belongs to all of us, and that's where it will remain forever."

Pancho smiled and held the trophy up high. Roberto looked at Marcel and hugged him like he was his own son.

Train broke the seriousness. "All right, you two Mexican jumping beans, let's get back up to Match Point. We got a whole new group of kids coming early in the morning."

Train shook Marcel's hand, congratulated him on his victory, and said he would be praying every day and night for Marlene. Irma told Marcel to call every day and to tell his mama they were thinking and praying for her.

"We'll come to see her soon when she is feeling better," Irma said.

Annie drove Marcel to the airport and dropped him off at curbside. He only had twenty minutes to get to the gate. She kissed him and told him she loved him dearly and told him to give his mama a kiss for her.

When Marcel arrived, Marlene had already been released from the hospital. He got in about ten thirty Sunday night, and Viola was right there at Marlene's bedside. They were both asleep when he entered the room. Viola awoke and they exchanged quiet greetings and hugs.

"How's she doing?" Marcel asked.

"She's been sleeping a lot lately," Viola said. "She's very weak from the chemo. It's been very exhausting for her."

Marcel told Viola he would be home for a while and she should go on home and get some good rest in her own bed. He would see her tomorrow. Viola told Marcel that Irma called Marlene early that evening to give her the news of his victory. Viola said she was so happy, she'd cried and cried for joy.

Marcel drifted off to sleep after a long and grueling day. He awoke the next morning and couldn't wait to see his mama. He walked into her room, and she was sitting up in the bed. She smiled a great big smile and stuck her arms out for him. He walked over to the bed and put his arms around her and kissed her on the cheek. Viola had gotten there earlier and already served Marlene breakfast, given her a bath, and prettied her up. Marlene was wide awake, talking nonstop, and asking question after question about the tournament, Annie, Irma, and on and on. Viola hadn't seen her this happy in a long, long time.

My father walked in to the room. "Well, what do we have here, Miss Marlene?" he asked. "Would you happen to be in the presence of the new Pacific Palisades Open champion? Let's just call him the California gunslinger, why don't we?"

They all broke out into laughter. My father congratulated Marcel. He said that Train had called him every week to give him updates on Marcel's progress. Train knew my dad loved tennis more than anything, except my mama, of course, though Train used to joke that maybe my father might just love her a little bit less on Memorial Day during the Oyster Bay Classic.

My father took Marcel out to the back porch to explain Marlene's condition. She had finished the treatments several weeks ago and was now in the recurrence phase of the treatments. The outcome hadn't been good. They were only able to eliminate 90 percent of the cancer. The threshold for a more favorable nonrecurrence was 95 percent. My father explained that the rest was up to God. The nurses and Viola would keep her as comfortable as possible, but Marlene would have to stay home. There would be no crawfish boils, fais do-dos, music festivals, or piroque rides down the Bayou Vermilion. Marcel stayed by her side all day and night.

Two weeks later, when Marcel was returning from praying at St. John's Cathedral, he heard Viola call him into the bedroom. Marcel walked over to the bed and held his mother's hand.

"It's going to be all right," Marcel said.

His mother didn't open her eyes.

"Mama, it's me, Marcel. Please wake up. I don't want you to leave me. Please be okay."

Viola walked up behind him and put her hands on his shoulders. She started praying. "Our Father, who art in heaven, hallowed be thy name . . ."

Marlene slowly opened her eyes and smiled at Marcel. She put her hand out to Marcel and mumbled, "Now where's that sweet girl, Annie? Why didn't you bring her to see me?"

Marlene weakly pulled him down and rested his head on her chest. She whispered into his ear, "I love you so very much, my sweet Marcel," and kissed him on the forehead. "Viola, take care of my boy until I get better, okay?"

Viola held out her hand and nodded. He was like a son to her, too, Marlene knew. His mama asked for a kiss before she went back to sleep, so Marcel leaned over and kissed her gently on the cheek. She closed her eyes and smiled. He laid his head back down on her chest and stayed there a while. He listened to her breathing for about an hour and then got up and left the room. He sat in the hallway and cried. A short time later, Viola called him in and told him his mother had passed.

Marcel let out a loud cry, then he quietly sobbed, holding her tightly as if he could keep her from leaving. He rose up and put his arms around Viola.

A memorial service was held for Ms. Marlene Jackson at the St. John's Cathedral where Marcel had seen his daddy memorialized years earlier. A group of about fifty children, all of whom were Marlene's school music students, performed the music. The church overflowed with people.

My father and mother had presented a five-foot-tall sculpture of a violin—Marlene's favorite instrument—atop which would rest her ashes in a floral vase. Marlene had written her final wishes and had given them to Viola months earlier. After the service and reception, Viola drove Marcel back to her house and gave him the note. He asked Viola if Blind Willie's piroque was still down by the bayou.

"Yes, Marcel, you take all the time you need, honey," Viola said.

Marcel took his guitar and the floral vase holding his mother's ashes down the bank of the bayou to the piroque. He drifted down the Bayou Vermilion and began to play an old Cajun spiritual waltz. His mama had wished for Marcel to spread her ashes in the slow waters of the Bayou Vermilion, so they could float into the Vermilion Bay, leaving behind her beloved Lafayette and Acadiana, and be carried away into the deep blue waters of the Gulf of Mexico to be with her beloved husband, Melvin. There would never be a cemetery for him to visit his father and mother, but the peaceful quiet of the Bayou Vermilion would always be there for him.

Marcel stayed in Lafayette another two weeks to attend to Marlene's affairs. He told Viola he'd made the decision to return to California. There were opportunities there, not only for his tennis but a chance to explore a career in music. He also told her he had fallen deeply in love with Annie. He explained that he deeded his mama's house over to the Acadiana Parish school system to be used as a musical workshop building for underprivileged kids in honor of his mama.

"Oh, Marcel, you are one of God's chosen angels," Viola said. "Your mama would be so proud of you."

Au Revoir á Lafayette

Marcel decided to hang around Louisiana for another week. He came to visit me to discuss his future tennis career after winning the tournament. He was more confident in his tennis but also more confused than ever. I told him to head on back to California, and things would work out over time.

He played some fundraising exhibitions for Simone at Beaver Park and spent a lot of time hanging around with Bones. He was asked to return to New Orleans for the annual Tulane fundraiser for the tennis team. He was big news in New Orleans from his California victory. He was certain to one day be a Green Wave Hall of Famer.

He agreed to go on another fundraising auction block while at Tulane, and the winning bidder was the recently divorced millionairess, Ms. Crystal Bratteur. As Marcel nervously went over to congratulate her, rather than request his services, Ms. Bratteur asked a favor from him. When he returned to Santa Barbara, she expected him to ask his good friend Train to pinch hit in Marcel's place. Marcel was breathlessly relieved. She had planned a trip to California. With her winning bid, she expected Train to be her tour guide for a couple of days. Marcel was off the hook, and he said he could absolutely grant her wish. Marcel knew that Train would do whatever she requested.

Marcel drove back the next morning to Lafayette. It was Friday, and Annie called. She had some great news for Marcel to deliver.

"Go over to Crowley and tell the painter and carpenter that fixed up your house years ago that their two children were awarded the Kersh Scholarships at the University of Louisiana at Lafayette," Annie said.

Marcel went to Crowley to deliver the big news. They all celebrated with a crawfish boil, jambalaya, gumbo, and red beans. Later that afternoon, still a little hungry and savoring his short time left to relive his childhood memories, Marcel went to one of his and his mama's favorite places, Borden's Ice Cream Shoppe on Johnson Street, which had been in business since 1940.

He got his childhood favorites, the Frito pie made with chili and Fritos, and the Skyscraper, a banana split with walnuts and pineapple chunks. He went for one last boudin at Johnson's Boucaniere and washed it down with a couple of beers over at The Filling Station. Marcel had dinner plans with my father and mother and Viola at Pamplona. Marcel had saved room for his favorite Spanish dish, paella valencia—a rice dish with chicken, rabbit, and snail—and some apple bread pudding.

Marcel's appetite for the sunlit hours of Lafayette had been filled, but he would be even hungrier for the moonlight hours of Lafayette and Acadiana. This is when his other passion, music, magically came to life. He made all the stops during his last couple of nights to sit in with the bands at some of the dance halls around Acadiana. The end of his last night in Lafayette was heavenly. His mother's house had already been emptied of all the furniture, and he spent the night in his old room at Blind Willie and Viola's house.

His room was at the rear of the house. The windows were opened up to the view out back, the Petite Bayou. He was still awake with thought and his memories of Blind Willie. He took his guitar and walked out to the bench beside the bayou where he had spent many hours listening to the stories and teachings of Blind Willie. He thought of a song he and Blind Willie had played here many times, Blind Willie on the accordion. The song was for their old buddy, Tabasco Joe. As soon as he and Blind Willie would hit the first couple of notes in the song, Tabasco Joe would glide through the water and rest his chin on the bank, quite the appreciative audience.

Over and over Marcel played on into the night, but Joe never made a ripple in the moonlit waters of the Petite Bayou. Maybe it was too late, Marcel thought, or maybe he played too softly, or just maybe the real magic was missing: Blind Willie.

Viola woke Marcel early Sunday morning. His flight was at noon. She cooked him his favorite breakfast, crawfish-tail biscuits with tasso gravy, an andouille-sausage-and-shrimp omelet with artichoke bottoms, and finished with a slice of Viola's homemade pecan pie. Marcel told her he might miss his flight.

"Why do you say that?" Viola asked.

"I might be too heavy for the plane," Marcel said, and they both broke out into uproarious and uncontrollable laughter.

Viola told Marcel that if sweet young Annie was anything like her grandmother, he didn't need to be wasting his time around no more California girls. He wouldn't find one any better than her. The luckiest thing about Annie, Viola explained, was that she had Cajun blood running through her. She was always going to be happy, sweet, and fun.

"That's what yo mama was wishing for you," Viola said, "a happy life. You need to be thinking 'bout jumping the broom with Miss Annie."

As Marcel was leaving Viola's house, he heard the loudspeaker from just across the Bayou Vermilion at Beaver Park. He decided to take all his tennis trophies over to Beaver Park to remain in the trophy case as inspiration and motivation for all the young players around Acadiana. He thought it a better place than sitting around in some old pirate's chest hidden away somewhere. Marcel went back to his house, boxed up his trophies, and went down to the bayou. He jumped into Blind Willie's piroque and paddled his way across to Beaver Park.

He was surprised to see a couple of pickup trucks at his house as he walked up the street. As he got closer, he heard hammering coming from the backyard. He stopped short in the driveway. There over the front porch and door was a sign, reading "Mama Marlene's House of Music." He walked out back, and there they were, the painters and carpenters from over in Crowley. They were surprised to see him. They thought he had already left. Viola told them about him giving the house to the parish's school system for all the kids in Acadiana. They knew it was God's plan, and they wanted to pitch in and start fixing the place up real good to honor Miss Marlene. Marcel thanked them and said he knew his mama was smiling down from heaven this Sunday morning.

Marcel heard his name called out. It was Bones. Bones went around back and told the painters and carpenters that God knew they were playing hooky from church today, but he was sure they were forgiven because they were doing God's work. As Marcel and Bones were walking away, the Crowley men asked Marcel to be sure and thank Miss Irma and Miss Annie for the scholarships. And just like Viola, they told him he was a crazy Cajun if he didn't go back and ask Miss Annie to jump the broom with him before somebody else got there first. He smiled and said he was going to start looking for that broom as soon as his feet hit the ground in California.

Marcel got into Bones's pickup truck with only one possession in hand, his mother's violin. He wanted to give it to his future daughter if he had one. Bones got out of the truck at the airport and gave Marcel a big hug.

"You one of dem special people, Marcel," Bones said. "Ever since Louie brought you to see me dat time we spend over at dat old Heyman Park tennis wall, well, you always be makin' me proud. When you get back at Match Point, you tell Train dat old Bones said he need be calming down those ways of his. You know what I'm talkin 'bout, don't you, Marcel?"

"I know what you talking 'bout, Bones," Marcel said.

"You tell him I say get back over here soon and see old Bones."

"It might be sooner than you know, Bones," Marcel said.

Marcel's plane back to Santa Barbara took off southwest out of Lafayette. As he looked down he felt an emptiness of leaving the land he loved so much. The plane traveled a route over the Bayou Vermilion, the Vermilion Bay, and over the Gulf of Mexico. A smile came to Marcel's face as he looked down out of the window. He closed his eyes. How strange, he thought, leaving the beauty of Lafayette and southwest Louisiana to find a new life in the beauty of Santa Barbara and southwest California.

As the plane taxied up to the gate, he felt fresh, ready to get back to Match Point, ready to see Train and Roberto and Pancho and Irma and all his other friends. But he was especially ready to see Annie. A new life indeed.

Soul-Searching

Annie surprised Marcel at the airport. She was standing in the waiting area with a big sign in red letters that read "Chauffeur for Mr. Marcel Jackson." Marcel smiled. Annie dropped the sign and ran to him and kissed him on the lips. She missed him and felt so sorry and sad for him about the death of his mama. He told her he was okay. His mama was at peace now. He told her his mama spoke of her in her final hours. Annie didn't know how to respond.

Thinking Train was picking him up at the airport, Marcel told Annie he was flattered she would be his personal driver. Annie knew Marcel would still be thinking of home when he arrived, and she had something special planned for the afternoon, something he was not expecting. She told him she was taking him to the Bayou Palace and treating him to a crawfish etouffee and gumbo Cajun afternoon—a little quiet late afternoon lunch, just the two of them.

They walked into the restaurant to cheers and applause. A big banner on the wall read "Marcel Jackson the Pacific Palisades Open Champion." The room was full. Irma, Train, Roberto, Pancho, some museum members, and the Ladies Lawn Tennis Club were there. Charles and Jerry, Joe, Cappy, Freddie, and even Tiny, who closed his restaurant for the afternoon, were also in attendance. Annie reserved the whole restaurant for Marcel's homecoming victory celebration.

The party lasted until seven. Irma decided to go back to Bel Air on Sunday night. Annie had volunteered to help set up a new exhibit at the Santa Barbara museum for the week and would stay in the guest house at Irma's mansion.

Marcel went to work at the Match Point tennis camp with Train and Roberto and walked up the trail to spend the evenings and the nights with Annie. The next Sunday, Annie left to go back to Bel Air and flew out Monday morning to Barcelona, Spain, to spend two weeks with her mother. As they sat beside the pool Saturday afternoon before she left, Annie asked Marcel if he would still be here when she got back. He hadn't told her of any of his plans for the future and was really just unsure right now and not in a big hurry. He told her he had decided to stay at Match Point with Train at least for a while and chill out. The future could wait. Train was pushing him hard to qualify for the US Open in a couple months at a tennis club just west of LA, but Marcel really didn't know if he wanted the grind of the tennis tour in his future.

As Annie was leaving to drive to Bel Air the next morning, Marcel told her that he didn't exactly know what his future was all about yet, but there was one thing he knew he wanted in his future for sure. He told her to have a good trip and come back safely.

For the next two weeks, Train and Marcel worked daily on Marcel's tennis game, preparing for the Open qualifier. Train knew Marcel could qualify. Train knew Marcel had the full arsenal of shots and the mentality to strategically play the game.

There were no tennis camps for two weeks. Roberto and Pancho had gone to visit relatives in Mexico. The daily workouts with Train, staying in shape on the mountain runs, were grueling.

"That's what it takes," Train frequently said. "Every day you have to bust your ass to stay in the top twenty on the tour."

Marcel finished every day exhausted. He chose to relax and spend time writing songs and playing his guitar. Every night, another new song idea came to mind. He enjoyed the exciting and adventurous musical journey. Some nights he was awake until one or two in the morning, writing and playing the guitar. The music began to take over his every waking moment. By the end of the second week, he knew he was losing his focus on tennis. Train noticed it too. Marcel told Train when his mind was on his music he felt happy, relaxed, and motivated. He enjoyed everything about it. That wasn't the case with tennis and the pro tour.

Train told Marcel about of all his experiences on the pro circuit: the travel, the planes, the cars, the hotels, the autograph sessions, and all the women. He told Marcel all of this not so much to brag, but to explain the reality of it all. Marcel wasn't really interested or excited about any of those things, especially not all the women. He was a one-girl guy, looking for Mrs. Right and a couple kids. He wasn't the playboy type like Train. The best tennis he ever played was against Harrison to win the Pacific Palisades Open, but the sad part of his victory was not that he enjoyed the win. His motivation to beat Harrison came from hatred. He knew he couldn't continue to play that way. He had always played for the enjoyment and skill of the game. He wasn't a warrior like Train.

Marcel showed up at the tennis court the next day around lunchtime. Train was already there, hitting balls against the wall. Train had just returned from Bel Air that morning. More doubles lessons, Marcel guessed. He thought about what Bones had said about Train's ways and laughed. It would be impossible — not a chance — for Train to give up his ways.

As Marcel approached, Train smiled. Marcel didn't have his tennis racquet or his tennis clothes on. He'd finally made up his mind, and Train knew it. He told Train he was very fortunate for what the game of tennis had given him, and he had been down the road with pretty good success, but he was always thinking that the journey ahead for him was in music. When he was into his music, the spirit of his people back in Louisiana seemed close by and made him feel happy and alive inside.

Train put his hand on Marcel's shoulder and told Marcel he should do what would make him happy. "The *joie de vivre,* Marcel," Train said, "that's what this life is all about, young man. I'm just happy you finally made up your mind."

Train told Marcel he was going to change into his beach clothes. They were going to cruise down Highway 101, spend the rest of the day on the beach, and grab some food and drinks at The Hawaiian Surfer at Malibu Beach. Marcel could only laugh. He remembered what I had told him about Train. He would work you hard, but when the work was done, you'd have the time of your life. They spent all afternoon on the beach, partying and talking about the training, the championship, Irma, and, of course, Annie.

That day in Malibu with Train marked a shift for Marcel. He drove Train's Gullwing back to Match Point alone that night. Train met up with Irma's two lady friends on the beach later that afternoon and went back to Bel Air with them. Marcel went back down to LA for the weekend to play with the house band at Cozy's and talk to some guy named Clive about a contract. Marcel invited Train to go with him.

"I'd love to go," Train said, "but you already made plans for me this weekend."

Marcel looked at Train, confused.

"I have to go down to Beverly Hills this weekend on your behalf and entertain Crystal Bratteur of New Orleans, Louisiana. I'm quite sure she'll want a long rodeo ride."

Jumping the Broom

Annie returned from Spain on Friday. Marcel picked her up at the airport, and they drove up to Santa Barbara. They had plans to spend the weekend at the mansion. Marcel dropped her off at the mansion and told her he would pick her up again around seven.

Marcel dressed in a pair of white linen slacks, a pink pin-striped dress shirt, and a cobalt-blue blazer with a white silk pocket square. Annie came to the door dressed in a green knee-length spaghetti-strap dress, high heels, and a necklace of white pearls. This night in Santa Barbara was especially beautiful—clear skies, a cool ocean breeze, and twinkling stars. Marcel had a big night planned for them. They stopped at the White Whale restaurant for a couple of glasses of red wine, perfect for walking down to the end of Stearns Wharf, the old wooden pier built in 1872 by John Stearns.

Marcel asked Annie to have a seat on the bench by the pier railing. He smiled and took a moment and looked into her eyes. She smiled back, and he lowered himself to one knee. He told her he had always dreamed of this moment, but it was more than he ever imagined.

He reached into his jacket pocket and put a red ring-box in her hand. She began to tremble. She had always dreamed of this moment. Marcel made her so happy, and he was so loving. She wanted to spend the rest of her life with him. She accepted his proposal and they kissed. They touched their wine glasses together, took one last sip, and threw them into the glistening waters of the Santa Barbara Harbor.

They had dinner at the Café del Sol in Montecito. Marcel had reserved a table across the little bridge in the back corner garden area. After dinner, he suggested they go to the Bayou Palace to have a couple of Cajun toasts to christen their engagement. Annie happily agreed. They walked in, and everyone was there. Marcel knew how to plan a surprise too. Irma, Train, Joe, Freddie, Roberto, and all their other friends were there. Annie put her hand over her mouth and ran over to hug Irma.

"Annie, my dear, we're all wanting to know. What was your answer?" Irma asked.

Annie nodded her head. Everyone clapped and congratulated the newly engaged couple. Every table had a floral arrangement as a centerpiece—a rose for love and a magnolia, the state flower of Louisiana, for happiness.

After a few drinks, Irma rose to present a toast, wishing the newly engaged couple a happy life together. Train then laid a broom decorated with flowers on the floor. He explained the age-old Cajun custom of a couple jumping over a broom to let everyone know they were going to be married. Annie and Marcel jumped over the broom and everyone cheered, raised their glasses, and toasted the couple with champagne.

Irma went to the back of the room and found Train.

"I wonder if you'll ever jump the broom," she said.

"One day I might be jumping away from some crazy woman's broom, but never over one," Train said.

Much to the delight of Irma and Train, Marcel and Annie had decided where they wanted to get married. When Annie first asked Marcel where he would like to be married, he sang to her a verse of the very first Cajun song ever recorded in 1928 by Joe and Cleoma Falcon, "He wanted to take her back to Lafayette to change her name . . ."

The day of the wedding, Irma had an early morning breakfast planned for the wedding party. When she was a little girl, she and her grandfather, Maurice, would head out early just about every Saturday morning from New Iberia for breakfast. Their destination was the Café de Amis miles away over in Breaux Bridge. Every Saturday morning along with the great breakfast, the young Irma and her grandfather chose to start the mornings off dancing to a Zydeco band.

"What better way to begin a great wedding-day celebration?" Irma said.

The wedding party arrived at eight o'clock sharp, grabbed some tables, drank mimosas and bloody marys, ate breakfast, and danced until the band stopped at eleven thirty. There must have been more than three hundred people standing on the banks of the Bayou Vermilion on that beautiful May afternoon in southwest Louisiana. The priest, Marcel, Irma, Pancho—the ring bearer—and Train—Marcel's best man—stood under a trellis covered in magnolias.

The faint sound of an accordion and a violin accompanied the ceremony. The guests looked down toward the bend in the Bayou Vermilion. They saw Blind Willie's piroque floating toward the dock. Annie was seated in the front, and Bones paddled from the rear. Bones stopped just a little ways downstream at the gravesite of Blind Willie. Annie placed a bouquet of magnolias on his headstone. The vows were spoken in French and English. The rings were exchanged and a final prayer said. Marcel took a rose from his lapel and a magnolia from Annie's hair. He knelt down on the dock and placed them in the slow currents of the Bayou Vermilion. They drifted to the Vermilion Bay and into the blue waters of the Gulf of Mexico in remembrance and in honor of Marcel's mother and father.

There were so many guests for the wedding that the traditional Cajun wedding reception known as the La Bal de Noce—the wedding dance—had to be held at the cavernous Grant Street Dance Hall in downtown Lafayette. Just before Marcel and Annie were to begin their wedding dance, Viola brought a chair to the center of the room, a seat for Annie. Viola handed the gift box to Annie. Annie opened it, and inside were the red cowgirl boots Annie had seen at the foot of Marlene's bed in the hospital on her earlier visit. Annie grabbed her heart. She couldn't speak. Marcel knelt down and slipped off Annie's silver wedding shoes and put his mama's boots on her. He looked up and whispered to Annie

"There, my beautiful Annie. Now she can dance with us."

The band—of course, Blind Willie's Bayou Boogaloo Band—began playing.

Annie chose her bridal dance partner, much to the delight of Irma, to be Train. Marcel's choice to be his dance partner was Viola. Later, all the guests got into the age-old Cajun tradition of pinning on money. The honor of dancing with the bride required pinning money on the bride's dress to help pay for the couple's honeymoon and future expenses. The night was filled with music, dancing, food, and laughter.

All the ladies from far and wide across Acadiana lined up to dance with the ever-so-handsome and charming Train. Train's favorite dances of the night were with Simone, and that dance lasted into the wee hours of the next morning. Marcel and Annie walked out of the Grant Street Dance Hall into a shower of rice. They were whisked away by Maurice in his limousine. It was strange how life worked sometimes. Only a short time ago, Marcel had watched as Annie, not knowing his name, had been whisked away from Papa Mojo's Roadhouse in the same limousine that was now carrying them both to their new beginnings and a new life.

They were going to spend their honeymoon in Paris, France, for two weeks in May during the French Open at Stade Roland Garros. Paris was full of street side cafés, wine, dinner, desserts, champagne, music, plays, moonlit boat rides down the Seine, late-morning breakfasts in bed. Marcel was happy knowing that he wasn't traveling to Paris to compete in a pro tennis tournament.

Love-40

Irma, Train, Marcel, and Annie had lunch in New Iberia the Sunday morning before the newlyweds headed off to Paris.

As they were riding to the airport, Marcel asked Train where he first started playing tennis. When they passed through the little town of Broussard, Train drove down East Railroad Street and stopped in front of a vacant house. It had a haint-blue porch ceiling and a faded name on the mailbox. Marcel could barely make out the text.

"This is where I was born and raised," Train said. He drove on down the road and turned right, stopping short of the railroad tracks for the Louisiana and Texas line, just across from the sugarcane warehouse. Train showed them the warehouse wall where he practiced his tennis. He left his backyard every day and hit balls into the wall.

"That splintered old wooden door there," Train explained, "that was my practice target for serving. I hated that door. The train engineers gave me a new tennis racquet and balls for Christmas one year. I got mad at a tournament one year and tossed that old racquet over a fence. Never saw it again."

Train told them that Bones would walk down that road and watch out for Train and his mama. Irma's granddaddy, Mr. Maurice, would sometimes take them down to his grandmother's house in New Iberia when they were having some bad troubles with his daddy. He said when his daddy was alive, he felt like he was waking up to Love-40 every day. He was always fighting back at him. Train apologized to them. He didn't mean to get so lost in his past.

As the L&T train slowly passed by in front of the car, Marcel smiled, patted Train on the shoulder, and said, "Train, 40-Love."

Irma decided to lighten the mood and said it was time to get the two lovebirds to the airport. When they got out of the car to go into the airport, Marcel told Train there was something in the trunk for him that Train could look at later. They all wished Marcel and Annie a good honeymoon.

"Marcel, don't spend all your time at the French Open," Train said and laughed. "It's only a game, you know."

Train then took Irma to the other side of the airport where Roberto, Pancho, and the Kersh company jet were waiting for departure back to Santa Barbara. Train told Irma he would see her back in Santa Barbara in a couple of weeks. Maybe she could arrange a lunch with him and her two young golfing lady friends. She glared, waved a finger at him, and then softened and kissed him on the cheek.

Train had one more nostalgic stop to make. He left the airport and drove across Surrey Street on to Fisher Road, cruising parallel to the Bayou Vermilion. He pulled in and parked under the palm trees beside the old blue tennis wall at the Beaver Park tennis courts. There was no one here this Sunday. They were closed for repair work on the courts.

Train parked the car and opened the trunk. Marcel had left a guitar case in the trunk, which Train thought was strange. He wondered why in the world Marcel gave him a guitar. The guitar case was old and worn, so he opened it carefully. There inside was an old tennis racquet, and wrapped around the neck and handle was black duct tape. He couldn't believe what he was seeing. At the very top of the neck he could see the letter T scratched in. He unwrapped the duct tape and down the broken handle were the letters R-A-I-N and at the bottom, L-O-V-E-4-0. It was the Christmas present from the train engineers so many years ago, broken and lost, the one he threw across the court right here at Beaver Park when he lost the Acadiana Amateur Championship so many years ago. He was overwhelmed. This racquet, this old missing broken racquet, a symbol not of broken dreams or a broken childhood but of dreams fulfilled beyond his wildest expectations. This racquet was the instrument, the symbol that gave him the strength to fight.

His head was still cupped in his hands and his eyes were closed, when all of a sudden he heard a voice.

"Hey, Mister, are you okay?"

Startled, Train looked up to see a young boy about the age of six or seven sitting on a bicycle.

"Are you okay, Mister?" the kid asked again.

"Yeah, kid, I'm okay," Train said. "Where did you come from? The park is closed today."

"I know all the secret paths around Beaver Park," the kid said defiantly. "I can always find a way in when I want to. Why are you here, Mister, with that tennis racquet if the courts are closed?"

"I used to play here a lot when I was growing up. Do you play tennis here?"

"I never played any tennis before."

"You play baseball or football?"

"No sir, I don't play nothing. I just ride my bike around."

"Your dad doesn't play any sports with you?"

"I ain't got a daddy no more. He left me and my mama one day. He told me I was going to be trouble and nothing but a pain in his ass and drove off. He ain't been back since."

"So you never played tennis before?"

"No, I ain't got no tennis stuff, but I can hit rocks all the way across the Bayou Vermilion with a broken boat paddle. I can aim and hit the trees on the other side."

"Kid, go get those balls off that court and come up here to the blue tennis wall and let's see if you can hit those balls with my old, taped-up, broken tennis racquet."

Train bounced him the balls and was amazed. The kid was a lefty. Train told him to hit from the other side of his body. He put two hands on the racquet, a natural two-handed backhander. The kid never took his eyes off the ball. His swings were a little wild, his style a little rough, but Train thought there was enough there to work with.

"How'd you like that?" Train asked.

"That's not bad," the kid answered. "Beats hitting rocks across the bayou."

"If I got you a tennis racquet, do you think your mama would let you come over to the park and play? I know a thing or two. Where do you live, kid?"

"Just down the road in Broussard near the sugarcane warehouse and the railroad tracks. What's your name, mister?"

"They call me Train."

"That's a funny name."

"It sure is," Train said and chuckled. "So what's your name?"

"I got a French name, Mister Train. When my mama was a little girl, she came to Beaver Park a lot and saw this man play tennis, and he was real good. She said he was always nice to people and was very handsome, and if she ever had a son she would name him after that man.

". . . My name is Rene, Mister. Rene Pierre."

Game. Set. Match.

Acknowledgments

Lafayette, Louisiana

Many thanks to all the people of Lafayette and Acadiana who, on my first visit for research of the book in the fall of 2012, were so friendly and welcoming. By chance I was there during the annual Acadiens et Créoles Festival in Girard Park. It was my first introduction to many things: boudin, Zydeco music, and the dancing of people of all ages—but especially the women and young girls loving the dance and the cowgirl boots they wore to push-push and waltz. They call New Orleans the Big Easy; I hereby christen Lafayette the Big Happy. *Joie de vivre,* y'all, and *laissez les bons temps rouler.*

My grateful thanks to the McIlhenny Company and owners of the restaurants and establishments in and around Lafayette who gave permission to use their names, products, and menu items: Pamplona Tapas Bar, The Filling Station, Randol's Seafood Restaurant, Johnson's Boucaniere, The French Press, Dwyer's Café, Don's Seafood and Steakhouse, Café Des Amis, Borden's Ice Cream Shoppe, Red Lerille's Health and Racquet Club, and the Blue Moon Saloon.

Santa Barbara, California

In memory of my cousin, Charles Craig, who invited me to spend the summer of 1970 in Santa Barbara, a paradise I'll never forget and revisit whenever possible. Charles was a banker and a major art collector who introduced me to the world of art, and a scholarship endowment still exists in his name at his alma mater, Louisiana State University. I thank him for all the breakfasts he bought me at the Copper Coffee Pot on State Street and the #22 at Tiny's Mexican Restaurant on Milpas Street.

And to the memory of Charles's dear friend Irma Kellogg, who that summer treated me like royalty on many occasions: museum exhibits, dinner parties at her mansion in Montecito, and enjoying wine and "avocados" by the pool overlooking the Santa Barbara Harbor.

My Publisher

None of this would have been possible without the encouragement, advice, and support of the staff at BookLogix, a professional publishing house that supports authors and independent publishers. A very appreciative and grateful thanks for his guidance and patience during this writing to my Ace, my editor.

My Family

Most especially, thank you to my family. My creative writer and producer son, who said the story and characters would make a good movie, was the motivation for writing this story. The game of tennis certainly deserves a good movie: take one—action. To my wife, who encouraged me over the last three years to keep going, you are a rock, sweetheart. And to my beautiful and inspiring daughter, who told me that I couldn't give up. I had to finish the story.

To the three of you, all my love.

About the Author

Victor Cauthen was born and raised in a small textile town in North Carolina. After graduating from the University of North Carolina-Chapel Hill, he moved to Atlanta, Georgia, where he still lives today.